HELSGAARD'S HEROINE

BOOK ONE OF THE HELSGAARD CHRONICLES

GEORGE TOFT

DIGITAL GRID

Helsgaard's Heroine

Book One of the Helsgaard Chronicles

George Toft

A NOTE TO THE READER
(OR THE UNINITIATED)

Forget the hearth fire and the hero's journey. You are about to step into the Helsgaard Chronicles, a saga forged in ash, blood, and the black, cynical humor of a twenty-year military scar.

This isn't a book; it's a butcher's floor, and you're the next one in line.

Within these pages—stretching through Helsgaard's Heroine, Helsgaard's Fury, and the rest—you'll find the grim truth of a world populated by warriors, Seithr (witches), dragons, necromancers and the monsters men make of themselves. It is a world of dark, visceral power, where the only thing cheaper than a life is a promise.

We deal in violence ranging from petty, soul-crushing degradation to the wet work of battle. Swearing is in the tradition of the Old Norse—so yes, you'll be exposed to the coarseness of warriors. There is also cost and consequences for the cold reality of child abandonment, hazing, post-traumatic stress, and mental illness.

Still clinging to fairytales? Bless your soft, unscarred heart.

You won't find kindly wizards, noble swords, or damsels in distress. Here, the damsels are the ones causing the distress. This isn't heroes versus villains—it's raw politics, cold betrayal, fire in your face and the taste of mud (or worse) in your mouth. Peace is bought with the last thread of hope you dared to keep.

DO NOT CONTINUE IF:

- You like your sieges tidy. Expect tactical maneuvers, ambushes, and one-on-one melee fights.

- You prefer your battles clean. Swords stick in ribs, shields splinter, limbs scatter, and heads roll. Don't look for a neat cut; this is a desperate, ugly mess.

- You squirm at a slow, ugly death, the bite of a corrosive, sarcastic joke, or socially unacceptable harassment.

- Your version of 'roughing it' involves a campfire and a sing-along.

If you crave torchlit keeps, scarred Rangers, and a half-Aelf girl with a blue blade and a red-hot temper—then welcome. You're twisted enough to survive.

A full glossary is provided for those too soft to infer, but frankly, if you need a Rosetta Stone to decipher a little Old Norse, you're already behind. Time to catch up.

Now, pack your armor. Pour a strong drink. When it all goes to Hel, don't say I didn't warn you. I honestly don't care.

CONTENTS

Acknowledgements

Thank you for all my friends and shipmates who unwittingly inspired much of the content of this book. They say every book has a piece of the author in it, and this is no exception.

And a special thanks to Donelle, who kept me humble when I needed it the most, kept my characters in line ("No, she wouldn't say that"), and boosted me up on this journey.

INTRODUCTION

What if the old myths and sagas were not merely stories? What if enough of them were true that humanity bent their lives around them?

In the north, the sagas whisper of Hel: A place of fire beneath the earth, ruled by Hela, her Dragons and populated by Valhalla's rejects—those who died of cowardice, sickness or old age. Imagine such a place not as fable but as fact—a volcanic plain, a lair not for serpents of dream, but for Dragons of flesh and scale, and the people knew exactly where it was and named that plain "Hel." The mouth of the lair was called Helgrindi.

When humankind pressed too far into the neighboring areas, the hunting grounds of the Dragons, blood was the inevitable price. To hold their ground, men raised a fortress of stone at the very edge of Hel and named it Helsgaard Keep.

This tale will not flatter you. It is not safe. It is meant to amuse only those who laugh at gallows humor, drink sarcasm like mead, and stare into the black pit of culture, society, and nature itself—finding something monstrous and true staring back.

The chapters are short, sharp cuts—meant to be taken like quick draughts of strong drink. And throughout, you will find the old tongue: Words half-familiar, half-forgotten. Fear not.

Their meaning is revealed by the tale or by the moment, as it would be in life. Many sound like English, because England itself was carved by Scandinavian hands.

So draw close, adventurer. Step through the gates of Helsgaard Keep. Here the dead do not rest, the living fight to survive, and the old gods still linger—whether we will them to or not.

CHAPTER 1

STREETS OF RAVNBORG

THE SWEET FLAVOR OF MUCK ON THE TONGUE

W ITH THE PRECISION OF a master thief, Lozen slipped the lockpick from her sleeve, its slender blade glinting faintly in the moonlight. The tool danced in her hands, coaxing the stubborn lock with a silent, methodical rhythm as the city's murmur faded into the stillness of night. A soft click signaled her success, and she swiftly pocketed the prize—only to freeze as a vice clamped onto her left shoulder. She was wrenched around to confront a towering figure with blonde hair and blue eyes that were as hard as flint. The Ravnsríki Raven, embossed on his worn leather armor, caught the dim light and marked him unmistakably as a guard.

Fear surged through her veins—she had never been seized like this. The sudden pressure of his grip was nothing like the rough tussles with drunken fools who tried to take advantage of her in the taverns, nothing like the scuffles she'd won with sharp elbows and quick fists. She locked eyes with the man towering over her, his jaw a rigid line of authority, his narrowed gaze brimming with suspicion.

"Caught you red-handed, little thief," he growled, his words reflecting his upbringing in a disadvantaged part of society. "And you has a bow—and black pants and cloak? Looks like I gots the Shadow Archer! The King has a big bounty on you."

Lozen struggled to remain composed as her heart pounded in her throat and eardrums. The stench of human and animal waste in the streets made her want to vomit. She feigned innocence. "I don't know what you're talking about, sir."

The guard's scrutiny intensified. His gaze swept over her, taking in her delicate features and seeing the tips of her pointed ears peeking out from her hair under her black hood. "You look... interesting. Like an Aelf, but too short and too thick."

Lozen's breath hitched. Her Aelfinn heritage was revealed, a dangerous secret in a kingdom at war with the Aelfs. Once a haven of anonymity, the marketplace now felt like a trap, the encroaching shadows closing in.

He continued, "Short, stocky, red hair like a Dwarf? Wait, that makes you—"

"—Don't!" she warned.

"A Dwaelf!" he said, referring to her mixed heritage.

The word "Dwaelf" rolled off his tongue with casual venom, a slur that dredged up the emotional weight from the prejudice Lozen had carried since her pre-teen years in Aeldoria. The insult twisted in her gut like a blade, igniting a blaze of fury that coursed through her veins. Her blood burned hot, her vision sharpening with the singular clarity of rage.

She flattened her right fist. Muscles readied. Furious! Anger! Strike!!!

But he was no novice. With a sharp snap of his left arm, he deflected her attack, his speed throwing her off balance. Before she could recover, his fingers clamped around her wrist—controlled, unyielding. In an instant, the fight shifted. His skill wasn't just impressive; it was dominating.

He drove his foot behind her left leg and shoved. She went down hard, crashing onto her back, his weight slamming into her as he landed on his knees, straddling her. The impact crushed the air from her lungs, leaving her gasping.

Her stomach churned under the pressure of his weight.

She thrashed, clawed, and fought.

But he was faster. He lifted just enough to twist her arm, flipping her onto her stomach. A blaze of agony seared her joint as he wrenched her arm behind her back. Her face slammed into the slimy cobblestones, the taste of piss and animal filth immediately coating her lips. He pressed down hard on the back of her neck, grinding her mouth into the muck. The sudden, wretched taste of feces triggered a dry heave that convulsed her body, and she spat desperately to clear her mouth.

"Feisty one, aren't you?" he chuckled.

Lozen strained against his grip, every muscle locked in defiance, but he didn't budge. Fear, anger, and the crushing weight of confinement tangled inside her, trapping the energy she couldn't unleash.

The guard pulled back her hood with a rough tug, revealing her Aelfinn ears, a pinkish face dotted with some freckles, red hair, and a stocky build inherited from her Dwarfinn father. He was surprised. "A real Dwaelf! Here, in Ravnborg?"

"*Tharnak!*" she spat. The word a curse in her mouth, and her chest heaved with fury. "Don't call me that."

"An Aelf in the capital city would be a concern, given the ongoing war with Aeldoria. Suspicious. The King put three Odin's Merks bounty on the Shadow Archer, and RIOS made it six Merks if the archer is a Dwaelf. Three more Odin's Merks will buy mamma some clothes and a new bed—one of those fluffy kind like the Jarls have."

"Like I care? Let me go!"

He hesitated, a flicker of uncertainty crossing his face. "Didn't mean no offense, little thief," he mumbled, releasing his grip, standing, and stepping back. As she rolled over and sat up, he offered her a hand and pulled her to her feet.

"We were told to look out for a Dwaelf, but no one ever seen one."

"Really. Stop calling me that."

Lozen straightened up, her anger fading and giving way to curiosity. This guard was different. He hadn't drawn a weapon or called for help, but still held her wrist. She hoped she could get out of this situation.

"Why does RIOS want you so bad?" He asked.

"What is RIOS?"

"Royal Invest—no, Royal Inter—no, Royal—I dunno Service. A nest of spy-skitr, stinking all the way to Hel. We don't ask—we just stays clear. Why are you here?"

The question hung in the air, heavy with unspoken truths. Her eyes locked with the guard's. Should she trust him—reveal her secrets to a stranger? But something lingered in his eyes, empathy, that she couldn't ignore. Her whispering voice carried the burden of a lifetime of rejection. "I'm here because I was exiled from Aeldoria."

"Exiled? Kicked out? But why? You're so young."

Lozen spat on the ground, taking a harsh breath. "Fine, you want the story? They judged me. Said I was some half-breed piece of skitr—a Dwaelf. A stain on their pure bloodlines! They kicked me out."

"Go on," he said, pushing her.

"I ended up living in the forest, then scrapping on the streets of Skjaldarhöfn and finally Ravnborg, just trying to find a decent score. An Elder told me about Helsgaard Keep—said they take anyone, no matter who you are. Never left, just trying to make a life."

"Here's the deal. You're mine." He grabbed her just above the right elbow with a vice-like grip, his thumb searching for the nerve bundle, causing extreme pain to the joint and sending a shock down her lower arm. "And I'm taking you to RIOS. Six Odin's Merks!"

"Ow! That was rude!"

"Jus' makin' sure we stays together." The guard's grip was iron on her arm, dragging her through Ravnborg's filth.

Lozen staggered once, twice, boots sliding in muck, bile sharp at the back of her throat. He hauled her into a narrow side street where the city noise thinned and shadows thickened.

"Hold still," he muttered.

She coiled to strike.

He didn't draw steel, instead, he twisted her arm to inflict a shot of pain. He rapped his knuckles on a blank stone beside a low, unmarked door.

A glass orb the size of a fist flared to life inside the wall. A face resolved in the glow—hard, sleepless eyes, no patience to spare.

"*What do you want?*" the orb said, the voice flat and disembodied.

The guard shoved Lozen half a step forward. "Shadow Archer. She has a bow, ears and all."

"*Turn her head so we can see her ears.*"

He reached to turn her head, but she ducked away.

"Don't touch!" she snapped, presenting her ear to the orb, street muck drying on her cheek and chin like war paint.

The eyes in the glass studied her. "*Name.*"

"Lozen," she said. "From nowhere you'd like."

A pause. "*You've been busy, Lozen-from-nowhere, Shadow Archer.*"

The guard squeezed her arm, angling for his bounty. "Six Odin's Merks. Dwaelf bonus."

Lozen's teeth bared. "Call me that again and I'll take your tongue."

The man in the orb almost smiled. "*Nice! We prefer bite. Here's the offer. You walk free tonight. At dawn you go west. Helsgaard Keep. You belong to the King. Do what we tell you, when we tell you.*" His gaze cooled. "*You don't show? We name you Skaldvárr—oathbreaker. Double bounty. The kind of hunt that ends with fights over who wears your pointed ears around their neck.*"

Silence thickened.

Lozen weighed the filth under her feet, the iron grip on her arm, the noose in every alley. West meant a chance. Here meant a dungeon and an intimate relationship with a sadist.

"Terms?" she asked.

"*Take the coin. Walk out that gate. Be at Helsgaard within the half-moon. You will be contacted after arrival. That's all.*"

A drawer in the stone slid open with a wooden scrape. Gold flashed.

The guard snatched up six Merks; one remained, waiting.

Lozen looked at it—looked longer—then took it. It felt heavy. She looked at the image of the Nordlund god Odin.

"*Done*," the orb said. "*We'll know if you run.*"

The ball went dark.

The guard with the vice grip released her. For a heartbeat they just stood there, looking at each other.

"Gate's that way," he said roughly. "Don't make me regret bringing you here."

She wiped her mouth with the damp rag, spat the last of Ravnborg's taste onto the stones, and watched as he walked away.

"Good luck, kid," he called over his shoulder.

Lozen stopped, confusion clouding her face. After a few paces, he yelled, his voice booming through the alley. "Hey! Come back! Halt! In the name of the King!"

Shouting as he ran down the empty streets, Lozen's eyes widened in disbelief. Realization dawned on her—this was the deal she had signed up for. The guard did his part and got paid. She got paid and now it was her turn. With a rush of adrenaline, she dashed around the corner and pressed up against the wall.

"Halt! Come back!" echoed through the streets.

The main gate, her gateway to freedom, was ahead. Gratitude washed over her for being given a new chance in life.

She grinned. The guard was too busy focusing on his bounty to notice that he'd left her with everything she'd stolen. Ravnborg's shadows stretched behind her, but beyond lay Unter-Ravnborg—the dark streets where patrols feared to tread. Tomorrow, she'd buy a new pack, supplies, sell the stolen goods and find a moneychanger to break the Odin's Merk. Then—Helsgaard—the red rock fortress on the western ridge.

A new future. A place where she can stop hiding and finally call home.

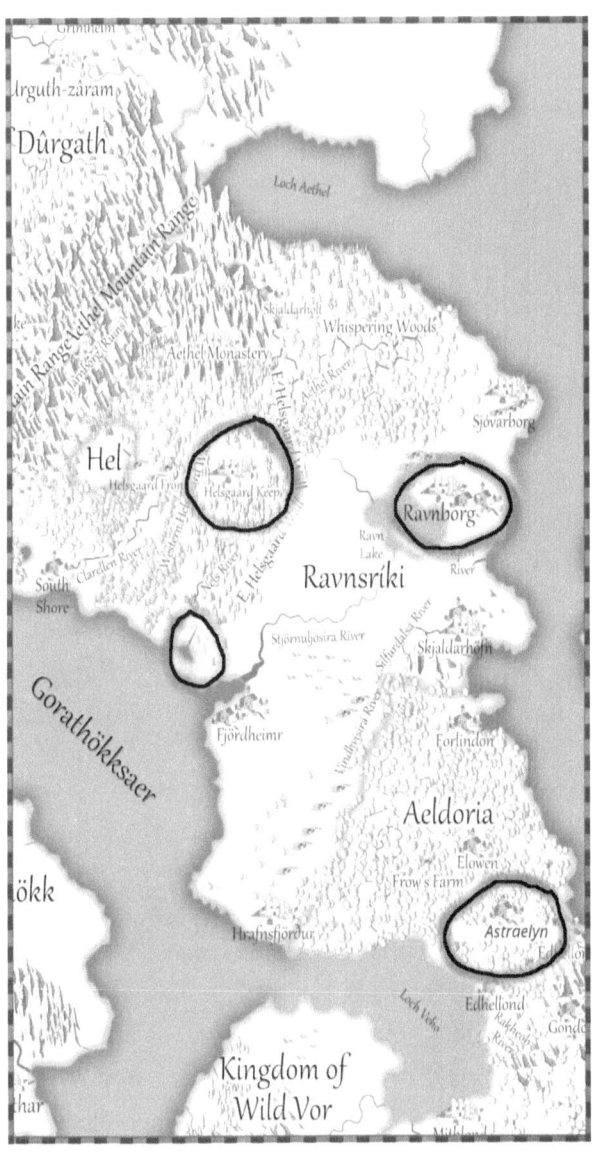

Ravnsríki With Areas of Interest Highlighted

CHAPTER 2

HELSGAARD KEEP

TWO WEEK'S WALK TO NOWHERE

HELSGAARD KEEP STOOD AS a solitary, imposing barrier of red rock on the western edge of Ravnsríki. Time and conflict had scarred its weathered walls, which overlooked cleared fields and the fledgling town of Helsgaardborg to the northeast. The stark fortress lacked grandeur, serving as the kingdom's shield against Hel's Dragons and securing lumber for the growing settlement.

A biting late winter breeze whipped across the plains as Lozen stopped before the Keep's open gates. She wore a black cloak and hood to conceal her Aelfinn ears, aiming to blend in with the passing locals. Hesitantly, she approached the entrance, where a burly, gray-streaked, red-haired Dwarfinn guard named Rylen monitored the traffic. Suspicious of the newcomer, he called out in a gruff challenge, "State yer business!"

Helsgaard Keep

Lozen met his stare and responded with a voice that attempted to mask her apprehension. "I'm looking for refuge. I am a traveler." Feeling anxious after her arrest and journey, she took a deep breath and pleaded her case. "Please. I come from afar. I was told to come here. I seek a place where I can offer my skills in exchange for protection." Rylen looked up at her stocky form. "Doff yer hood, lass."

She revealed her fiery red hair and the telltale pointed ears of her Aelfinn heritage.

"An Aelf, then?" He stared in disbelief as he took in her features. "Ye've come from distance. But ye measure short compared to their kind."

Curious at Rylen's conversation, the other guard left his post to join the discussion, eyeing Lozen's pointed ears. "Another Aelf? Why she so short? This is weird. Think she's a spy?"

Another Aelf? she wondered.

"If she's a spy, she's doing a poor job of it, lad," Rylen said, his tone sharp with suspicion. "If I know Bryn, the lass will be here soon enough. If this one is a spy, she'll sniff it out." He paused, leveling a firm gaze at the other guard. "Mind yer post. If Bryn shows up, tell her I've taken our guest to the Commandant."

The other guard, visibly disgruntled at being left behind, grumbled. "Stickin' me with the gate while you take our guest on a tour?"

"Rank holds the coin, lad," Rylen said. Smirking, he scratched his right ear with two fingers.

The other guard nodded at the covert signal, turned his attention to Lozen, and said, "So tell me. Aelfs are supposed to be good archers. But you? Don't make me laugh, girl. You look more like something the wolves dragged back to their cave."

She stiffened, temper flaring. "That your way of greeting travelers? I've spent a half-moon slogging through swamps with bounty hunters on my heels. I'm worn thin, out of patience, and I don't need your skitr on top of it."

While she was distracted by the other guard, Rylen stepped beside her and grasped her right hand with his left, clamping onto it with a firm grip, his thumb in her palm.

"What the—" she exclaimed.

He squeezed and twisted her wrist behind her back, pushing into her back, using his right hand as a fulcrum on her right shoulder joint, eliciting a sharp gasp from the young Aelf. Lozen, angry, tried to pull her hand free, but he put more pressure on her shoulder joint while twisting with his left hand, amplifying the pain and halting her struggle.

"Be still, now. Until the matter of yer purpose is clear, I'll keep ye bound to my hand."

Lozen realized the futility of resistance and relaxed her arm with grudging acceptance.

"Rasshole!" she spat.

Rylen glanced at the other guard and said, "Ye need to sharpen that tongue."

"Hey! It worked, didn't it? Did I not distract her?" The other guard retorted.

"I'll grant ye the point, lad." Rylen put some pressure on Lozen's hand and shoulder, urging her forward. "Now move it!"

"Pikk!" Lozen yelled as Rylen drove her though the gates.

Beyond the gates, the courtyard teemed with motion, a controlled chaos of steel and sweat. Warriors circled each other, wooden axes striking with sharp cracks that echoed off the stone walls. Each clash sent vibrations through the air, a rhythm of strength and precision. Nearby, the forge roared, its heat pressing against Lozen's skin as the blacksmith's hammer struck iron, each blow ringing like a battle cry. Sparks burst with every impact, flaring and dying in the midday sun. The tang of scorched metal and sweat mingled in the air, thick and tangible.

Lozen's sharp eyes tracked the flow of movement. Training, crafting, tending to duties—but not enough defensive vigilance. If someone wanted to strike Helsgaard, now would be the time.

A figure emerged from the shadows.

Her long legs carried her swiftly across the courtyard, black pants and tunic blending into the shade while her blonde hair, bound in a high ponytail, caught the light like spun gold. Her approach was deliberate and confident.

The moment Rylen saw her intercept course, he and Lozen slowed their pace. It was clear—her presence meant something.

"Ah, Bryn," he greeted her with disdain. "I knew ye'd come snuffling 'round. Couldn't keep away."

Bryn, looking over Lozen, responded with a snide remark. "A mouse doesn't skitr in this keep without me knowing how many turds it dropped. Looks like you found a little bird. What's your name, Little Bird?"

Lozen remained quiet, her jaw clenched, her lips pursed, and her eyes defiantly narrowed.

"Oh, the silent treatment?" she taunted, stepping closer to Lozen and bending over to match heights. Unfazed by her silence, she stepped up her verbal assault. "Well, Little Bird from Aeldoria, I presume you are from Aeldoria with the pointed ears? You'll have to find your voice and start tweeting messages of love and friendship real soon."

Lozen hesitated, breathed, and said, "I come seeking refuge. Someone in Ravnborg said I should come here."

Bryn straightened up, her demeanor shifting from playful menace to focused intensity. "Little Bird can tweet after all. Now we're getting somewhere. Let's see what else she tweets."

Lozen, growing impatient, responded with a defiant stare. She asked, "Why all this bullying? I got this pikk twisting my wrist and you're looming over me like I'm some thrall. What!? You don't know about manners?"

Bryn, unfazed by Lozen's outburst, leaned in closer. "Let me set you straight, Little Bird. We've been at war with the Aelfs for sixteen years—that would be most of your life, am I right? And here you come, strolling up to our doors, and you expect us to roll out the King's red carpet? For you?"

She stopped and looked into Lozen's eyes. "Not how it works, Little Bird. We'll take some time to get to know you first. If you don't like it, Rylen will show you the gate. So what's it going to be, Little Bird?"

Lozen glared at Bryn with defiance. "I'm from Aeldoria. I'm seeking refuge as I was exiled by the Council of Elders. I've been living on the streets of Skjaldarhöfn and Ravnborg ever since."

"An Aelf from Ravnborg interests me." Bryn straightened up and looked at Rylen with raised eyebrows. "She told you all that?"

"Just that she wanted the Keep's shelter, aye." He shrugged. "The rest of the matter is new."

"So Little Bird only tweets for me," she said, returning to Lozen. "Maybe she likes me."

Rylen shook his head, grinning. "Hmph. Just ye wait till the lass ken ye."

Bryn moved in close to him and spoke in a menacing tone. "Maybe I need to get to know you and your Aelfinn wife. Hmmm? Uncover some dark secrets, maybe? Watch your step."

The other Aelf is the guard's wife?

By this time, the warriors practicing in the courtyard stopped, their curiosity piqued by the arrival of the young Aelfinn girl and the ensuing exchange with Bryn. All eyes were focused, awaiting the unfolding events. Bryn's interactions were always entertaining, as long as it was someone else, and this one promised to be particularly spicy.

After tending to a minor injury, Anja, an Aelf with blue eyes, graying platinum blonde hair, dressed in a brown tunic without a cowl, rose and approached Lozen and Bryn. At five arm-spans distance, she paused, her eyes meeting Rylen's in a silent question.

With her patience dwindling, Bryn assumed a sharp, authoritative tone and asked, "Before I waste the Commandant's time, what exactly are you offering us? Look around you—everyone here contributes. No refugees waiting for a better life. You work, or you fight, or you sell, or you're gone. Which is it?"

Lozen confidently responded, "I'm a good archer!"

Bryn, unimpressed, pointed at Anja. "The healer is an archer! Give me more!"

Lozen's eyes snapped to follow the direction of Bryn's finger. She found the silver-haired woman instantly and their gazes locked for a brief, tense, measuring moment. Undeterred, she met Bryn's challenge with determination. "I can learn anything, she said. I learned the Common Tongue while on the streets. I learned skills to survive. Just give me a chance!"

Bryn paused. "Begging is good. It shows humility. I don't need a translator, so learning a language doesn't mean anything." Bryn glanced at the growing crowd of onlookers interested in the exchange. "We've got eyes on us. Come."

Rylen applied firm pressure on Lozen's arm and shoulder, guiding her to follow Bryn.

Pained by the coercion, she scolded, "Owww. You don't have to do that!"

The path across the grounds felt endless, and Lozen's frustration rose with each step. She matched Bryn's pace, refusing to be rushed, and held her chin high despite Rylen's agonizing grip on her wrist and shoulder.

The crowd's murmurs grew louder as they approached the towering stone structure housing the Commandant's office. After they entered the building, Bryn paused and faced

Lozen, "Remember, you have one chance to impress the Commandant. Choose your words wisely."

Lozen met her gaze unflinchingly, defiance in her eyes and unwavering voice. "Now, you want to help me?"

Bryn nodded. "Maybe I see something in you. Maybe I know something you don't. Maybe I know a lot you don't and you should make a good first impression. Maybe—turn down the fire a bit."

She turned and walked down the hallway to the Commandant's door, with Lozen and Rylen trailing behind. The heavy wooden door, adorned with intricate carvings that depicted scenes of battles and victories, bore witness to the proud history of the warriors who had lived within its walls.

Bryn raised her hand to knock. "It's showtime."

CHAPTER 3

COMMANDANT'S OFFICE

BARK LIKE A DOG

R YLEN, LOZEN, AND BRYN stood at a formidable door, its surface reinforced with iron bands. Bryn delivered three precise knocks before pushing the door open. As they crossed the threshold, Rylen released Lozen's hand, slid his left hand to the back of her neck, and squeezed to remind her to behave as he guided her into the room.

Rohand hurried down the hallway, his long black hair tied back in a low ponytail. At twenty, he was lean and sharp-eyed, his storm-gray eyes steady above a short-cropped black beard. Like Rylen, he wore brown leather armor over a tan tunic and matching pants. Slipping through the door, he shut it behind him.

Inside, Commandant Günther sat at his desk, his battle-worn face unreadable as his gaze shifted to the unexpected visitors.

"Rohand, good," Bryn greeted him. "You might want to hear this. Rylen, thank you for your escort. You can go, but please send the Mission Commander here on your way back to the gate."

"Aye," he acknowledged, releasing Lozen and hastening down the hallway, closing the door as he left.

With Rylen gone, Rohand, Bryn, and Lozen stood in the Commandant's office. Rohand, mindful of security, moved close to Lozen, ready to take control of her if necessary. Rising from his seat, Commandant Günther greeted Bryn with curiosity and resignation.

Günther wore blue pants and an orange silk tunic, highlighting his elite status, and spoke as eloquently. "Bryn? You knocked? That's different. What do you have for us?"

Bryn focused on Lozen, and she prodded the young Aelf forward with a sharp poke in the shoulders. Bryn and Rohand followed, watching the newcomer closely.

Bryn said, "This Little Bird comes all the way from Aeldoria. Says she seeks refuge. Along the way, she claims to have lived on the streets of Ravnborg."

Looking disgusted, she leaned in close to Lozen, wrinkling her nose as she sniffed. "By her smell, she probably hasn't had a bath in a moon or more."

Günther smiled slightly at the graphic display of body odor. He asked, "Well, does she have a name?"

Bryn looked at Lozen, poking her in the chest. "That's your cue to speak."

"I am Lozen from Elowen in Aeldoria." Lozen said abruptly.

"Great!" Günther said. "I suggest we all take a moment to sit down and get to know our guest."

The assembled group moved to the table with four chairs tucked underneath. They settled into their seats, their postures reflecting curiosity, apprehension, and guarded anticipation.

Looking at Lozen, Günther began the introductions with a warm and welcoming voice. "I'm Helsgaard Keep's Commandant Günther. You met Bryn. And over here is Rohand, our lead melee combat trainer."

Lozen glanced at the three individuals, maintaining a polite appearance to hide her inner turmoil. She nodded after each introduction, her silence revealing the uncertainty gnawing at her heart.

"Would you kindly begin from the top?" Günther suggested. "I understand you are from Aeldoria and have made your way here. I would appreciate it if you could share more about your journey."

Lozen closed her eyes to steady her nerves. "I was born in Aeldoria and grew up in a cottage outside the small village of Elowen. Orcs killed my real parents in a raid, and Elder Faelar facilitated my adoption by my new parents when I was a baby."

"Orcs? I didn't know they were seafaring." Bryn commented.

Lozen looked at her questioningly.

Bryn motions for Lozen to continue.

"Ah, so you know some of the Council Elders?" said Günther, steering the conversation.

A shadow of pain that flitted across Lozen's features. "Until I was thirteen."

Sensing the shift in her demeanor, Günther held up a hand, signaling for her to pause.

Three sharp knocks resounded through the chamber. The door swung open, revealing Mission Commander Hrolf. A man of fifty years, his once fiery red hair was now fading to gray, matching his longer-than-average beard. He wore a dark blue silk tunic, a mark of his rank, though it lacked the undeniable panache of Günther's attire. He walked inside and closed the door behind him, his presence adding a new layer of authority to the gathering.

Bryn, used to standing in the shadows and apart from others, rose from her chair and gestured for Hrolf to take her place. "Mission Commander, please."

He accepted the offered seat. "The Helsgaard spy is giving me her chair? To what do I owe the honor?"

With a growing smirk, she retaliated with a playful jab. "Age before beauty."

Hrolf chuckled as he settled into the chair.

Eager to resume their discussion, Günther turned his attention back to their guest. "You were telling us about a the Council Elders when you were thirteen..."

Pain and anger contorted Lozen's face. Her eyes were now cast downward, hidden from view. Her arms crossed her chest as if trying to protect herself from the onslaught of memories that threatened to overwhelm her. With a deep sigh, she closed her eyes, her body tensing as if preparing for a battle. She took a steadying breath to prepare for the arduous task ahead. Her voice trembled as she began to speak, yet she remained determined to tell her story, to release the burden that long oppressed her heart.

"When I was thirteen," she whispered. "We were outside playing—"

⚠⚠⚠

Young Lozen, a thirteen-year-old girl with red hair, had struggled to keep up with her Aelfinn companions as they had darted through the trees of Elowen Forest, their movements like a graceful dance. Their tall, lithe forms, resembling fleeting shadows, had starkly contrasted her shorter, robust build. Amidst the verdant tapestry of emerald foliage, her fiery red hair stood out like a radiant beacon, signifying her distinctiveness within her social circle.

"Look at the Dwarf trying to keep up!" Gildor sneered, his green eyes dancing with cruel amusement. The wiry boy, draped in a finely woven emerald tunic with silver-threaded cuffs, pointed and giggled, the sound light and mocking—like birds chirping before a storm. His platinum hair, always a little unkempt, caught the sunlight as he leaned forward, reveling in the laughter of the other Aelfinn children.

The other children joined in, and their laughter rang like wind chimes in the breeze.

Lyriel, a girl with a sharp tongue, mocked, "Maybe she'll trip and roll all the way to some filthy Human village!"

"She's half-Dwarf and half-Aelf, making her a Dwaelf!" Gildor's laughter grew louder.

Lozen clenched her fists at her sides. Her anger boiled like molten lava. The taunts burned like a brand. Rage consumed her. She lashed out. Impact!

With a swift, unexpected movement, her finger knuckles connected with Gildor's breastbone in a failed throat punch. The force of the blow, though lessened by his sternum, reverberated through his body and caused him to stumble backward, clutching his throat.

"Don't call me that!" Lozen screamed.

Gildor gasped for air and sputtered a curse. "Dwaelf bitch!!! What's wrong with you?"

Elder Faelar arrived and interrupted their argument. Her normally calm face showed disapproval. Her dress and cloak marked her as politically important, demanding respect. Her speech was equally demanding. "That's enough. There's no place for that language here. Leave the girl alone."

The children scattered like leaves in a gust of wind. Their laughter faded into the rustling of the trees. Faelar bent over beside Lozen, her ancient blue eyes sad with regret.

"Lozen," she began. "I have a hard message for you, and I need you to listen."

She looked at Faelar with apprehension. "I'm not a Dwaelf. Gildor deserved that punch."

"I'm not saying he didn't. He needs to learn to control himself so that punch may teach him something. But I'm not here to discuss Gildor."

Her heart sank with growing dread. What was the Elder about to say?

"You do not belong here, Lozen," Faelar declared. "You are not one of us. This much is obvious, yes?"

Nausea rolled through Lozen's stomach and nose. She felt as if the forest floor had shifted beneath her feet, and her once familiar surroundings were now alien and hostile.

"Wh-what do you mean 'do not belong?'" she stammered.

Faelar hardened. "You don't fit in. It's time for you to go."

Lozen stared in disbelief. "Go? Where? Where will I go?" She cried, tears welling up.

The Elder sighed. "It's not about what you've done," she explained. "You have met every requirement and have excelled with every training exercise—"

"But why? But—why? This is the only family I have. What did I do?"

Faelar looked Lozen in the eyes, her expression stoic. "Lozen, it's about who you are. You're not like the rest of us. We took you in, cared for you, and raised you, but you are not like us. Your physical attributes—your ears, your stature, your size—all indicate you are something else—and they are becoming more pronounced as you mature."

"But what about my parents?" Lozen pleaded with anguish. "Did they agree to this?"

Faelar's face remained impassive, and she chose her words carefully to help divorce Lozen from her parents. "The decision has been made. Your guardians, who are not your parents, have been informed they are no longer responsible for your care. They knew this day would come. I had hoped this would not be the case."

Lozen's legs buckled beneath her, her sobs crying out through the silent forest. Pain racked her voice. "It's not fair. I tried. I did what you asked. Why can't you accept me?"

Faelar reached out and placed a soft hand on Lozen's shoulder. "You must find your own path, Lozen. Your own path, not with us. Perhaps with the Humans. Their warriors need someone like you. Maybe even Helsgaard Keep—I've heard they'll take anyone. Now go home. Your things are already packed."

Faelar turned and walked away. Left alone, Lozen began her walk home.

Upon arriving at her former home, the modest cottage nestled in a sun-dappled clearing, Lozen felt a quiet solitude. The gentle rustling of leaves accompanied her as she approached the front door, her thirteen-year-old face etched with confusion and hurt.

Her worn backpack, trusty bow, and overflowing quiver stood by the door alongside a large stash of neatly arranged food. Together, they signaled the grim finality of the situation.

"Why?" Lozen's voice, a whisper, trembled with the raw pain of abandonment, "I didn't do anything!"

Only the chirping of birds and the wind in the trees answered her desperate question. Tears welled in her eyes, blurring her vision as she knelt to gather her belongings.

Young Lozen slung the backpack over her shoulder. The weight of the bow and quiver felt familiar. She took one last look at her lifelong cottage home, turned, and disappeared into the woods, determination burning in her tear-filled eyes.

⚠⚠⚠

The tragedy of Lozen's tale permeated the stillness in the room. The revelation of her abandonment, leaving her exiled and homeless, with the added intrigue of a hidden identity stunned everyone in the Commandant's office. Rohand, face flushed with shock, broke the silence. "Víd hamri Thors—by Thor's hammer— the very people who are supposed to protect you tossed you out like a piss pot!"

Hrolf nodded, sharing Rohand's outrage, and he addressed the outburst. "Thank you, Rohand, for the colorful language in front of our guest. Remind me why you are here?"

"Evaluating the new recruit for training, sir!"

"Very well. Try evaluating with more understanding and less judgment of those you don't know." He motioned for Bryn to continue the conversation.

"She's not a recruit yet. She hasn't told us what she has to offer." Bryn's voice remained calm and analytical. "All I've seen so far is a troubled girl with a heartbreaking story who shows up here. Why? What brought you here?"

Lozen took a deep breath to steady her nerves and looked at Bryn with resolve. "There was a merchant who had a map," she explained. "She let me copy it and showed me how to get here, suggested I come here to get off the streets before the guards caught me. I was developing a reputation."

Bryn smiled and finished Lozen's sentence, "Because the Shadow Archer was robbing the rich, feeding the poor, and stirring up the people into rebellion." Bryn looked at Gunther. "The bards were singing her tales."

Her words hung in the air, the implication clear. Lozen's expression betrayed her surprise, curiosity, and apprehension. Sensing the unspoken connection between the two women, Hrolf turned to Bryn, puzzled. "Am I missing something?"

Bryn continued. "Not at all. It's just an amazing coincidence that an archer shows up in Ravnborg, upsetting the merchants who are losing inventory and distressing the poor because her charity highlighted their plight. Tensions bordered on rebellion, and King Valdissen had to nip that in the bud before it got out of control. So he put a bounty on our girl."

Bryn stared at Lozen, boring into her Aelfinn inner being. Lozen stared back, reeling on the verge of a panic attack, wondering how she knew these details.

Günther interrupted the stare-down and leaned toward Bryn. "So now I'm hearing we have a RIOS-bountied fugitive in the room? I know everyone here is running from something, but RIOS? I don't want any RIOS entanglements. Bryn?"

"As you suspect, RIOS has taken care of the situation. The bounty was paid. She's bounty-free, gone from Ravnborg and the King is happy. Well, happier."

Günther smiled and leaned back. "Please, continue."

"She seems to know everything," Lozen snipped. "Being RIOS and all. Let her tell."

Bryn glared at Lozen's outburst. "I have the raven's eye view. Tell us what's happening on the ground."

Lozen sighed. "I got caught by a guard one night. He dragged me to this talking crystal ball called RIOS. He got paid his bounty. He let me go and I took the hint and disappeared."

She kept her attention on Bryn. The unspoken question amplified the tension in the room. Feeling their stares, Lozen explained. "I'm not saying I am the Shadow Archer, but getting caught at night in a black cloak with a bow was pretty damning. So I took the deal and got out."

The intensity in the room remained as everyone focused on Lozen.

Bryn commented, "The deal was she comes to Helsgaard Keep or have a lifelong stay in the dungeon—however short that may be."

Lozen took a couple breaths before continuing, "Not wanting to be branded an Skaldvárr—oathbreaker—and have a blood eagle carved in my back or my ears swinging on someone's necklace, I left. A half-moon later, slogging through swamps and dodging bounty hunters, here I am."

"There shouldn't have been any bounty hunters—RIOS paid your bounty."

"Don't know what to tell you," Lozen glared at Bryn. "And this is not quite the welcome I had expected with your goon twisting my arm and you in my face, poking me. Lemme guess—you're my contact? If so, you suck at introductions."

Bryn's demeanor shifted, becoming more businesslike. "Here's how it works. You give us a skill we need, and we let you stay. No skill and the Little Bird is out of the nest flying somewhere else. What I've got is maybe you can shoot a bow. And you might have some healing ability—not sure how much you learned by thirteen. So far, I am not impressed, and you're halfway back to the gate right now. I'm sure Rylen would love to hold hands with you again."

Günther and Hrolf glanced at each other, silently amused that Bryn took command of the meeting and dominated Lozen.

Lozen grimaced at the thought of Rylen's strong arm and looked down at the table, defeat settling in.

Bryn, noticing her reaction, pressed on. "How old are you?"

Lozen stared at her. "Sixteen."

Bryn felt a sense of relief. "Sixteen? The streets have been rough on you, Little Bird. At sixteen, you're still trainable—maybe—almost too old. I'll give you a chance. Are you ready to hang with the big dogs?"

Lozen, confused by the idiom, furrowed her brow. "Sorry, my Common Tongue may not be so good—you want me to hang a dog?"

"Are you ready to run with the big dogs?"

Lozen pondered the question, realization setting in with a mischievous grin spreading across her face. "Woof!" she exclaimed, sparking a playful challenge.

Bryn, mirroring her enthusiasm, barked back. "Woof!"

The room erupted in laughter as everyone joined in with a "woof," dispelling the tension. She assessed Lozen. "So you're an Aelf," she said, stepping forward and examining the newcomer. "But what else? Maybe Dwarf? Red hair, stocky build, smaller ears? I'm betting on it. That will make you a good melee warrior. Maybe even kick Rohand's rass."

Rohand stared at Bryn with a challenging look, mouthing the words, "Bring it."

Bryn asked, "Where did xenophobic Aeldoria find a Dwarf to mate with an Aelf seventeen years ago, right before this war started? It's an enigma, to be sure."

She turned to Günther and Hrolf. "All right, she amuses me. Let's see if she can actually shoot that bow."

Günther and Hrolf nodded in agreement, their curiosity piqued.

Hrolf ordered Rohand to go with them. "Rohand. Based on Bryn's assessment, you will take Shadow Archer to the gate or bring her back to me. You are dismissed."

Bryn headed for the door, Lozen following, with Rohand trailing just behind, his eyes never leaving her. Behind them, Günther and Hrolf remained, silently weighing the fate of the young Aelf who had unexpectedly become part of their world.

CHAPTER 4

THE TEST

THRICE IS SKILL

ROHAND AND LOZEN, FOLLOWING Bryn, navigated the bustling courtyard of Helsgaard Keep. The air reverberated with the sounds of combat training—the clack of mock axes, the grunts of exertion, and the rhythmic hammering from the blacksmith's forge. The atmosphere crackled with an intensity that spoke to the ever-present threat of war and the constant need for vigilance. The pine trees out past the field blew gently in the westerly winds from the Helsgaard Frontier valley.

The trio entered the training yard, a wide stretch of hard-packed earth bordered by rows of sturdy wooden poles, each standing about an arm-span tall. Faces were painted on them, with lines marking where legs would be, and some bore shields strapped to their sides.

Bryn, watching Lozen, gestured towards the targets with a challenging smirk. "This is where you'll prove your worth, Little Bird. Show me what you've got."

Lozen reached back and unshouldered her bow, a simple yet well-crafted weapon fashioned from polished yew wood. It lacked the ornate decorations and intricate carvings that adorned the bows of Aelfinn archers. Still, its unassuming appearance belied its deadly effectiveness.

Bryn's eyebrows arched in surprise, and she examined the bow. "Yew wood? Nice!"

Lozen strung the bow with confidence, her movements fluid and practiced. "It may not look like much, but it gets the job done."

Bryn, amused by the young Aelf's self-assuredness, nodded her approval. "Very well. Let's see if your aim is as sharp as your tongue."

She pointed at the furthest target, a small wooden figure ten arm-spans away. "Hit that."

Lozen hesitated momentarily, eager to demonstrate her prowess yet hoping for a brief respite before being thrust into the spotlight. "Any chance of a warm-up first?"

Bryn firmly shook her head. "You won't have a warmup in battle! Go!"

Lozen nocked an arrow and controlled her breathing, her muscles taut as she pulled back the bowstring. She narrowed her eyes with unwavering focus, aligning her sights on the distant target. The arrow, released in a fluid motion, soared through the air in a graceful arc, finding its mark. A hush fell over the crowd, broken only by the satisfying thud of the arrow embedding itself in the wooden figure's chest—a perfect bullseye. Astonishment replaced Bryn's initial skepticism.

She applauded slowly, although still hesitant to acknowledge Lozen's skill. "Impressive, very impressive. I call it luck. Do it again."

Rohand nodded in silent agreement as he studied the young archer.

"You want me to do better than a bullseye?"

Bryn's lips curled into a sly grin, daring Lozen to prove herself again. "Shoot the next target. The one in the back."

Pissy at being asked to repeat a perfect shot, she nocked another arrow, took a couple breaths, and drew back the bowstring. With a smooth and effortless release, the second arrow pierced the air, finding its mark with unerring accuracy in the middle of the target's head. Her pride was evident as she smiled at Bryn.

Rohand, witnessing the display of skill, stared in disbelief, his initial doubts about her fading.

"Again," Bryn demanded.

"I hit the furthest target."

"Maybe you aimed too high and that's why you hit the head. Do it again!"

Accepting the challenge, Lozen nocked a third arrow and aimed carefully at the distant target. This time, she placed her shot just over the shield, embedding it deep within the target's chest.

"I told you I'm not just any archer."

"Indeed, you are not."

Lozen, curious about the purpose of the exercise, asked, "But why did the test consist of three arrows?"

"If you hit the target once, it's luck. Twice is coincidence. Thrice is skill. Get it?"

"Got it."

Bryn walked towards Lozen, hands outstretched in a welcome gesture. "First test is complete. Now the second." Looking at Rohand, Bryn said, "Push her hard. We need to know what she's truly capable of."

Rohand raised his eyebrows at Bryn as she backed up, then shifted to stare at Lozen with a predatory intensity and offered a curt greeting. "Little Bird."

Lozen stared back.

Why does everyone call me Little Bird?

She stood isolated in Rohand's presence, aware of his intense scrutiny. Bryn observed from a distance.

He rushed her with a fierce tackle, followed by a swift and unexpected thumb-punch to the ribs. "You're dead. I just knifed you in the ribs."

Their fierce duel at the training ground differed from the typical practice sessions. The other warriors couldn't help but stop what they were doing and gather around to enjoy the surprising clash. They were all curious about the new trainee.

Caught off guard by Rohand's sudden charge, she muttered in his face, "Pikk move. You like hitting girls?"

"There's no gender here," he said. "You're a warrior. Get up and act like one."

He stood up and extended a hand to help her. Though still wary of her attacker, she accepted his arm and rose to her feet.

"Now fight me," Rohand commanded, letting her go with an arrogant and dramatic flip of his hand and wasting no time resuming their sparring session. He rushed towards her with renewed vigor. With a graceful sidestep, she evaded his charge, spun, and delivered a swift kick to his rass.

The unexpected move sent a ripple of laughter through the assembled warriors. Stunned by the blow and the ensuing mockery, he stumbled forward. Lozen, with a mischievous smirk, stood a couple arm-spans away, looking amused and defiant.

"Oh, Little Bird..." Rohand growled, his pride wounded by the humiliating display.

Determined to regain the upper hand, he lunged at her once more. But Lozen's agility and quick reflexes, honed by life on the streets, were more than a match for her larger opponent. She ducked under his outstretched arm with the grace of a seasoned dancer, her movements fluid and precise. Circling him warily, she scanned for an opening, constantly watching his hands and feet.

Mocking her with a sneer, he jeered, "Is that all you've got, Little Bird? You dance well enough, street rat, but all I see is a stray trying to dodge the boot." His words were sharp and calculated, meant to undermine her confidence and divert her focus.

Lozen's smirk widened. She faked to the left, drawing Rohand's attention, and pivoted to the right, delivering a swift kick behind his calf and dropping him to the ground. Hopping out of the way as he fell toward her, she taunted, "I'm just getting started."

Rohand got back up, glaring at Lozen. His respect for her begrudgingly grew.

The crowd roared approvingly, their laughter and cheers resounding through the training yard. Even Bryn, observing the sparring session with a critical eye, couldn't help but smile at the street rat's audacity and skill.

Rohand's pride burned from her earlier victories. With a growl, he lunged again, determined to put her in her place. But this time, Lozen didn't dodge—she met him head-on.

Their clash was a storm of speed and strength. Rohand swung, but Lozen was already inside his reach, deflecting his strike and slamming her fist into his guts. He staggered but recovered fast, launching a brutal counterattack. She ducked under his wild punch, driving an elbow into his chest before spinning away.

She was smaller, but that was his mistake—underestimating her. Dwarfinn blood coursed through her veins, and every hit she landed felt like a smith's hammer striking iron. Rohand's eyes flickered with surprise when she caught his wrist mid-swing and twisted hard, nearly wrenching his shoulder from its socket. He barely tore free before she could lock the joint.

The fight became a blur of movement. Rohand relied on raw power, but Lozen was relentless. Her Aelfinn grace made her a shadow, slipping past his defenses, striking with precision, and vanishing before he could retaliate. She wove around him like smoke, forcing him to swing at air. Each time he missed, her counters landed harder—fist to ribs, knee to thigh, a ruthless barrage that sapped his strength.

He gasped for breath, sweat dripping from his brow. His muscles screamed, his lungs burned—he wasn't used to fights dragging out this long. Lozen, however, barely looked winded. She stood ready, eyes locked on him like a predator waiting for its prey to falter.

He took a shaky step back, chest heaving, frustration twisting his face. For the first time, doubt crept into his eyes.

"Enough," he panted, his voice drowned in the din of the cheering crowd.

He looked at Lozen with respect, his initial skepticism replaced by admiration. "You're not half bad for a Little Bird. I think we're going to craft a special training plan for you."

She bowed her head in acknowledgement of his praise. However, her confidence, bolstered by her impressive performance, gave way to a surge of aggression and a desire for revenge.

"You mean a plan where you always have the upper hand? From where I stand, the Big Dog is looking pretty ragged. Maybe the Big Dog needs training?"

"One that will divert your energy to fighting and not quipping, Little Bird."

"How about you agree I am good enough?" Lozen said.

"You're the type that always has conditions, aren't you? How about you're just a curiosity, not a combatant? You fight better than I expected for a half-Aelf street stray, but your worth isn't decided by you or your dancing tricks. Now shut up and let the adults decide your schedule."

Vengeance for being marginalized overwhelmed her. Emotions boiled and seethed. She rushed him. Hit low. They fell to the ground.

Rolling off him, she hammered him in the groin and bounced into a standing position. "Were that my knife, you would squat to piss for the rest of your worthless life."

The warriors cheered and laughed, recalling how Rohand had struck most of them. Now, sprawled in the dirt holding his crotch, he glared at her in stunned disbelief. Annoyed by her unexpected attack, he couldn't help but admire her audacity.

Bryn walked up to Lozen, who, still high on adrenaline and ready for the next attack, braced for the next enemy.

"Relax. I've been watching you for some time. I'm the real reason you're here, and it wasn't some merchant and a map."

Rohand, nursing his nethers, got up, looking at Bryn with confusion and curiosity.

Bryn continued with cold assertion. "Thank you for responding to my invitation. Welcome to Helsgaard Keep, Shadow Archer."

Though grateful for the acceptance, she hesitated to use her former moniker. "Thank you. It was an offer I couldn't refuse.

But I'm not Shadow Archer anymore. This is a new path. New path, new name."

"Very well. Welcome to Helsgaard Keep."

Rohand stepped forward, a faint crease formed between his brows before he quickly smoothed it away, masking his recognition of the swamp smell and stale sweat that still clung to her. "Welcome to Helsgaard. Let's get you a bath. First thing, though—back to Hrolf's office for House assignment."

"No. Günther's office," Bryn interrupted, her voice cutting through his assumption.

Rohand looked quizzical.

"Her success was predestined. Elara, Hrolf, and Torsten are waiting for us in Günther's office."

"Then why the test," Rohand asked.

"I wanted to see a little bird kick your rass."

Rohand smiled and flipped a Blótstafn at Bryn.

As they walked back, Lozen asked, "What is RIOS?"

"Royal Intelligence Operative Service. It's a spy organization that supports the King in his ambitions to control all of Nordlund through strategic intelligence and pacification."

"That's it?"

"That's it. What makes us special is—" Bryn looked back and saw Rohand was within earshot. "Rohand, go ahead. I need to brief our Little Bird alone."

Rohand glared at Bryn for being excluded as he passed by her, but he recognized her autonomy and authority as the King's Agent, and continued back to Günther's office.

"It took you fourteen days to walk here. It takes a Griffin less than half a day. I can talk to RIOS in Ravnborg like we're in the same room. Sometimes I help Günther with faster communications, sometimes not."

"So you spied on me from here?"

"Not quite. Ravnborg saw what you were doing and asked the remote stations, like me, if we wanted to take on a project. Or should we stand aside and let royal justice take its course. Your destination was the dungeon, because, you were going to get caught."

"So I'm your project?" Lozen said.

"Yeah, and these are your first of many RIOS secrets. Keep them to yourself."

CHAPTER 5

FOUR HOUSES

EVERYONE GETS A FEATHER MATTRESS

INSIDE GÜNTHER'S OFFICE, GÜNTHER, Elara, Hrolf, and Torsten were seated. Bryn opened the door and walked in without knocking. Rohand, Bryn, and Lozen entered. Rohand stood behind Hrolf. Bryn walked around and stood behind Günther, leaving Lozen alone. Bryn leaned over and whispered in Günther's ear.

Günther nodded and said, "As Commandant, I want to welcome you to Helsgaard Keep."

Everyone at the table smiled and welcomed her.

Günther explained, "Helsgaard is different. We don't have kin here; everyone chose to be here. So we organize people into Houses based on skills: Elara heads the Merchants, Torsten the Trade House, Hrolf the Warrior House. I take Höfn House, which is a haven for everybody else."

"Got it," she nodded.

Hrolf added, "We rely on Ravnborg for food now, but homesteading in the valley is making us self-sufficient."

Günther continued, "We debated where to put you. You were stealing from merchants, so Elara's House was an option. You're clearly a warrior, so Hrolf's House was an option. But in the end, we decided you belong with the warriors, and Bryn confirmed that for me."

"Welcome to the Warrior House," Hrolf said as he stood up. "In ten years, you will be known as Lozen of Helsgaard. Now you have a House. Rohand, show her the bath and get her a blanket and fur from the equipment room. New boots, too, if she needs them."

Lozen said, "Thank you, sir. I won't disappoint you."

Relief washed over her. She had passed the test, but the journey ahead promised greater challenges and more profound mysteries. Hrolf's words lingered in her mind, the name "Lozen of Helsgaard" carrying both expectation and possibility. As she followed Rohand, the clamor of the courtyard fading behind her, she felt the first stirrings of acceptance and belonging.

⚠⚠⚠

The smoky warmth of the longhouse enveloped Lozen as she stepped inside, clutching her backpack. The hearth fire crackled in the center, its light flickering against the polished surfaces of the long-used shields and weapons that adorned the walls. Along the walls were wooden platforms with fine wool feather-filled blankets and furs sitting atop feather-filled mattresses. The air carried the mingled scents of woodsmoke, roasting meat for the evening meal, and the faint tang of lye.

Feather mattresses and blankets? If the Ravnborg Karls—commoners—knew about this luxury, there would definitely be a revolution, she thought. *Or there would be more recruits than they could handle.*

They walked to the far end of the longhouse, where Rohand gestured to a narrow sleeping space near the edge. "That's yours—the bed furthest from the central fire because you're the newest. As you rise in the House, you'll get more choices in where you want to sleep. For now, put your pack there and take out anything you need to launder."

She nodded and removed a tunic, pants, and a high-necked wool shirt before dropping her pack onto the platform. "Beats the streets of Ravnborg," she said.

"Follow me."

He grabbed a mug filled with lye soap on the way out and led her to the back of the Keep, where the mountain loomed close. There, a pool of water, with mist and steam rising from its surface, came into view—a natural hot spring channeled into the Keep. Nearby, wooden racks for drying clothes leaned to one side, and a stack of rough-spun towels rested on a bench.

"Here's the bathing pool. You just missed our normal bath day."

"Is there... somewhere private I could—" she began hesitantly, her voice barely audible.

Rohand chuckled, shaking his head. "What is this 'private'? Private is for rich people, the Jarls. This is how it's done in Ravnsríki," he said, his tone kind but matter-of-fact. "Take off your clothes, get in, wash up, make sure you get the crevices, and I'll ensure no one bothers you. If you want anything, let me know."

She shifted uncomfortably, gripping her spare clothes tighter. The thought of shedding her layers in front of strangers was foreign—a stark reminder of how different her upbringing in Aeldoria had been. There, privacy was a given, even for the lowliest wanderer.

"Look," Rohand added, softening his tone as he noticed her discomfort. "You're among kin here. Nobody's staring at you. It's just another chore—like mending a tunic or sharpening a blade."

Lozen glanced around. By the longhouse door, an older man with a weathered face hummed an old tune as he stacked freshly chopped firewood. A woman seated on a stool repaired a blue wool dress, her hands deft and practiced. None of them so much as glanced in Lozen's direction.

"Once you're in, figure out which clothes need washing the most," Rohand said. "You can soak and scrub them while you bathe. Then you can join the regular bath-day routine."

Taking a deep breath, Lozen set her loose clothes down. She slipped off her boots, surprised at the warmth of the black stone surrounding the hot spring. Realizing it might take some time, Rohand sat down on a boulder near the edge, keeping his back to her and facing the Keep's courtyard. Slowly, she peeled away her layers, her cheeks burning despite the late winter chill. Finally, she stepped into the pool, sinking into the warm water that seemed to embrace her like a second skin.

Rohand set a mug of soap on the pool's ledge, within easy reach. His smile was reassuring but casual, offering neither pressure nor pity. "See? Not so bad," he said before turning away. "I'll grab you a towel."

She exhaled slowly, relaxing backward as the tension eased from her shoulders. The sharp yet cleansing scent of lye soap filled the air as she worked it through her hair, unraveling her braids with deliberate care. To her surprise, this unfamiliar, communal way of life was beginning to feel almost... tolerable. Maybe even comforting.

He returned and set the towel on the rocks next to her. "I have to get you a blanket and fur for your bed. You can let your clothes dry here or bring them to the longhouse—it's warmer there. When you're done, I'll be in the training yard."

"Thank you," she said.

As the warm water soothed her and the sharp scent of lye lingered in the air, Lozen found herself watching the quiet rhythm of the Keep around her. The clatter of a spoon against a pot, the murmur of voices discussing the day's work, the rhythmic scrape of metal against a whetstone, the milling of wheat—it was all so ordinary, so unguarded.

△△△

The Warrior longhouse was alive with the warm glow of the central fire, its flickering light casting shadows on the polished shields and weapons adorning the walls. The scent of roasted meat and simmering herbs wafted through the air as Lozen stood at the far end, her heart pounding in her chest. Her bow and backpack were safely stowed beneath her bed, leaving her hands free but restless. Her fingers brushed the fabric of her tunic as she tried to ground her feelings.

Hrolf, the HouseFather, stepped forward, his broad shoulders illuminated by the firelight. His deep and commanding voice carried easily over the quiet murmurs. "Tonight, we welcome a new member into the Warrior House. Lozen, a skilled archer and brave spirit, now stands among us. Let her be known, not as an outsider, but as kin." He gestured toward her, his steady gaze offering both authority and reassurance.

The warriors rose from their benches one by one. The first to step forward was Bjorn, a burly man with piercing gray eyes and a jagged scar cutting across his brow. He moved slower than the others, his gaze cool as he regarded Lozen. When he finally extended his hand, his grip was firm but brief, a mere formality. "Bjorn," he said flatly before stepping away without further acknowledgement.

Next came Hans, a young and eager Junior Warrior of fourteen, his Nordic blonde hair falling just past his shoulders. His blue eyes shone with excitement, and his grip was surprisingly firm for someone still growing into his strength. "H-h-hans," he introduced himself, grinning. "I'll try to k-k-keep up." His enthusiasm was contagious, though his attempt at confidence wavered a little under the influence of tradition.

A tall, broad-shouldered man followed, his blonde hair neatly tied back. His light-blue eyes, calm and assessing, met hers with quiet approval. "Petr," he said in a measured tone. "Welcome, sister. Strength is earned here—you've already proven you have it." His grip was solid, his acceptance sincere.

Next was Siv, a musclebound shield-maiden that looked like she could crush the skull of a Fjord bear between her thighs, followed by Freydis, a sharp-eyed woman whose intricate leather armor was laced with small, sharp bone fetishes, her gaze carrying the cold, measuring intelligence of a hunter who waits by the water's edge.

One by one, the warriors stepped forward, each clasping her arm in recognition before moving to ladle a bowl of stew from the great iron pot near the hearth. At the end of the line, Olaf hesitated. His expression was unreadable, but when he finally stepped forward, his armclasp was brief, his grip impersonal. He nodded, almost imperceptibly, before moving past her without a word.

Though there were thirty, the ritual felt intimate, each greeting carried acceptance, except for Bjorn and Olaf.

When the last warrior had taken their seat, Lozen followed suit, ladling a portion of the rich, steaming stew into her own bowl. She carried it carefully to her place near the end of the longhouse, settling onto the bench as the quiet murmur of anticipation filled the room.

Hrolf stood by the fire, raising his hands in solemnity. The flames danced behind him, their glow casting his face in sharp relief.

"Odin Allfather," he intoned, his deep voice resonating through the longhouse, silencing the room. "Watch over this house, its warriors, and the battles to come. Grant us strength, courage, and wisdom as we stand together. Skål."

"Skål," the Warriors echoed, their cups and cheers rising like a wave down the table.

As the first spoonfuls of stew were lifted, the murmur of voices filled the longhouse once more. Lozen sat with them, her bowl warm in her hands, the knot of tension in her chest slowly loosening. For the first time in years, she felt more than just tolerated but indeed seen and accepted. Among these warriors, her new kin, she was no longer a wanderer. Maybe this was home.

Yet, it felt extraordinary to her. For the first time in as long as she could remember, she wasn't passing through or surviving on the outskirts of society. She was here, part of this bustling, imperfect whole. The strangeness of their customs still made her cheeks flush, but beneath the surface, a tentative sense of belonging began to take root, warming her as much as the firelight and the bath.

CHAPTER 6

PARENT'S HOPE

THE MENTOR'S GUISE

A<small>N OIL LAMP, SMALL</small> and defiant, flickered in the infirmary of Helsgaard Keep. Its light danced, dragging sharp, shifting shadows across the rough-hewn stone walls. Brightly colored tapestries, perhaps looted from a distant time, offered a fragile warmth and muffled the room's natural, cold echo. Seated upon a thin straw mattress, Anja worked, her movements precise and automatic. She was sharpening her arrows, the steel whispering against the stone. Her face, though once delicate, was now a map of hardship, reflecting a life of quiet resilience and an unwavering commitment to the task at hand.

Rylen opened the door, a rush of outside cold preceding him, and stepped into the room. His expression was heavy with the visible weight of weariness. He lowered himself beside Anja, his hand settling gently on her shoulder—a silent comfort. "You didn't return to the longhouse. You are missing the night meal," he said, his voice soft but edged with an undeniable question.

Anja's features were shadowed, a profound apprehension tightening her jaw.

"Ye saw the lass," Rylen stated after a pause, his tone dropping to a certainty that needed no confirmation. "Bryn pointed ye out. True enough."

Anja nodded once, her attention locked fiercely on the arrow in her hand. She attempted to suppress the sudden flood of emotion, and failed. "I did. Do you believe it's her? You were there. You escorted her."

"Maybe so. Look here." He began to enumerate the compelling reasons, ticking them off against the tips of his thick fingers. "She's the right age, aye. She's got my stout frame and the true red crest. Ye see yer own shadow, twenty years back. And this—her ears are too small to be a full Aelf."

He paused again, his voice gaining animated force as he arrived at the crux of his desperate argument. "How many teenaged, short-eared, red-haired children of forbidden lineage are breathing in Aeldoria right now?"

Anja could not contain the sudden surge of desperate excitement. "It might be her! It must be her! What is her name?"

"I dinnae hear. Bryn sent me back to my post once they reached the Commandant's door."

They stood and embraced. They clung to each other tightly, the brief, fragile flame of hope flickering back to vibrant life between them. The guilt, the constant ache of loss, and the sixteen-year-long shadow of uncertainty lingered heavily, but for that moment, they found deep solace in their connection and the desperate promise it carried.

The fierce, relentless determination of a mother drove her next words. "We have to know. We have to confirm her name.

We have to find out what happened to her life, and how she was brought here."

Anja turned, clasping her hands behind her back, and paced the small stone room, each step reflecting the storm of emotions churning within her. Rylen watched her closely, his expression a quiet mix of concern and deep empathy. He felt the vastness of her love for their lost daughter and shared the gut-deep longing for the child they had been forced to leave behind sixteen years ago.

Pausing mid-stride, Anja straightened, her resolve hardening like cooled steel as she faced him. "We need to see her. We have to tell her the truth."

Rylen approached her with slow, measured steps, his gaze steady and utterly reassuring. He gently took her hands in his, the simple warmth of his touch grounding her from the wild momentum. "I understand this deep ache to finally touch our lass, aye. I feel the weight of it, too. But we must proceed with prudence."

Frustration sliced across Anja's face as she looked up. "With prudence? After all these years we sacrificed? She deserves the truth. She deserves to know we never once stopped loving her. We did what we did because we loved her."

"Aye, my love. But we must have prudence, now. She believes us lost. When she finds the truth, she'll read it as a lie—a hard one. She'll harbor anger, maybe enough to sever the thread. We risk losing her entirely."

"I know that cost. But I can't bear the thought of her being alone in this vast world, thinking we simply didn't care enough to survive for her."

"We will find a safe path to the lass, I swear it." Rylen pulled his wife into a gentle embrace, his heart aching for her familiar pain. Resting his forehead on her shoulder, he held her close, offering comfort and his own steady strength. "But we must go slow, aye, with a good measure of heart. We need to give the lass the stone she needs to steady herself against this terrifying truth, and then the time to decide if she wants us in her life, or not."

Drawing strength from him, she clung to her husband, feeling a sense of safety and powerful warmth. "I hope she can find it in her heart to forgive us."

His hand stroked the length of her hair, and he offered the low, quiet assurance. "She will, my love, aye. We only need the patience to let her reach us on her own terms."

Anja pulled away from his embrace, now sparkling with renewed determination. Energized, she began to pace the room, her mind racing, seeking a subtle solution to their impossible challenge.

"I have an idea," Anja announced, her eyes flashing bright with excitement.

Rylen raised a curious brow, inviting her plan.

"We approach Lozen not as the parents who left her—but as mentors."

"Mentors?"

She nodded. "Yes. We guide her in Helsgaard culture, help her find a safe place in this cold Keep. We can build trust without crushing her with the truth."

A practical flicker of hope caught in Rylen's eyes. It was a clever solution—one that might finally bridge the gap between them.

"And," Anja continued, warming to the idea, "since she was exiled at thirteen, she will have virtually no healing skills. I can teach her the healing arts she was denied, and you can teach her about the Dwarfinn ways. Helsgaard will have a strong warrior healer."

They looked into each other's eyes. Both reflecting on Anja's commitment to never take up a sword. She was a healer, not a warrior.

"Aye, now that's a clean-forged path!" Rylen nodded, his admiration growing. "A fine plan, true enough. We use that."

A subtle smile tugged at her lips as she revealed the final piece. "And if we approach the Mission Commander as weapons trainers—you, the former Captain of the Guard, and I, the bow master—we'll have undeniable reason to be near her. We can train the others in the Keep and show her, implicitly, that she is not alone."

He took her hand, his grip firm but gentle. "Ye are bloody brilliant, m'love." His expression immediately darkened, the shadow of reality falling over him. "But the thread is tangled. Bryn from RIOS has her hooks in yer path."

Anja stiffened, Bryn's name cutting her confidence short. "Why would RIOS take an interest?"

"I don't know. If Bryn's weaving her in, if those RIOS shadow-spiders hold the thread, this road is naught but a trap." He exhaled, letting the grim reality settle. "We'll hold to yer own plan for now, aye."

She squeezed his hand, the renewed determination hardening in her eyes. "We can face this challenge. We can finally bring our family back together."

Rylen managed a weak smirk. "I am forged for the close fight—shield, spear, axe—not the feather of the arrow. And this mending is yer craft, not mine."

Anja chuckled, a sound of fragile hope. "You'll learn the bow and she will learn how to heal wounds."

"Come now, let's go fill the belly," he said, pulling her toward the scent of roasting meat drifting faintly from Höfn House. "Give that heart o' yers a chance to stand down."

Hand in hand, they walked toward the warmth of home. The road ahead was uncertain, but for the first time in sixteen years, they faced it not with dread—but with hope.

CHAPTER 7

HELSGAARD ARCHERY TRAINING

A PROPOSAL OF AELFINN SKILL

S UNLIGHT FILTERED THROUGH A narrow slit in the stone wall, casting a soft glow across Hrolf's austere office. Maps woven into tapestries adorned the walls. A heavy wooden table, its surface scarred from years of use, was scattered with rune-carved copper sheets and small pieces of wood etched with messages. Hrolf sat on a simple, high-backed, solid oak chair, its carvings plain but sturdy. His fingers traced slow, deliberate circles on the armrests as he contemplated the tasks at hand. Anja and Rylen stood before him, their hands clasped together in front of them. Anja, filled with a mother's love and longing, spoke first.

"Mission Commander," she said, her voice steady despite the knot of anxiety that tightened in her stomach. "We have a proposal."

Hrolf raised an eyebrow, glancing between the two. His expression remained inscrutable, his thoughts concealed behind a well-practiced veil of stoicism. "A proposal? And what would that be?"

Anja inhaled deeply, drawing the strength to calm her voice as she confronted her swirling emotions. "We have heard much about the young archer. We believe our combined Aelfinn experience could greatly benefit Helsgaard Keep's archery training."

Rylen stood beside Anja, nodding in agreement, his voice exuding a quiet authority that reflected his past experiences in the King's Guard. "Since we don't have a formal archery training program, we propose creating one," he added, echoing Anja's sentiment. "The focus will be on developing the archery skills of all warriors in the Keep, regardless of their background."

Hrolf leaned back in his chair, and his fingers steepled as he considered their offer. Using their expertise to bolster the Keep's archery training intrigued him. "A noble idea, to be sure," he said. "But she has only just arrived and must first complete basic warrior training before we consider any new duties."

Anja's shoulders slumped from disappointment. Hoping for an enthusiastic response to their proposal, Hrolf's cautious reply reminded her of the challenges ahead.

She quickly regained her composure. "Of course, Commander. We understand the importance of following protocol. We are confident that she has the potential to excel as a trainer. She's an Aelfinn archer, and her natural talent and dedication, combined with our guidance, would make her a valuable asset to the Keep."

Hrolf remained silent as Anja spoke. He sensed the depth of her belief in Lozen's potential and admired her motivation. He cleared his throat, his voice more conciliatory. "I see. And where do you fit into this, Rylen?"

Rylen said, "The flight of the arrow isn't my craft. I'll turn my hand to any honest work from m'lass."

Hrolf nodded, his mind racing with the possibilities of their proposal. He recognized Lozen's talent as an archer and witnessed her resilience and determination firsthand. The combination of Anja and her years of archery experience would be a game-changer for the Keep's archery training.

A slow smile spread across Hrolf's face, his initial skepticism giving way to anticipation. "Very well, I'll give your proposal some thought. In the meantime, she will continue her basic training. Bryn also commented on her healing abilities, saying that we need more healers. Based on what I've heard about her ground combat, I don't think her training will take long. Before we begin archery training, I want you to get Lozen up to speed on healing."

Rylen stiffened, and Anja jerked at the sound of Lozen's name, but quickly recovered.

Hrolf asked, "Is there a problem?"

Anja nodded and said, "No, sir. No problem. Understood."

Hrolf continued, looking at Rylen, "And if we move forward with this idea, you'll become an archer. I don't see any reason to make exceptions."

"Aye, that's what she said," Rylen indicated to Anja.

"That's what she said," Hrolf mimicked Rylen. Everyone laughed, relieving the tension.

The couple exchanged looks of shared joy and relief. Their proposal was met with a positive response, and they were eager to begin their new roles in Helsgaard Keep. They knew the road ahead would be challenging, but they were confident their combined efforts would impact the Keep's future.

Hrolf leaned back in his chair, his sharp eyes fixed on Anja. "And maybe someday," he said, his tone deliberate, "you can tell me the real reason you're so interested in Lozen."

Anja's heart raced, but she forced herself to appear calm. She offered a neutral response, her voice steady. "First Aelf we've seen in years."

Hrolf raised an eyebrow, clearly unconvinced. "Uh-huh. That excuse could use some polish. And while you're at it, you might include how a Dwarf and an Aelf ended up with such a strong bond. Or why Lozen seems like she could be your daughter."

Anja froze, her composure slipping for a fraction of a second before she regained it. Hrolf wasn't asking outright, but his words cut close to the truth.

"Now I'm not prying," Hrolf continued, his voice softening. "Everyone in Helsgaard has a story. I just hope yours isn't one that'll put us in danger."

His gaze bored into her, searching for cracks in her facade. Anja stared back, willing herself not to flinch. She bowed her head—not only out of respect but to conceal the relief that washed over her.

"Thank you, Commander," she said evenly. "We are grateful for this opportunity."

Hrolf studied her for a moment longer, pausing before waving them off. "You are dismissed."

Anja turned and walked away, her shoulders stiff but her mind whirling. She knew this was far from over. As they left his office, comfort washed over them. They took the first step to reuniting with their long-lost daughter. Though the path ahead remained uncertain, they clung to the hope that this marked the start of a new chapter in their lives.

They closed the door to Hrolf's office behind them, standing in the corridor, silent, the air between them thick and heavy.

Anja pressed a hand to her chest, as if trying to steady the pounding of her heart. Lozen. Their daughter. The girl they had seen fight and beat the lead trainer—now within arm's reach after all these years.

She breathed, barely a whisper. "It's her. It's really her."

Rylen's jaw clenched, his hands balling into fists at his sides. His eyes, usually sharp and calculating, were unfocused—caught in the past, in memories of a child they had left behind.

A child they thought they would never see again.

Anja turned to him, her blue eyes shining with urgency. "We have to tell her. Now."

He inhaled slowly, deliberately. "Anja. Hold fast, now."

She blinked, stunned by the command in his voice. "Hold fast? After all these years? After all we—"

"—Hold. Think with yer head." His voice was firm but not unkind. "We tell her the truth this minute, and what stone does that set in place?"

"She knows the truth."

Rylen shook his head. "She'll call it betrayal. We walked away from her on Elowen's border, and that score won't be settled easy."

Anja flinched at the word "betrayal."

"We didn't have a choice," she whispered.

He exhaled, rubbing a hand over his beard. "I know that. Aye, ye know that. But the lass has no bedrock to stand on."

Anja's fingers curled into her tunic.

The truth sat between them like a blade—sharp, inevitable.

"I won't lie to her," she said, voice hard.

Rylen met her gaze. "And I'll not ask it. But we must use our minds. She's built a life on stone and grit, without our shield. We burst in and claim we're kin—then what? Ye think she'll just—run to us?"

Anja swallowed hard but didn't answer—because she didn't know. She wanted to believe Lozen would understand, that she would hear the truth and recognize the love behind it. But Lozen wasn't a child anymore. She was a warrior—a hardened survivor. And survivors don't trust easily.

She turned away, staring down the dimly lit hallway. "She deserves to know."

"She deserves to not have that poison in her heart. We must grant her that peace."

Anja spun on him. "And keeping it from her won't change that."

Rylen held her gaze. Worn. Tired. Knowing.

"Not locking the truth away, Anja. Just choosing the minute to give it to her."

Anja's chest rose and fell, frustration twisting through her. But deep down, she knew Rylen wasn't wrong.

He sighed, stepping closer, resting a hand on her shoulder.

"We will tell her, lass. But we don't dump the score in her lap. We earn her sight, first. We stay. We want her—not because of the name she carries, but because she's ours, true enough."

Anja closed her eyes, pressing her lips together.

"I hate waiting."

Rylen's mouth twitched in the barest ghost of a smile. "Aye, I ken it."

She exhaled, nodding. "Fine. But not forever."

"Not forever."

The decision settled between them, uneasy but solid.
They would wait.
But the truth was coming.
And when it did, there would be no going back.

CHAPTER 8

THE CRUCIBLE OF MUD

THE UNAVOIDABLE PROXIMITY

T HE MIDDAY SUN BEAT down on the training yard, turning the mud pits into a hazardous mix of slick grime and firm footing—a perilous arena. Lozen, covered in a thick layer of muck, struggled to maintain her balance as she sparred with Rohand. Anja stood nearby as the Keep's medic.

"Come on, Little Bird!" Rohand barked, unfazed by the slop. "Dig deep! Find your center! Show me what you had a few days ago."

Lozen's muscles strained. She tried to throw him, but he countered, sending her sprawling face-first into the mud. "Easy for you to say," Lozen retorted, spitting out a mouthful of mud. "I've never fought in this filth before! How can I fight if I can't stand?"

Rohand grinned, extending a hand. "That's the point. Use your Aelfinn blood—agility, balance, speed. The mud is your trial, not your cage."

Bryn watched from the sidelines, impressed by the grit beneath the grime. Rylen, leaning against a wall, felt the familiar gnawing guilt of their past choices.

Lozen surged with renewed resolve. She parried his next attack, landing a series of well-placed strikes that elicited a grunt from the seasoned instructor.

"Precisely! Now you grasp the essence of combat!" he said.

A triumphant grin spread across her face.

Without warning, he shattered her reverie with a brutal tackle and a vicious blow to the eye. "You are dead!" he snarled, pinning her. "You let your guard down! Never relinquish your guard. Never!"

Lozen recoiled, anger coursing through her veins. "You pikk! I thought you were coaching me!"

As the ordeal drew to a close, Rohand helped her up. She crouched low, anticipating another attack.

Anticipating her move, he stepped into her personal space, raised a knife-hand, and pointed directly at her face, halting her advance. "We are done."

She stood tall, adrenaline fading. "Yessir."

Anja rushed forward, her Aelfinn healing hands hovering over Lozen's swollen eye. "Rylen, get me some snow."

As Anja's touch eased the pain, Lozen whispered, "Will you teach me the healing hands? I didn't get the chance in Aeldoria."

"Yes, I will," Anja promised. "The Mission Commander expects it. You've seen it, you've felt it. You're ready."

Anja took a handful of the snow Rylen delivered. "Hold this on your eye."

Lozen flashed a playful grin. "Hey, Rohand, are you always such a rass?"

Rohand chuckled. "Better a rass to you in training than praying for your soul's journey to Valhalla."

"Aelfs don't go to Valhalla. We have the Halls of Mandos where we can reflect on our life's mistakes before coming back."

Muttering, Rohand turned, walking around the mud pit with a slight limp. By the time he finished three laps, he flicked a glance her way and jerked his chin toward the bathing pool.

"Come on. Mud trainers get special permission to bathe outside their normal bath day," he said.

Steam curled into the cool evening air as the natural hot spring bubbled gently. Lozen stepped in, hissing as the warmth seeped into her bruises. Across from her, Rohand leaned back, rubbing his leg, his usual sharpness dulled by exhaustion. For once, silence was peace.

The moon, a luminous pearl, cast an ethereal glow over the training yard. Torches flickered along the edges of the pits.

△△△

A few evenings later, Lozen and Rohand stood facing each other in the mud pit again, their bodies glistening with sweat and mud beneath the moonlight. A few warriors circled the pit watching the show.

"Remember," he said, his voice low, "darkness is your ally. Use it to your advantage."

Rohand launched his attack. Lozen reacted with lightning speed, sidestepping his charge and landing a swift kick to his thigh.

He grunted, spinning around. She parried his blows, but the slippery mud made it difficult to maintain her balance.

Seizing an opportunity, Lozen dropped to the ground, sweeping Rohand's legs out from under him. Landing hard beside her, he yelped.

"Agh! My ankle!"

Lozen, forgetting their adversarial roles, looked into Rohand's eyes, concerned. "Are you alright?"

Rohand's ankle buckled as he attempted to stand, sending him back into the mud. His face contorted in pain. "Fukk!"

Anja rushed to the sidelines. "Warriors! Two of you, into the pit! Retrieve Rohand, carefully!"

Rylen arrived instantly. Anja knelt beside Rohand. "It's a sprain. Rylen! Get a bucket of snow and meet me outside the infirmary."

Anja turned to Lozen. "Help me get his boot off."

Lozen knelt beside him, her fingers trembling. Once the boot was removed, Anja directed her, "Remember what I taught you. Apply the touch to his ankle. We need to get control of the pain and swelling."

Lozen pressed her palms against his leg, the faint blue glow of her healing touch bringing instant relief.

Anja nodded. "Good. That will hold for now. Let's get him moved to the infirmary."

The warriors carried Rohand away. Lozen grabbed his discarded boot and followed.

At the infirmary entrance, Anja ordered the warriors to strip Rohand of his muddy clothes. Lozen hesitated.

"Don't get shy on me now," Anja muttered, rolling her eyes. "Get in there. He's a patient."

Lozen, along with the muddy Rangers, quickly stripped Rohand and rinsed away the muck. Anja sent the others away.

Anja then tossed Lozen a thick cloak. "Take off your muddy clothes outside, wash up, and wear this. Consider it a test of endurance."

Lozen stepped outside and strode past the cold water trough to the bathing pool. She stripped off her armor, boots, and soaked clothes before plunging in. Once she had scrubbed away the mud, she threw on the cloak and sprinted back to the infirmary, hissing at the cold and muttering curses in both Aelfinn and Common. When she entered the infirmary, Anja was stoking the central hearth.

"Good. Now, back to the healing. Like I showed you."

Lozen took her place beside Rohand, setting to work. Rylen entered, hauling snow, before leaving to deal with the armor.

Lozen fought to keep her expression neutral. It was hard to concentrate when his bare chest was right there, all toned muscle and battle scars. She felt something stir within her that she had never felt before.

What is that? What's wrong with me?

She moved closer to his feet and redoubled her healing efforts.

Anja watched, amused. "You're doing fine. Get the energy flowing."

Rohand groaned dramatically. "Better," he admitted with a slow smirk. "But I'm not saying much—don't want to get on her bad side."

Lozen rolled her eyes and sighed as the glow faded. "Good plan, Hersir. There, done."

Anja retrieved the bucket of snow and asked, "What's next?"

Lozen, now fully in her medical apprentice role, explained, "Cool the injury to keep the swelling down."

As she knelt to pack the snow around his ankle, the towel draped over his hips shifted slightly. For a fleeting, sharp moment, she saw too much. Heat instantly rushed to her face, a sudden, scalding flush. She slammed her attention onto the snow, willing herself to ignore Rohand's quiet, infuriating amusement.

Anja finished the immobilization. "Lozen, you should get some rest."

"Hey," Rohand called after her. He gave her a rare, genuine smile. "Thank you."

Lozen nodded. "Try not to break anything else."

Rohand grinned. "No promises."

She slipped out, her thoughts a tangled mess as she ran barefoot toward the pool for her armor, then to the longhouse. The intense, emotional exhaustion of the day finally setting in.

CHAPTER 9

BLOWING OFF STEAM

CAMPFIRE STORIES TO SCARE THE CHILDREN

T HE FLICKERING CANDLELIGHT OF a hundred flames cast a warm glow across the bustling tavern, the first building outside the Keep's gates. Lively conversation filled the space, blending with the strains of a bard's melody. Spilled mead left a fruity scent hanging in the air. At the far end of a bench table, Anja, Rylen, and Lozen sat close, voices lowered beneath the tavern's din.

"So, Mission Commander is considering our suggestion about a training team," Anja said, excitement barely contained.

Lozen tapped a finger against the rim of the mug. "Sounds interesting. I'd rather train archers than have Rohand beat me daily. That guy is pissing me off. It's like he wants me to quit."

Rylen chuckled, amusement flickering across his face. "It is his function, friend, no great conspiracy. He finds pleasure in testing the recruits. Ye struck him in the seat and told him, 'I do not yield.' That's the reason. Now your training is quite... 'special.'"

A scowl crept onto Lozen's face. "I just want to run my fingers through his ponytail, grab hold, and smash his face with my knee. A few times."

Anja reached over, placing a hand on Lozen's arm. "Sounds like you're in love with him. Is there something you'd like to share?"

A faint blush crept up Lozen's cheeks. "He's my trainer, nothing more."

Rylen sensed the charged atmosphere and, with a dramatic stretch, attempted to shift the mood. "Hmph. All this loose talk has made me thirsty. Anything for the table?"

Before either could respond, he was gone, leaving the two alone. The murmur of the tavern filled the space, but any further conversation was cut short as an old woman approached. Cloaked in shadows, a hood obscured most of the weathered face, except for unsettling red eyes that gleamed like embers. Without hesitation, she slid into Rylen's vacant seat, movements fluid yet unnervingly deliberate.

Something primal stirred in Lozen's gut. A warning. Muscles tensed as unease crawled up her spine and up her arms. Across the table, Anja straightened, a glare sharpening in ice-blue eyes.

"Can we help you?" Anja asked, voice taut, like a bowstring ready to snap.

The woman ignored the question, red eyes locking onto Lozen with a quiet intensity. When she spoke, the words were like steel wrapped in silk. "Lozen," she said, the name sliding off her tongue like a curse. "You are the one from the prophecy."

Lozen's breath hitched. "What prophecy?" A scowl darkened her features. "Who are you? And how do you know my name?"

Lips curled into a sharp smile, the kind that unsettled rather than reassured. "My name is Alva, and I've been watching you longer than you know—since your time in Elowen," the old woman said, voice smooth as ice. "You are destined to walk a path no one else can. A warrior forged from two worlds."

Lozen recoiled slightly. "I don't know what you're talking about."

Anja scoffed, breaking the tension. "A prophecy? You're kidding me. Campfire tales to scare Aelfinn children—that's all it is."

The eerie smile never faltered as Alva's gaze shifted. "You know better," she murmured. "You've heard the stories. Half-Aelf, destined to walk a path no one else can. A warrior forged from two worlds."

Lozen shifted, discomfort curling in her stomach. This felt wrong. Like a story she hadn't agreed to be part of. "What do you want from me?"

"I want to help you embrace what lies dormant within you," Alva replied, voice soft yet chilling. "The power only you possess."

Lozen jerked back, pulse hammering. "I don't understand any of this. Get away from me!"

A firm grip tightened on Lozen's arm. Anja's knuckles whitened as she pulled Lozen closer. "Don't listen to her," she warned, voice steady but forceful. "She's a mad Seeress whispering riddles and feeding on fear and manipulation."

Alva's attention shifted back to Anja. A knowing smile lingered. "Three years, Momma," she whispered, low enough for only Anja to hear. "She needs to know."

The old woman stood, the movement eerily grace-ful. "You'll come to me eventually," she told Lozen. "Not to-day. Not tomorrow. But you will. The truth is coming, and I will be waiting." Without another word, she turned and exited the room, vanishing into the night.

A tense silence settled between the two women.

"What did she say to you?" Lozen asked, suspicion thread-ing through her voice.

Anja's expression hardened as she watched the door swing shut. "Nothing important. She doesn't like me."

Moments later, Rylen returned, setting a fresh drink down with a curious glance. "What's with the mood? And who was that old lady? That the forest Seeress?"

Lozen exhaled shakily. "I don't know," she admitted. "But I think my world just got a lot stranger."

Anja dismissed the concern with a wave. "Yeah, that was that crazy forest Seeress trying to scare Lozen with Aelfinn campfire stories."

Still shaken, Lozen pressed further. "What's with the red eyes? And how does she know about Aelfinn stories? And she knew about when I got kicked out of Elowen. Who is she?"

Rylen, eager to shake off the tension, offered a reassuring smile. "Forget the woman. Here, take my drink—I'll get an-other."

As he walked off, the two women exchanged uneasy glances. Alva's visit had left an unwelcome chill in the air, and the once-warm tavern now carried an undercurrent of unease nei-ther could ignore.

CHAPTER 10

ARCHERY TRAINING PROCEEDS

FUGITIVES, FANATICS, AND PROPHECY

S UNLIGHT FILTERED THROUGH A narrow window, cast-ing a golden streak across the worn map sprawled over the heavy oak table in the Mission Commander's briefing room. Despite the dim torchlight, the chamber felt oppressive, its stone walls lined with tapestries woven with maps and intri-cate strategic diagrams. At the table's head, Hrolf sat in quiet contemplation, his sharp gaze locked onto a detailed map of Ravnsríki, its inked lines on stretched animal skin telling the story of countless battles and shifting borders.

Lozen and Anja stood before Mission Commander Hrolf, their attentive yet relaxed posture contrasting sharply with the usual tension in the room. Bryn stood tall, her arms crossed over her chest, her face revealing no hint of emotion.

Hrolf addressed the two Aelfinn women with a measured and authoritative voice, scanning their faces. "I've called you both here today at Anja's request to discuss a proposition that I believe will benefit Helsgaard Keep. The seventeen-year Aelfinn war has been escalating. Their raids on our farms and travelers have become more frequent and brazen. I'm not saying the war is coming here, and I'm not saying it isn't, but we need to protect our residents as Helsgaardborg is being built. The King is encouraging homesteading in the valley to the west, so we're about to become a hotspot in Ravnsríki as settlers come in for some free land."

Bryn frowned. Although Helsgaard's remote location shielded it from the direct impact of the war, the conflict took a toll on its people through their families near the border. The thought of further escalation filled her with dread. Lozen and Anja, however, remained stoic, their expressions neutral.

Hrolf noticed Bryn's attitude change but continued with renewed determination. "We must strengthen our defenses, including improving our Warriors' skills. I've heard impressive reports of your abilities, both of you. Working together, we can enhance the archery skills of our Warriors to new heights. This won't be difficult since the two of you have been trained by the best archers in the world—the Aelfs."

Lozen and Anja exchanged a glance, an understanding passing between them. They hoped for this opportunity to work together and contribute to the defense of Helsgaard Keep. As they were the only two Aelfs in the Keep, they needed the camaraderie of a common background.

Anja, calm and confident, addressed the Mission Commander. "Thank you for your confidence in us, Commander. We are eager to begin this training program and believe we can significantly improve the Keep's archery capabilities."

Hrolf nodded. "Good. Ravnborg just shipped us 40 bows and some arrows. The Trades House will make more arrows for us. You will start training all warriors tomorrow at dawn. Concentrate on enhancing their accuracy, speed, and tactical awareness. We need them to be prepared for anything. The threat of war looms large over us. We must be ready."

Lozen and Anja straightened, their determination evident in their posture. They fully grasped the gravity of their role and duty. The future of Helsgaard Keep—and perhaps even the survival of the entire kingdom—rested on their ability to forge a new generation of expert archers.

Lozen looked at Hrolf. "We will not disappoint you, Mission Commander."

Hrolf, satisfied with their response, disengaged with a curt nod. "You are dismissed."

As they turned to leave, Lozen smiled at Anja with a questioning look.

Bryn interjected, "Anja? A word, if you please? Wait outside the door." Looking at Lozen, she continued, "Just Anja."

Lozen and Anja exchanged glances and left, closing the door behind them.

"Hrolf," she said, using his name rather than his title. "If I may?"

Hrolf sighed, recognizing her tone's shift in formality and the challenge. "Speak your mind," he said.

She smiled with arrogant amusement. "You know I will. That's the beauty of serving the King and not the Commandant. I can say what I want and do what I want, and none of you can do skitr about it."

Hrolf's patience dwindled, and he glared at her. "Please, your thoughts?"

Bryn's smile faded. "Are you certain this is wise? Putting Aelfs in charge of our archery defense—potentially and maybe even likely against other Aelfs, if they ever come this far?"

The Mission Commander leaned back in his chair, a wry smile on his lips. He anticipated this objection and stood ready to address her concerns. "A valid concern," he said. "Thank you for being so forthcoming. I appreciate it. But I trust their loyalty. And who better to teach us how to defeat the Aelfs than those who know their capabilities best?"

She nodded, conceding that Hrolf's logic held merit. The potential benefits of having Lozen and Anja train the archers were clear. Yet, a sense of unease lingered, a doubt she couldn't dismiss.

Before she could voice her thoughts, Hrolf interrupted her. "As a point of accountability, I would like you to record each archer's scores and track their progress over time. There must be improvement."

"I was going to suggest the same thing," she said.

"Seems like there was something else. I saw you frown. Anything you want to share?"

"Not really. I lost my whole tribe to the Aelfs when I was not much older than Lozen. And now I have to train her for RIOS and monitor our Aelfs for training reports? Not sure what I did to anger the gods. if it's the Norn sisters, or Loki, but somebody hates me."

Hrolf, a rare chuckle escaping his lips, shook his head. "Now, go and prepare for tomorrow's training. We have a lot of work to do."

Bryn smiled and bowed her head in acknowledgement.

As she turned to leave, Hrolf cleared his throat. "I know I didn't take the opportunity to tell you. Thank you for finding

Lozen. Your spy-skitr is beyond my understanding. I think she'll turn out to be a good asset."

She grinned at his unexpected praise. "I'm not going to tell you how much it cost to convince that guard to let her go. The King put a bounty on her, so we had to top that with a hefty premium. Just because we work for the King doesn't mean we tell him everything we do. In this case, he discovered what we had done and allowed it, as he wanted to eliminate her one way or another. This way, she's helping the Kingdom and not dividing it."

Hrolf, about to dismiss her, paused for a moment. "You are dis—," he started. Before he could finish his sentence, Bryn was gone, leaving him with his thoughts. He leaned back in his chair. The day's events left him with a sense of anticipation, feeling that something momentous would unfold as he trusted Lozen and Anja, two unexpected heroes with the potential to save countless lives. As he contemplated the challenges and opportunities ahead, he was hopeful. Perhaps, Odin willing, Helsgaard Keep could survive and even thrive in the face of the unknown.

△△△

Anja stood alone outside the Mission Commander's briefing room when Bryn exited. Bryn closed within Anja's personal space and assumed an aggressive stance.

"You've been here for quite a while—much longer than I have. Strangely, I have no reading on you or Rylen. No intel from Ravnborg, nothing. It's like you two are ghosts. So how about giving me the Monk's Digest version of who the fukk you are, ghost?"

Anja stared back and remained silent, which irritated the spy, who was accustomed to compliance with her demands.

"I'm not asking. You know who I am and who I work for."

She reconsidered, glaring at Bryn, and took a deep breath. "The Monk's Digest version. I was the Junior Emissary to Ravnsríki for the peace negotiations eighteen years ago. Rylen was a Captain of the Royal Guard—Valdissen's Guard—and was assigned as my bodyguard. We fell in love. We were exposed on the day of the peace treaty signing, the negotiations failed, and this seventeen-year war resulted."

Bryn's expression softened, and she took a couple of steps back. "So Anja and Rylen, deep in the politics of each kingdom, came here to disappear?"

"Something like that."

"So, how does Lozen fit in? Maybe she's... your daughter? You and Rylen knotted together in the dark, made a baby, and that's her?"

A long pause.

"Yes," Anja said softly.

Bryn froze. "Yes?" she repeated. "You left her behind in Aeldoria and fled here?"

The two women stared at each other for a moment.

"Tell me the story."

Anja took a slow, measured breath. "There's a death bounty on our heads from both sides—Aeldoria and Ravnsríki. We gave her to a family friend to raise—a Council Elder. We thought she had a better chance in the elite political environment in Elowen than with us—two fugitives pursued by two kingdoms."

Bryn listened intently. "A death bounty? Gods! So, the girl is a target, too. Why?"

"Are you familiar with the prophecy of the warrior of two worlds uniting the warring races?" Anja asked.

"No. Go on."

"The prophecy says a half-Aelf, born of two races, will unite warring kingdoms. Our Council of Elders is usually split, but for years, the conservers—the fanatics—held the majority. They believe the halfling is an abomination that will destroy Aelfinn superiority."

Bryn's lips pressed into a thin line. "So they will kill an innocent half-Aelf to prevent it. And you left her behind with that threat hanging over her?"

Anja exhaled sharply. "Faelar is a loyal progressor, an emissary of peace for all kingdoms. We believed Lozen would be safe under Faelar's protection. We couldn't keep her as we were on the run with a death bounty on our heads."

A heavy silence fell. Bryn ran a hand through her hair, then sighed. "One more thing—'Anja' is not an Aelfinn name. What was your name in Aeldoria?"

"It was 'Anyael.' I dropped the 'el' and tweaked the 'a.' It passes."

Bryn absorbed the weight of everything. Finally, she nodded. "Your secrets are safe with me." Then, her voice shifted to business. "And with that, I have things to do."

Anja pleaded, "Do you know Lozen's history? Why did she leave Aeldoria? What led her here?"

"I do, and her secrets are safe with me, just like yours. I appreciate your honesty." Bryn turned to walk away.

"I know you work for the King. Are you going to report us?"

She stopped and looked at Anja. "I'm not a puppet. I have wide latitude. The two of you have been missing for sixteen or seventeen years—I don't see any reason for you to show up now. And for what it's worth, not telling Lozen you're her mother saved her from feeling abandoned twice, and I need her focused. If you have any thoughts of telling her, don't!"

Turning, she continued down the hallway, boots echoing as the footsteps faded.

CHAPTER 11

THE BETRAYAL

THE DAGGER OF UNSPOKEN TRUTH

A s the last light of the spring day spilled over the Helsgaard Keep, its gentle warmth embraced the training ground, casting long shadows across the surrounding landscape. The air rang with a melodious birdsong while the delicate fragrance of sping flowers drifted through, promising vibrant months ahead. Lozen practiced her archery, her focus absolute, each arrow finding the heart of its target with a satisfying thwack. Anja watched her from afar, feeling a mix of pride for her skill and sorrow for her lost years.

As Lozen released another arrow, Anja slowly approached, carefully closing the distance.

"Your form is impeccable," she complimented, a bittersweet smile gracing her lips. "It reminds me of someone I once knew, long ago."

Lozen lowered her bow, her posture shifting from fluid grace to cautious interest. "Oh? And who might that be? Someone I know back in Aeldoria?"

Anja paused, her smile tinged with a hint of sadness. "An old family friend from Elowen. Faelar. She was the finest archer I'd ever seen."

The name landed like a stone. Lozen's body instantly stiffened; her grip tightened on the bow until her knuckles were stark white. A dark cloud passed over her face, twisting it into a rigid mask of outrage and pure anger. When she finally spoke, her voice was sharp and cutting, stripped bare of all warmth. "Faelar? Council Elder Faelar? That vile woman? She's dead to me."

Anja's heart plummeted. She physically cringed as Lozen's composure shattered, years of pent-up rage and hurt erupting in a torrent of accusations.

"She abandoned me!" Lozen raged, her voice shaking. "Worse—she turned on me and kicked me out of Aeldoria. She told my parents to pack my stuff, and they left it on the porch—I didn't even get to say goodbye. Exiled me to rot in Ravnsríki!"

Each word pierced Anja's heart like a dagger. She yearned to reach out, to cradle her daughter and finally tell her the truth that burned like a fever in her soul. But the fear of breaking the fragile trust they had just begun to build, coupled with Bryn's implied threat, paralyzed her. "So Faelar isn't your mother?"

"No way!" Lozen spat the word. "That bikkja stopped me while playing and told me I didn't fit in and had to leave, and my parents, who she called 'caretakers,' had been informed. Just like that—kicked out. Exiled! I was only thirteen!" she shouted, the last word ringing with years of raw pain.

"Lozen, I—"

"—Don't," she snapped, raising a hand. "Just—don't!"

With a final, furious glare, Lozen whirled around and stalked away, her retreating figure a monument to broken trust, leaving Anja alone in the waning evening light of the training yard.

Lozen's accusations, a bitter symphony of betrayal and abandonment, reverberated in Anja's ears. She stared at her daughter's vanishing shadow, tears suddenly welling in her eyes. The profound pain of Lozen's rejection, the agony of her enforced silence, overwhelmed her. Crumpling to her knees, Anja's sobs were muffled by the rough fabric of her tunic and the soft dirt of the practice field.

△△△

The flickering oil lamps cast elongated shadows that stretched and twisted across the stone walls, their restless movement reflecting the turmoil in Rylen's chest. He paced the length of the infirmary, his heavy boots scuffing against the wooden floor, his fists tightening with each heavy step. The air was thick with the aroma of healing herbs and old parchment, but it did nothing to settle his growing unease.

The door creaked open, and Anja entered, her face pale, her eyes raw and swollen from weeping. She barely made it two steps before her legs wavered. Rylen was there in an instant, catching her in his arms, his grip firm, steady, and utterly grounding.

"Anja! What's the trouble? Speak plainly!"

She collapsed into the nearest chair, her shoulders trembling as silent sobs wracked her frame. Her breath hitched, and her voice came in a broken whisper. "She hates her."

Rylen knelt before her, his pulse hammering a warning rhythm. "Speak the names, Anja. Who hates whom?"

Anja squeezed her hands together as if trying to keep herself from unraveling. "Faelar. Lozen hates her."

The words struck him like a physical blow. His breath stilled. "What did the lass tell ye, word for word, aye?"

Anja inhaled sharply, trying to steady herself. "She said Faelar abandoned her. Cast her out of Aeldoria. Left her to fend for herself. She's the reason she's been living on the streets for three years."

Rylen's grip on the seat tightened until his knuckles went white. His jaw locked, fury burning white-hot in his chest. "That treacherous viper," he growled, the Captain-of-the-Guard discipline momentarily dissolving. "She gave us her word, the snake. She promised to guard our own kin. And instead, she—" He swore under his breath, the rage twisting inside him, sharp as a blade. "Leave it to politicians to fukk us."

Anja wiped her face with the back of her sleeve, her hands unsteady. "I should have told her the truth. I was afraid—afraid she'd reject me."

He took her hands in his, his rough palms against her trembling fingers. "Nay. Ye found a wound on the mend. No need to pour the salt in." He brushed away the tears on her cheeks with his thumbs, his voice gentler now. "This weight isn't yers, my heart. We sealed the decision, together, believing it held the best chance for her."

Anja swallowed hard, but crushing doubt still darkened her expression. "But what now? How do we ever make this right?"

Rylen exhaled slowly, his eyes dark with deep thought. "I don't think that stone can be moved. Not in her eyes, lass. We gave her to Faelar; Faelar broke the trust; and she was driven out. To her, it's all one chain of betrayal. She'll hold the same debt of hate for us as she does for Faelar. And when the time is true, she'll be gone. If we push her too hard, she'll vanish into the black, and we'll never find the trail again."

The silence between them was heavy, filled only by the low crackle of the hearth. Anja's breath shuddered as she looked at him, searching his face for hope and answers.

"So what do we do?" she whispered, with pleading eyes.

His fingers tightened around hers, his grip unyielding. "As long as the truth is held, we stand here for her. She is our kin. We will not let the family break again."

Anja leaned into him, but uncertainty gnawed at her even as she found comfort in his presence. "How long can we keep the truth from her? If she ever finds out we lied—if she learns everything—will she hate us, too?"

Rylen inhaled sharply but did not answer right away. The terrifying truth sat between them like a blade waiting to fall. Finally, he whispered, "We'll face that if the day comes. But right now, she needs us to be the rock she never had. And we need to make certain she never counts herself abandoned again, aye."

Anja nodded, but the unease in her eyes lingered, flickering like the fire in the lamp. The road ahead was treacherous and uncertain, but they would face it together. They had to.

The wind rattled the shutters, the fire in the lamp flickering with the draft, but neither of them moved.

"I am still worried. She's just a girl."

"Right," he admitted, his voice barely above a murmur. "But she has true steel in her core. She's clever. The rough path didn't break her—it honed her edge. And her skill with the string—that is undeniable." He glanced toward the door. "We will stand watch over the lass. Give her a safe haven to return to. She is home now. And we will not let the line break again."

The flames from oil lamps steadied, its golden light stretching across the walls. Anja exhaled slowly, the tension in her shoulders easing. The doubts remained, but for the first time in years, a calculated, desperate hope burned brighter.

CHAPTER 12

FIRST MISSION

HEL'S YARD AND THE FINAL FRONTIER

THE SUN SHONE ON the Helsgaard Keep training yard. The air was warm, and a slight westerly breeze carried the scent of lush plant life from the valley below. Rohand and Rylen strode purposefully toward Lozen, each wearing brown pants and tan tunics with leather armor. Rohand called out to her, his voice booming with authority. "Come on, Little Bird, we have a mission."

Irritated, she scowled. "Name is Lozen. When are you going to stop calling me 'Little Bird?'"

Both men, unfazed by her protest, turned and kept walking. Rohand smiled over his shoulder. "When you can fly on your own. Catch up, Little Bird."

"You skitkarlr!"

"Unless you want me to call you Dwaelf—"

Rylen halted mid-step, his head snapping toward Rohand. "—What!? Come again?"

"—Stop!" she screamed. "I should have left that part out! You fukkar feel privileged to call me names?"

Rohand said, "Rylen, go ahead—I'll meet you at the equipment room."

"My shield stays put."

"Really, go ahead."

Rylen crossed his arms and puffed out his chest. "My shield stays."

Rohand stepped closer, lowering his voice. "Then you might want to give us some room."

"An' ye migh' wanna be careful throwing those words." Rylen took a few steps back but continued to watch.

Rohand turned to Lozen, his expression unreadable. "We would have found out eventually." He leaned in, his voice dropping. "You can't hide weakness from a Warrior. The problem with Warriors is they're like chickens—they peck at the weakest to see if they can make 'em snap. If you snap here, you'll die out there—maybe even get a team killed."

Lozen muttered, "Warriors are lunatic rassholes."

"That, and much more. But you need to toughen up, Little Bird. Lucky for you, I'm the only Warrior who knows about this. Me and now Rylen. My job is to toughen you up. And we're short on Warriors—we don't need you throat-punching any of them. I suggest getting over being called a Dwaelf."

Lozen hissed, "Rasshole!"

Rohand raised a knife-hand, stopping just short of her nose, and leaned in. "Get over it, Little Bird. Now."

The air between them turned electric. He held the position, unwavering. Then, in one swift motion, he jabbed her sternum—hard. Not enough to hurt her through the armor, but enough to make her step back. The shock of it cut through her self-control like a blade.

To be struck in training was expected. Outside of training made it personal.

She glared at his back while he walked away. Her blood boiled. Fists clenched. Rage!

The moment she lunged at him, Rohand dropped into a crouch, and she tumbled over him, grasping at air. He straightened his legs, launching her into a somersault. She hit the ground flat on her back with a thud, dust clouding around her. The impact knocked the wind out of her.

Rylen tensed as his daughter went down so fast. He took a couple steps forward.

Rohand moved in, dropping down on his knees, on each side of her head, pinning her braids to the ground. His knife-hand hovered just above the tip of her nose. "Control yourself! That temper is going to get you or my team killed. If you can't control it, I'll drag you out the gate right now. Self-control or the gate—decide!"

Lozen glared, her rage barely contained.

He thumped her sternum again, hard, pushing her toward the edge. "Decide!"

The adrenaline hit like a flood, and she fought to keep herself still, to force the anger down. Her chest rose and fell in rapid breaths, her muscles aching to lash out. She could flip him. Lock her legs around his head. Squeeze until he choked.

But reason stopped her.

Rylen moved next to them. "Rohand—"

"—Shut it and back off! My trainee!"

Rohand stood up, walked around to her feet, and extended his hand. "Let's go. We have a mission."

Lozen stared up at him, her body rigid with defiance. Every instinct told her to strike back, stomp his kneecap, but deep down, she knew what would come after. She clenched her teeth.

"Take my arm, or I'll drag you out the gate! Decide!"

A long, tense silence. Then, finally, she exhaled. "Yes, Hersir. We have a mission."

"Hear you?" Rohand barked.

"Yes, Hersir. We have a mission!" she snapped back.

He grabbed her arm, pulling her up in one motion. As she brushed herself off, he spun her around and dusted off her braids, shoulders, back, and legs. Then, without another word, they walked toward the equipment room.

Inside, they each took two waterskins and a backpack stocked with dried meats, vegetables, bread, and cheese.

Rylen asked, "Lozen, everything okay?"

She fastened the strap on her bag. "Fine. Why do you ask?"

"Mmmm... Just curious."

She turned to see both men watching her—Rohand, expectant. Rylen, cautious.

She squared her shoulders. "I'm fine. We have a mission."

Rylen nodded slowly, a small smirk forming. Many Warriors had been on the receiving end of Rohand's lessons.

With their gear secured, Lozen and Rylen followed Rohand out, stepping into the unknown, their purpose clear. There was no room for weakness in the face of the coming storm.

⚠⚠⚠

As they left the ancient stone walls of the Keep, the familiar road to Helsgaard Frontier stretched out before them, shadowed by the Western Helsgaard Wall. The red rocks bathed in the early morning sun, the harsh light illuminating the dust rising from their heavy boots.

Rohand, already holding a length of smooth, pale aspen, settled his weight against the road and began carving. Using his ever-present knife, he transformed the wood into the rough likeness of a raven, his hands moving with a focused intensity that spoke of years of honing his craft.

Rylen, looking out across the valley ahead, broke the silence. "What's the score, Hersir?"

Rohand divided his focus between his carving and the conversation. "A rancher on the frontier claims a Dragon stole a cow. We're going to investigate."

Rylen's brow furrowed in disbelief, and he scoffed. "A Dragoon takin' a cow? No true sighting for a century. Was the farmer blind with drink?"

"He wasn't drunk when he got to the top of the Western Helsgaard Wall to make his report."

Rylen, still unconvinced, said, "Dragons? I was sure they were cleared from the plain. Ragnar Valdissen cleaned the dirt, didn't he?"

"I don't know," Rohand admitted. "I've only been here for a few years, and the old guys never mentioned Dragons, except those that accompanied Hela, daughter of Loki, who attacked Ragnar Keep a hundred years ago."

"Sixteen years I've been rooted here—not a single shadow—only the steam of bad liquor and old tales from the taverns."

Rohand turned to Lozen. "Lozen, I have a little bit of history for you. Helsgaard Keep was originally named Ragnar Keep. Ragnar was the second son of King Valdissen a hundred years ago and came here to fight Hela and her Dragons. Then, suddenly, the Dragons disappeared and haven't been seen since. The black plain you see way off in the distance is Hel, where

Hela reigns over those who die from sickness or old age or cowardice."

He continued his carving. "Funny thing is, the name was originally Helsgardr Keep—Hel's Yard—a reminder this is where the Dragons play. But a runic error switched it to Helsgaard—Hel's Homestead. Over time, Helsgaard Keep became the outpost of last resort—the final frontier. It takes a certain type of person to live here—usually outlaws and society's outcasts. Generally we don't ask questions."

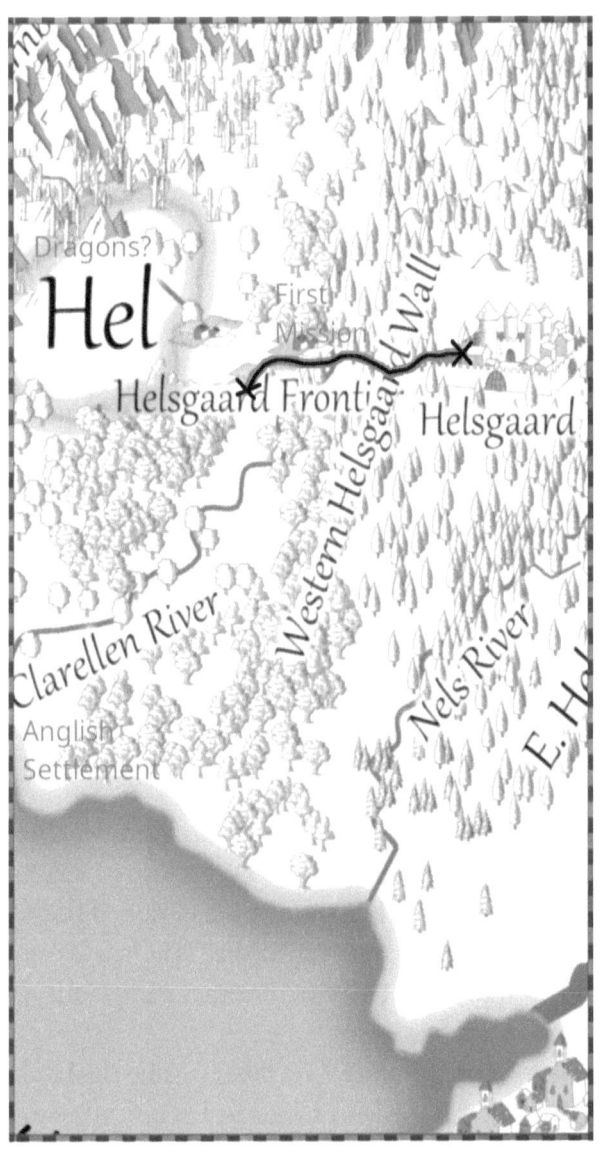

Path of Lozen's First Mission

Lozen retorted, "Well, you asked me a lot of questions in the Commandant's office." Looking at Rylen. "And you with the wrist-twist—was that your notion of courtesy?"

He calmly explained, "As members of the King's Guard, we were trained in pain compliance. I just used that on you to make sure you wouldn't do something we would both regret. I'm sorry for that."

Rohand's brows shot up at Rylen's revelation, his posture stiffening ever so slightly. He looked at both of them, as if weighing the unexpected information. "I've never seen you apologize to anyone before. And a King's Guard? I don't know which of those two surprises me the most."

A brief pause hung in the air.

Rylen changed the topic. "So what are we doing, exactly?"

Rohand's carving took on a more recognizable form, and he grinned. "Making a settler happy. He lost a cow and says a Dragon took it. We're here to investigate. Get some real exercise instead of Training Yard calisthenics."

Noticing Lozen's prolonged silence, Rylen turned to her with concern. "Lozen? You've been quiet, except for the wrist complaint."

Looking at the path ahead, Lozen shrugged her shoulders. Her voice dripped with petulance. "Never seen a Dragon. Glad to get out of the Keep. But since you mentioned it, the maps show this valley has a river called the Clarellen River. That name doesn't seem to fit in with the other names in Ravnsríki. Do you know why?"

Rylen spoke up this time. "We'll be crossing the headwaters soon. Clarellen was the lass of an exiled Briton royal in Breta; he sailed the Bretahaf and founded South Shore at the river's mouth, aye. They couldn't mouth his true name, so they settled for 'Jørgen,' which was close enough for the Common tongue."

Lozen grimaced at the word exile. "Any idea why he was exiled?"

"The talk says he was a wild thing, aye, couldn't turn away from a woman's touch, nor could they turn from his. He left his seed and took his pleasure with many a fair lass. So they asked him to step off—threw him clear of the kingdom—put him and his kin on a boat, and sealed the door behind him. That's why South Shore carries a Briton name, not a Nordlund one."

The trio strolled down the worn dirt road that led to Helsgaard Frontier. The air smelled earthy from the pine trees around them. The sounds of their journey included the rhythmic thud of their boots on the ground and the soft scraping of Rohand's carving knife as he shaped a piece of Aspen into a wooden raven.

CHAPTER 13

CHAT WITH A RANCHER

LIFE'S A BIKKJA, DON SOME ARMOR

T HE TEMPERATURES WERE SEVERAL degrees cooler than on the top of the Western Helsgaard Wall, where Helsgaard Keep overlooked the valley. The shaded settler's road, more of a widened trail than a road, was pleasant to walk along, as only a few settlers with their wagons used the road. The birds sang in the distance, and flying insects buzzed about. Flowing water could be heard in the distance.

The rancher, a weathered figure with sun-beaten skin and calloused hands, leaned against his fence, his expression etched with frustration. Rohand, Rylen, and Lozen approached him.

"Hail and well-met friend," Rohand began, using the traditional Norse greeting to ease the rancher's visible distress. "We heard of your troubles and have come to investigate."

"Hail to you as well, good sirs. I say... it's as strange as it sounds. One minute, Bessy was grazing with the rest; the next—poof—she was agone. No signs of struggle, nuthin'. Got some interestin' tracks and some burned grass, though." He ran a hand through his graying hair. "Appreciate you folks comin' out. Can't says as I've ever seen the like."

Lozen, amused, asked, "You name your cows? That's sweet."

The rancher relaxed and chuckled. "Uh, you're not a rancher, are you? Bessy is just a nickname for a cow, darlin'."

Lozen, realizing her faux pas, exchanged a sheepish glance with Rohand.

"So Bessy was taken?" Lozen asked, confused. "By whom?"

The rancher hesitated, looking at the distant horizon where the ominous dark ground of Hel loomed in the distance.

"Dragons," he whispered.

A tense stillness descended upon the group. The word "Dragon" evoked images of fire, destruction, and ancient legends relegated to children's stories and tavern tales.

Rylen asked, "Dragons? We haven't seen them in a hundred years, aye."

The rancher's face hardened, his jaw clenching with a stubborn resolve. "I don't believe in tales. I believe in what I see. And what I saw were tracks, big ones, leading right up to where Bessy was grazin'. Tracks that weren't there before, and tracks that weren't made by a hooved animal."

Rylen, sensing the tension dissipating, refocused the conversation. "Can ye show us these tracks?"

The rancher nodded and led them to a patch of scorched earth where the grass was trampled and singed. Large, four-toed footprints, each print the size of a shield, marred the ground. The tracks were unmistakable, chilling proof of the presence of a creature far more powerful than any they had encountered before.

Rohand knelt, examining the tracks with a practiced eye. He concentrated as he traced the outline of the massive footprints with his fingertips. "They are fresh. And deep. Whatever made them was big."

Rylen's skepticism faded in the face of the undeniable evidence. He combed a hand through his red beard, his expression thoughtful. "Dragons, then. It seems the deep lore holds the truth, aye."

"Yeah, and they're back."

Lozen stood, looking at the distant peaks past Hel. A chill ran through her body as she realized the enormity of the threat they faced. Dragons, creatures of myth and legend, were no longer confined to the realm of stories and songs. They were real, and they were here.

Sensing their apprehension, the rancher spoke up. "Welp, are ya gonna do somethin' about it?"

Rohand straightened to his full height. "We're here to investigate. And if these Dragons are responsible for the disappearance of your livestock, then we'll do everything in our power to stop them."

The rancher's face brightened, hope replacing the fear that had existed before. "Thank ya. We'all here are countin' on you."

"You can count on us. We'll do the best we can." Rohand placated the rancher.

The rancher bid farewell to the Warriors. "Well, I has to tend to the herd. Thanks for stopping by. You folks travel safe now, ya hear?"

As the trio walked away, once out of earshot of the rancher, Lozen spoke up, confused and dissatisfied. "So that's what you do? Just lie to the locals?"

Rohand faced her and said, "I didn't lie. I said 'we'll do the best we can,' which, sadly, is nothing." He stared at her. "Do you think it's better to tell him there's nothing we can do? This is the first evidence of Dragons in a hundred years. We collect a report, make them feel good, and take the information back to the Mission Commander, and make it his problem. Don't be the senior warrior with a secret."

She fell silent, understanding the logic behind Rohand's words but feeling uneasy about withholding the truth from the rancher.

"It still smells like skitr, Hersir." she muttered.

"Look," he said. "We have a war at our southern border with the Aelfs, and now we have Dragons? We report our findings and let the higher-ups figure it out."

Lozen, despite her feelings, gave in. "Yes, Hersir. I just think it's rude."

Rohand, sensing her lingering doubts, offered a gruff reassurance. "Life's a bikkja. Don some armor. Let's see what we can learn about the footprints."

Scanning the scorched earth and the massive footprints, he turned to Rylen, seeking his perspective on the scene. "What's your read?"

Rylen's analytical mind pieced together the evidence, pointing at the most prominent marks. "He set down here and claimed the cow here. Look at the marks—they are monstrous. A true elder wyrm."

Lozen asked, "Are we heading west to hunt down the Dragons?"

Rohand, frustrated, dispelled any notions of a Dragon hunt. "No. Not only no, but fukk no! Our mission is to collect and report. Put your spear down next to that track so we can accurately relay how big it is."

She placed her spear alongside one of the massive footprints. Astonishment washed over her as she realized the footprint nearly matched half the length of the shaft.

"Vid hamri Thors!" she exclaimed with awe and trepidation.

"Exactly! A warrior must know what they are up against. I thought I beat that into you. You need another lesson?"

Lozen, chastened by his words, shook her head. With fire in her eyes, she sniped back. "I don't need any more of your Special High-Intensity Training, Hersir."

Rylen, trying to dispell the tension, surveyed the scene thoughtfully. "And the bearing is the key. The Fire-Lizard wen' that way, as the man told us. It looks to have come from the black dirt of Hel."

"Hel?" Lozen asked.

"It's a viable theory," Rylen said. "Fire-beasts are known to hold their ground. The score from a hundred years ago said their source was Hel, deep in the earth."

Rohand nodded. "That makes sense. We will need to find Helgrindi—the lair. It may be the key to finding the Dragons."

Lozen asked, "What if we're in their territory? Nobody has seen them for a hundred years, but now you're settling in the valley, and they're back. A hundred years ago, Humans tried settling in the area and the Dragons attacked. Seems like whenever Humans move into the valley, Dragons show up. I know it's only two data points, but the trend looks obvious."

Rylen responded, "You should get the truth from Bryn on that. People were trying to live there, and the Fire-Lizards struck the villages and dirt-holds, which is why Ragnar brought his soldiers. I think no one has held that place until just now."

Changing the subject, Lozen asked, "Our mission is to investigate the attack and learn what we can. We have enough information for a preliminary report and even some conjecture to add to it. Wouldn't you agree, Hersir?"

Rohand agreed. "We do. Let's head back and make our report. Searching for Helgrindi—the mouth of Hel—can wait."

United by a shared purpose, the trio returned along the path, hearts racing with anticipation and unease about the upcoming briefing. Each step echoed in the stillness, heightening their excitement and reminding them of the risks ahead. The road remained shrouded in shadows, hinting at hidden dangers. Yet, despite the uncertainty, they were determined to uncover the truth, resolute in their commitment to move forward, whatever the cost.

CHAPTER 14

ARCHERY TRAINING

THIS IS ABOUT FAMILY

T HE SUMMER SUN CLIMBED high, cutting sharp shadows across the Helsgaard Keep training yard. Hrolf stood on the platform, his thoughts heavy with Rohand's recent report: four toes, a foot the size of shields, burned grass, and a missing cow. The sheer scale of the threat weighed on him. It was only when Anja and Lozen stepped up to join him that Hrolf's focus finally snapped back from the impossible reality of the Dragon to the present moment.

Looking toward Anja and Lozen stood on a raised platform, ready to address the assembled warriors. The westerly wind blew softly, keeping everyone cool as they gathered for the briefing.

Hrolf's voice, amplified by the courtyard's natural acoustics, resounded through the assembled ranks. "As your combat trainer has informed you, we will start a new training program. We have two of the best archers in all of Ravnsríki: Anja, who has been here for a while, and our newcomer, Lozen."

He gestured towards the two women with pride. "They are teaming up to train you… to become the best archers in Ravnsríki, too."

Surprised by the announcement, a murmur rippled through the ranks as the warriors exchanged glances and whispered amongst themselves.

Hrolf scanned the assembled warriors. "This Aelfinn war is escalating. They are renowned for their archery skills, and we need to match them—or come close."

He paused, letting his words sink in before delivering the surprise. "And with that, warriors, I give you a free day. Tomorrow, we begin The Feast of Miðsumarblót. After that, you train! You are dismissed!"

A cheer erupted from the ranks as the warriors, relieved by the unexpected reprieve, scattered in different directions.

Lozen approached Hrolf with hesitation and a thoughtful expression. "Mission Commander, they all seem to be so accepting of us. Us Aelfs, I mean. I expected someone to object."

Hrolf nodded. He turned to face her, his posture rigid. "We are not a club, Ranger; we are a shield line. You are judged by your service, not your blood. Individuals may carry their foolish prejudices, but they will never show them here." Hrolf put his fist next to his chest. "Discrimination is a failure of duty. A soldier who fails his duty here will be shown the gate, swift and hard."

He paused for a moment, searching her glacier blue eyes. "We rely on each other for life and death. If I can't rely on you to save them, you're out the gate. I'm sure Rohand has offered to show you to the gate, if I know him."

She said, "Uh, dragged to the gate, actually. He offered to drag me by my foot."

"Likewise, if I can't rely on any of them to save you, they're out. There is no room for that skitr in my Keep, and everyone knows it."

She nodded in understanding, her heart filled with gratitude. "Thank you, sir. I needed that."

Hrolf, a rare smile gracing his lips, nodded in acknowledgement. "You are welcome. Enjoy the free day. Take a walk outside the stone."

With that, he turned and descended from the platform.

Hans and Petr approached, grinning like boys released from chores. Petr carried a leather-wrapped ball under one arm, while Hans twirled a short stick between his fingers.

"K-k-knattleikr," Hans said, nodding toward the training field. "F-five on f-f-four. T-t-tradesclan v-v-versus us and we're sh-short one. T-thought you m-m-might want t-to help us out-t."

"Five on four? That's hardly fair—they'll need more than five."

"Yeah, right! You in? Come on!" Petr pleaded.

Lozen smiled despite herself, glancing toward the field where laughter and shouts were already rising. For a heartbeat, she considered it—the rush, the release, the simple joy of comradery and competition.

She shook her head. "Another time. I promised Anja I'd spend today learning something that doesn't end in bruises."

Petr blinked. "You? Passing up a chance to kick some ass?"

Lozen grinned, shaking her head, "If I'm going to keep us alive out there, I need to learn how to put people back together, too."

Hans snorted. "F-f-fair enough. We'll save you a p-p-place next t-time."

They wandered off, already arguing about teams, as Anja leaned closer to Lozen and murmured, "Meet me at the infirmary. I have something for you."

Lozen's brows lifted, curiosity sparking. "Sure. See you there."

⚠⚠⚠

The infirmary was unusually quiet. Sunlight streamed through narrow windows, casting a serene, almost sacred glow over the room. The usual bustling energy was absent. Lozen stood near a wooden table, her hands deftly braiding a spare bowstring. Each twist and pull was deliberate, a rhythmic act of focus that steadied her restless mind. Despite the calm, a subtle tension lingered in her stance—shoulders squared, prepared for the next challenge lurking beyond the silence.

The soft sound of footsteps broke the stillness. Anja entered the room, her presence as serene as the light yet carrying a tangible weight that seemed to fill the space. A long, cloth-wrapped object was draped over her arms, the fabric shimmering faintly in the sun's golden rays.

"I want to give this to you," Anja said simply.

Lozen looked up, curiosity in her glacier-blue eyes.

Anja stepped closer to the table and gently placed the bundle upon it. With deliberate care, she began to unwrap the cloth, first revealing the hilt of a sword—silvered and intricately etched with delicate, ancient patterns. The sheath, ornate and somehow glowing with a faint, light-blue ethereal shimmer, was a work of art. Anja drew the sword. The mírenstál gleamed, its surface flawless, a testament to the unparalleled skill of Aeldorian smiths.

Lozen's breath caught in her throat. "Is that—" she started, her voice faltering, "your sword? I've never seen you with it."

"Yes," Anja confirmed using the Aelfinn affirmation, a faint, nostalgic smile on her lips. "Since you left when you were thirteen—"

"—exiled," Lozen interjected, the correction automatic and bitter.

"You probably didn't know about the sword trial."

Lozen shook her head, mesmerized by the blade.

Anja continued, her gaze distant, fixed on a memory. "In Aeldoria, every Aelf owns a sword. It's part of who we are. When I was young, your age now, I faced a great trial. A test of my strength, my healing, and my spirit. It was a rite of passage, a sacred ceremony. I had to prove myself worthy—I fought with blade, healed with my hands, and conquered the spirits' trials in the ancient forest. When I emerged victorious, a sword forged in the fires of the earth and blessed by the stars was bestowed upon me. It was more than a weapon; it was a symbol of my power, my heritage, and my destiny."

She paused, her tone softening with a tenderness Lozen rarely heard. "And now, I want you to have it."

"Me?" Lozen's disbelief was raw. "Why would you give it to me?"

Anja met her gaze evenly. "You've proven yourself, Lozen. Not just as an archer but as a protector. You've faced challenges with courage and skill. You deserve this." Her voice grew quieter, sincere. "And more importantly—it feels right."

Lozen hesitated, her eyes flickering from the sword to Anja. "I don't understand," she said.

Anja stepped closer, placing a hand gently on Lozen's shoulder. "I am a healer, not a warrior. This sword has never seen battle, and I believe it will serve you well. It's made of míren-stál, a rare metal found only in Aeldoria."

At last, Lozen reached out, her fingers brushing against the hilt. She lifted the sword carefully. She felt its weight, its balance—it was lighter than expected, and its presence in her hand was both alien and thrillingly familiar. "It's beautiful," she breathed, her voice filled with awe. "I've never held a blade like this before. I'm an archer."

Anja's smirk was almost mischievous. "An archer who might one day need a sword," she said. "The world is unpredictable, and having options never hurts. You must name your sword."

"What did you call it?"

"Its previous name is no more as it's not my sword. You must name it as it is part of you."

Lozen paused, letting her breath steady as her fingers traced the intricate hilt. Her eyes closed as if communing with its spirit. "Her name," she said softly, her voice resonating with quiet determination, "is *Vonar Egg*—Hope's Edge. I shall wield her keen blade for the hope of a brighter tomorrow."

"Vonar Egg," Anja repeated, a profound warmth in her tone.

A single tear rolled down Lozen's cheek. She examined the sword again, its mirror-like blade reflecting her image, hinting at the warrior she might one day become. She saw a name on the hilt and looked closer, pronouncing the Aelfinn letters: "Anyael." She looked up at Anja. "You were Anyael in Aeldoria?"

"That's right."

"And you changed your name?"

"Right. Keeping a hood on and using a Human name helped us blend in. I assume they still teach that? How to blend in?"

"It is still taught. That's how I survived in Ravnborg. I thought of adopting a Human name, too. Lóssen. But nobody wants to know your name on the streets. So I was just Shadow Archer—someone with a bow blending into the shadows."

A silence settled between them, heavy with expectation.

Anja said, "You asked why I would give this to you."

Lozen looked apprehensive. "Yeah?"

"It's appropriate, in these circumstances, to—"

The door crashed open. Rylen stood rigid on the threshold. "Aye, did I miss anythin'?"

"No—just getting started." Anja exhaled, a slow, decisive release. "Lozen, I need to tell you a story."

Lozen stiffened. *A story?*

"Anja? What abou' Bryn? She said—" Rylen asked, concerned, bracing himself.

"—Fukk Bryn. This is about family."

Family? Lozen wondered, a cold curl tightening in her chest.

Anja continued, her voice taking on the clear, formal cadence of a record. "I was once the Junior Emissary to Ravnborg. The Senior Emissary, my mentor, was Soren. And Rylen," Anja continued, her voice quieter now, "was assigned to guard me. To protect me. My bodyguard, who went with me everywhere. It was a goodwill gesture."

The words felt detached, rehearsed—like something Anja had whispered to herself a hundred times.

"What does this have to do with me?" Lozen asked, her voice tight.

Anja hesitated, then pressed on. "We had an affair in Astraelyn, the capital city. We were able to keep it secret—until the day of the Peace Treaty signing when Soren exposed us. Everything fell apart. No peace deal. War erupted. The Conservors believe in a prophecy—one that speaks of a half-Aelf uniting the warring kingdoms. They fear losing their way of life."

Lozen scoffed. *A prophecy.* "That's just a campfire story," she muttered.

Anja nodded, though her expression was grim. "Maybe. But the new King, Aethor, didn't think so. He put a bounty on both of our heads. That's when we had to run."

"And?" she asked, voice sharper than she meant.

"One of the Elder Council members, Faelar, hid us," Anja said, her voice cracking on the name. "Until I could safely give birth."

Lozen flinched. *Faelar?* The same Faelar who had exiled her?

She wanted to laugh, to call it a lie. But deep down, something inside her whispered that it wasn't. She felt Rylen watching her closely, waiting for the pieces to snap together.

Anja swallowed hard and took a step forward. "Faelar hid us—all three of us."

Lozen's pulse hammered in her ears, a steady drumbeat. The infirmary walls closed in—suffocating.

The words hit like Thor's Mjölnir to the chest.

All three of us.

The room spun. The fire in the hearth crackled too loudly.

Her mind was screaming, telling her to deny it, reject it, run. But her heart—her heart already knew the shape of the lie.

Anja was still speaking, voice softer now. "We waited until you could process herbal milk. Then, Faelar smuggled us out of Aeldoria and promised to take care of you."

Silence. The world shifted beneath her feet.

Her throat tightened. Her fingers curled into fists at her sides. She couldn't speak. Couldn't breathe.

Rylen broke the silence. His voice was rough, almost hesitant. "We couldn't fix the right time to speak the matter. We were certain you would turn from us. And Bryn forced the silence upon us."

Lozen's ears rang. Her vision narrowed. She barely heard herself murmur, "So that's why Faelar told me to go to Helsgaard Keep?"

Faelar didn't exile her. It wasn't punishment. It was a path to her parents. And she wasted three years not doing it, living on the streets.

Anja sighed, rubbing her temples. "Lozen, it wasn't just fear. It was protection. You have no idea what it was like—hiding you, keeping you safe. If anyone had known—"

"—I did know!" Lozen cut in, her voice rising to a terrible pitch. "I lived it! I survived it! Alone! While you—" Her voice caught. She swallowed the lump in her throat and forced herself to continue, her tone dropping to a quieter, sharper accusation. "While you got to stay together, in a safe place."

"Two fugitives on the run with a baby? You think that was an option when we could keep you safe with a friend? A well-placed, political friend?"

Lozen turned away, running a hand along her braids, trying to pull herself together.

Anja's voice was softer now. "We thought we were doing what was best for you."

Lozen turned back, jaw tight.

Anja continued, "If anyone can understand the pain of decisions, it would be you. We did the best we could with the information at the time. Not a day has passed without me wondering what happened to you."

After a heavy moment, Lozen nodded, a small, involuntary twitch.

Anja exhaled slowly. "And Lozen?" She paused, meeting Lozen's eyes with pleading. "You don't have to figure everything out today. Just don't run from it."

Lozen didn't answer. She simply turned and walked out, leaving the mírenstál sword and the broken pieces of her life scattered on the infirmary table.

CHAPTER 15

PROCESSING THE NEWS

THE ANCHOR OF UNEXPECTED WARMTH

THE LONGHOUSE WAS BEGINNING to clear out after náttmál—supper—and the warmth of the roaring hearth was settling into the low drone of conversation. Petr approached the table where Lozen sat alone. Her bowl, still full of cold, heavy stew, sat before her.

"Lo," Petr started, sliding into the bench opposite her, his voice low and practiced. "We know that look. The one where you're tasting ash instead of roasted boar. You haven't touched the meal. What is it? Did the Commander give you a punishment detail?"

Hans sat next to Petr, his expression mirroring Petr's concern. He kept his comment short, his typical stutter present: "W-was it Rohand and h-h-his knife h-h-hand?"

Lozen slowly put down her spoon, the clink of metal against earthenware unnaturally loud. She met their gazes, her own eyes flat and distant. "No. It's nothing you need to score, or fix, or report." She gave them a dismissive, mirthless smile. "It's simply heavy. Leave me to it."

Petr looked at Hans, who gave a small, defeated shake of his head. They recognized the cold, professional barrier. This wasn't the usual grumpy Lozen; this was the wall.

"Alright," Hans conceded, standing up. "B-b-but the m-m-moment you s-s-stop looking s-s-so f-f-far away, you know wh-where t-to f-f-find us."

"Don't let yourself sink into the mountain, not when we're standing right here. We've got your back," Petr finished for him.

They left, and Lozen immediately stood, walking away from the light and the noise, out the door, leaving her full bowl behind. Hrolf watched her leave with eyes that see everything at once.

After the dishes had been cleaned up, Hrolf stepped outside. A breeze drifted across the Helsgaard Frontier, carrying the soft, familiar sounds of the night watch and the Keep settling down. Hrolf walked across the courtyard, stretching in the moonlight. The night meal had ended; the Warriors were bedding down, and Lozen hadn't returned.

He walked slowly, his sharp eyes scanning the darkened courtyards. He found her: a solitary female figure on the western watchtower, standing rigid against the vast, open wilderness beyond. Hrolf exhaled through his nose. He had seen that stance countless times—the posture of someone standing at an impossible crossroads, facing a choice that could break them.

He climbed the stone steps with deliberate slowness, the shuffle of his boots a warning, not wanting to startle her. When he reached the top, Lozen didn't turn. She stood rigid, arms crossed tightly over her chest, staring fixedly into the bottomless darkness.

For a long moment, he simply stood beside her, a companion in silence, looking out at the endless expanse of mountains and forest.

Finally, he spoke. His voice was low, careful, an anchor of normalcy. "You're upset."

She let out a slow, deliberate breath, her shoulders rising and falling. "Yes."

Silence stretched between them, thick and heavy.

He tried again, softer this time. "You don't have to talk. But if you need someone to just hold the silence—"

"—I don't." She glanced at Hrolf, and said, "Thank you."

The cold finality in her voice didn't surprise him. Hrolf studied her for a long moment, tracing the rigid lines of her silhouette. He had seen warriors break under lesser weights than whatever burden she carried. But she wasn't breaking. She was hardening, forging the hurt into a shield.

He sighed, stepping back. "Then I'll leave you to it. Don't fall."

And he descended the stairs, leaving her to the wind and the moon.

⚠⚠⚠

Lozen didn't know how long she stood there after Hrolf left, her mind an unrelenting, chaotic storm of why and how and what if? She almost didn't hear the second set of footsteps approaching.

"Are you going to stand out here all night, Little Bird?" Rohand asked, his voice rough and familiar.

She stiffened, but didn't look at him. "Maybe."

He sighed, striding beside her and leaning against the parapet. "Right. That's healthy."

She scowled, her anger immediately shifting to his unwelcome presence, but she said nothing.

He adopted the same defensive posture. "Want to tell me what's going on? Or do I have to guess?"

"No," she snapped.

He nodded, as if her refusal was confirmation. "Fine. Then I'll guess."

Lozen tensed, her gut clenching. "Don't!"

He ignored her, his eyes fixed on the moon. "It's Anja and Rylen, isn't it?"

Lozen's breath hitched, a small, involuntary sound of pain. *How did he—?*

He turned his head, watching her reaction with the critical eyes of a seasoned warrior. "Thought so."

She clenched her jaw, feeling completely exposed under his scrutiny.

Rohand exhaled slowly. "Hmmm... Let me guess again."

She whipped her head toward him, fire in her eyes. "I said, don't!"

A slow, maddening smirk spread across his face. "They're your parents, then."

Lozen's world tilted. She stared at him, stunned, taking a clumsy step back.

His smirk widened, a smug, brutal victory in his eyes. "Ah. Got it in two. Or was that one?"

Lozen's heart pounded, adrenaline flooding her system. "How—how did you know?!"

Rohand shrugged dismissively. "Everyone knows."

She blinked. "What?!"

He chuckled, a low, rumbling sound. "Think about it. You show up looking like a perfect mix between an Aelf and a Dwarf, and guess who's been living in Helsgaard Keep for sixteen years? An Aelf and a Dwarf. You're about as old as they've been here. And they look at you like a stolen relic. It wasn't exactly a bloody puzzle."

Lozen's breath came faster, shallow and ragged. "Then why didn't anyone tell me?"

"Everyone here has secrets. Not our place to flap our lips. They're your secrets." Rohand's smirk faded, replaced by a tough, uncompromising gaze. He studied her, then asked, "What did they say?"

Lozen hesitated, muttering the answer that broke her heart. "They thought I would hate them."

Rohand snorted, a sharp, disbelieving sound. "And you're proving them right."

Lozen's stomach plummeted, a devastating realization.

His voice was suddenly matter-of-fact, cutting through her self-pity like a blade. "They took a huge chance telling you the truth, and this is what you do? Run off, sulk, punish them for trying? Like a petulant little child."

Lozen's fists clenched, pure, protective anger surging. "You don't understand my—!"

"—Oh, I understand." He scoffed.

She glared. "Do you?"

He leaned in slightly, his face shadowed, whispering. "At least you have parents who want you."

Lozen froze. The words pierced straight through the center of her defenses, stopping her rage cold.

What?

Rohand's voice was quieter now, a deep, resonant rumble, but the edge of hard-won pain was unmistakable. "Mine dumped me into the Warrior Service when I was thirteen. And I haven't seen or heard a word from them since."

She swallowed hard, the years of her own abandonment suddenly feeling less unique, less isolating. She had spent so long feeling utterly alone, believing she had no one...

But she did.

And she had immediately shut them out, choosing the familiar comfort of fury over the terrifying uncertainty of hope.

Rohand took a deep breath and tilted his head toward the longhouse. "Come on. Sleep on it. It'll be better in the morning."

Lozen hesitated, her stubborn pride warring fiercely with the agonizing loneliness inside her.

Rohand didn't push. He simply waited, his presence a heavy, comforting anchor beside her.

And for the first time since Anja had spoken those fateful words, Lozen didn't feel like she was drowning alone in the abyss.

Without thinking, she turned toward him and wrapped her arms tightly around him.

Rohand stiffened in surprise—a momentary confusion—then slowly, deliberately, wrapped his arms around her in return, holding her fast against his rough hewn tunic.

His voice was barely above a whisper, vibrating against her temple. "You're important, Lozen. You're valuable. You're wanted here."

She squeezed her eyes shut, her throat tightening with unshed tears.

Maybe, but does she allow herself to believe in it?

But standing there, held together by the warmth of someone who refused to leave her alone, she could at least pretend it was true.

⚠⚠⚠

When they returned to the longhouse, the familiar warmth from the hearth greeted them like an old friend.

Rohand paused, giving the sleeping occupants of the longhouse a hard look. He nudged a few of the HouseBrothers and HouseSisters, motioning for them to shift aside. This close proximity, next to the hearth, was sudden change in the House rules, but no one challenged the lead trainer's unspoken command.

Lozen hesitated beside the bedroll. With a quiet exhale, she pulled back the fur and settled beside him.

As the longhouse settled into soft breathing, snoring, and the occasional creak of wood, Rohand wrapped an arm around her stomach, pulling her close against his steady warmth.

No words.

No expectations.

Only Human warmth.

And for the first time since leaving Elowen, Lozen let herself be held.

CHAPTER 16

HOUSE REORGANIZATION

NO SECRETS, NO LEVERAGE

THE MORNING SUN STREAMED through the infirmary's open windows, catching dust motes in the light. The air smelled of dried herbs, clean linen, and the faintest trace of antiseptic salve.

Lozen stood in the doorway, her heart pounding like war drums in her chest.

Anja stood across the room, her graying platinum hair loose, blue eyes watching Lozen with a quiet, cautious patience. She wore a plain brown tunic, sleeves rolled up, as if she were working, braced for impact.

Lozen took a slow breath, stepping forward.

Another step, and another.

Anja straightened, fingers twitching at her sides, but she didn't move.

Lozen stopped right in front of her, searching her mother's face.

Without a word, she wrapped her arms around her mother, burying her face in Anja's tunic.

Anja stiffened for half a breath, a shock of relief and joy seizing her. Then she melted completely into the embrace, her arms tightening around Lozen's back, her fingers digging in gently as if afraid Lozen might disappear if she let go. A shaky, silent sound escaped her throat.

Lozen pressed her forehead against Anja's shoulder, her grip firm, unyielding.

"You should have told me," she murmured, her voice muffled but steady, stripped of last night's rage.

Anja let out a shaky exhale. "We wanted to. Every single day."

Lozen pulled back a little, frowning. "Then why didn't you?"

Anja hesitated.

Before she could speak, Rylen's rough voice came from the door.

"Because we couldnae agree on the proper date. And Bryn told Anja she dare not tell you, or she would drop our truth right in the King's ear. Like so many who live here in Helsgaard, we are outlaws with a death bounty on our heads."

Lozen turned to see her father leaning against the doorway, arms crossed over his chest, expression weary but honest.

Anja nodded, rubbing a hand over her brow. "I wanted to tell you as soon as we realized who you were. I saw the eyes."

Rylen sighed. "And I argued for the delay. To let you root yourself here, lass. To let you secure your ground."

Lozen huffed, folding her arms. "So instead, I got neither. Years of a lie followed by shock."

Anja winced. "You're right. There is a cost to the choices we are forced to make, and we're sorry for the years we lost."

Lozen looked between them, her mouth twisting into a weary frown. "This is a hard truth to learn."

Anja's lips twitched despite herself. "Running with a baby and death warrants on our heads was not the answer. Leaving you safe in Aeldoria was the only choice we had. Your life was the priority, as painful as that decision was."

Rylen shrugged. "Cannae argue that."

Lozen sighed, rolling her shoulders as if shaking off the weight of the last sixteen years. "I'm glad to learn the truth of it, and as I've made my way to you, you're stuck with me now."

Anja smiled—a real one this time—full of fierce happiness. "Wouldn't have it any other way."

Lozen hesitated and nodded. "Good." She exhaled. "What now?"

Anja tilted her head, amusement flickering in her gaze. "I need to gather herbs before the sun gets too high. You coming?"

Lozen raised an eyebrow. "Since when do I gather herbs?"

"Since you're apparently stuck with me as a mother and mentor."

Rylen chuckled from the doorway. "Ye ran straight for the snare, daughter."

Lozen rolled her eyes but followed Anja outside. They walked together into the forest beyond the Keep, the earthy scent of damp moss and pine filling the air.

Anja knelt near a cluster of small, white flowers. "These are meadowsweet. Good for fever and nausea." She plucked a few, placing them in a small satchel before glancing up at Lozen. "Come on, help me look."

Lozen sighed but crouched beside her, fingers tracing the delicate petals before pulling a few from the stem. "I still think battle is more useful than brewing teas."

Anja smirked. "And yet, warriors still need healers when they take an axe to the leg."

Lozen huffed but kept picking. They moved from patch to patch, filling their satchels. The quiet rhythm of the task settled something in Lozen; the air between them felt lighter, less fragile.

As they reached a small clearing, Anja stood, brushing dirt from her hands. "You were always going to find out. But Bryn made sure it wouldn't be on my terms. She warned me that if I told you, she'd turn on us—tell the King where we were. Risking that meant risking our lives."

Lozen met her gaze. "And you're risking it now?"

Anja studied her for a long moment, her eyes steady and resolute. "Some things are worth the risk. You are."

Lozen exhaled, looked around eyeing a new plant and shifting her satchel. "So... what does foxleaf do?"

Anja chuckled, a sound of triumph. "Ah, now you're interested. Come on, I'll teach you on the way back."

Lozen groaned, but fell into step beside her, listening as her mother spoke. The forest felt different now—warmer, somehow. Less foreign.

⛰⛰⛰

The air inside Commandant Günther's office carried a weight of practicality and unspoken tension. The fire burned low, its flickering glow casting restless shadows across the large wooden table, where logistical items lay scattered.

At one end, Günther and Hrolf leaned forward, their expressions unreadable. Anja and Rylen stood side by side, their postures steady, their eyes sharp.

Lozen perched on the edge of a chair next to Anja, arms crossed, trying not to feel like a logistical problem being sorted out.

Bryn was there—casual as ever, arms folded, her knowing smirk setting Rylen's teeth on edge.

Günther exhaled, running a hand through his silver beard. "Well," he said gruffly, "normally, this would be simple. Family First. You should be together. But given the current housing situation, we need to decide."

Hrolf nodded. "Warrior House is full. Höfn House has open beds."

Anja folded her arms, her expression neutral. "So you're suggesting Lozen moves there?"

Hrolf nodded. "Yes. Moving you to Warrior House would mean displacing others. Höfn House has the space."

Lozen shifted uncomfortably. "So, I have to move?"

Günther cut in. "It's not a punishment. Höfn House isn't exile—it's a haven. You'll still train with the Warriors or work with your Mom." He paused, his gaze steady. "Can I say 'Mom'? This is about keeping family together."

Lozen sighed, rubbing her temple. Warrior House felt familiar—rough, brutal, sarcastic. Höfn House meant being under the same roof as her parents. "But that's my home. I don't want to move."

Günther said, "With Helsgaard's growth, we're going to get more warriors and there's no room for them in Warrior House. We need to stop segregating the houses anyway."

Bryn spoke, amusement dripping from her voice. "You realize, once this decision's made, the whole Keep will know. No more secrets. No more whispers."

Rylen, his gaze cold and hard as iron, cut Bryn a sharp look. "There is no shade where the light is strong. No truth is hidden. No lever to move us."

Bryn's grin widened, a silent acknowledgment of the loss of her power.

Rylen's hand twitched at his side. Slowly, deliberately, his fingers formed the blótstafn—the mark of profound contempt and damnation, a curse damning a soul as a breaker of oaths.

Bryn saw the gesture. Her grin vanished, replaced by a flicker of genuine shock, but she quickly recovered. "Charming as always. Let's see how that works out for you."

Günther cleared his throat. "Enough." His gaze swept the room, landing on Lozen. "Höfn House. Final decision. That a problem?"

Lozen hesitated and shook her head. "No, sir."

Hrolf nodded. "Good. Then it's done. And one more thing. Your friends Hans and Petr will move with you. This will help with the overcrowding."

Günther looked at her, eyes glinting. "Congratulations on your promotion."

Lozen blinked. "Sir?"

"Anja and Rylen are the most senior in Höfn House, having been here the longest, so they sleep next to the hearth." He gave her a pointed look. "You'll be with them. Warm and cozy in the winter."

Anja squeezed Lozen's shoulder gently. Rylen, having made his point, looked like he wanted to deck Bryn, but he kept his mouth shut.

As she stood to leave, Bryn nudged Lozen with an elbow, her voice quieter, lighter.

"Welcome to family life."

Lozen sighed but didn't argue. It would take some getting used to.

⚠⚠⚠

Inside the cramped RIOS communications room, no more than two arm-spans on a side, Bryn stood before a wall-length map of Ravnsríki. Each contour was expertly etched, every settlement and borg marked by fist-sized crystal globes. Within the softly glowing spheres, faces hovered—some looking in, some turned away—silent, living proof of the network's omnipresence.

Heavy tapestries softened the space, their intricate patterns adding warmth and muffling sound. The thick fabric, combined with the steadily floating pale lights, cast the room in an ethereal, cold glow—no flame, no smoke, just steady, living radiance—a silent echo chamber for secrets.

The face in the Ravnborg globe shifted, clarifying into the sharp features of Arne, the main operator. His voice crackled through the globe's inherent distortion. "*Bryn. Speak your trouble.*"

Bryn leaned heavily against the wooden table. "Our new arrival didn't exactly slide in quietly. Turns out she's pretty spicy. And get this—our Aelfinn healer and one of the Warriors are her parents. The whole Keep knows now. On top of that, she and her mother got the bright idea to teach all the Warriors archery. The Commandant and Mission Commander bought in."

She shook her head, the pressure mounting. "How did this situation go so far awry? We've got to regain control over this Dwaelf."

There was a pregnant pause, filled only by the ambient hum of the technology. "*Hold on...*" Arne muttered, followed by the faint sound of copper sheets shuffling far away. "*The half-Aelf Lozen's parents are there? The mother is an Aelf, but the father?*"

"He's a Dwarf, raise with Humans in Ravnborg."

A sharp intake of breath whistled through the line. "*Vid hamri Thors! We've been looking for them for almost twenty years. Why didn't anyone flag them?*"

Bryn's brows lifted in genuine surprise. "You said you had nothing on them. Now you do?"

"*We checked some local intel—old file data that was flagged for political sensitivity.*"

"In the taverns," Bryn guessed dryly.

"*Best place for secrets is the taverns and the brothels.*" Arne's voice turned smug, dripping with the satisfaction of a captured secret. "*Turns out your healer was the Aelfinn Emissary before the war started. Her bodyguard? A Captain of the Guard—*"

"—Rylen. Captain Rylen." Bryn's stomach dropped. The cold, political logic of the entire situation snapped into place.

"*And they are blamed for causing the war. The Aelfs put a death bounty on all of them because of some superstition about a half-breed Aelf bringing ruin to their kingdom.*"

They stared at each other in the globes for a tense moment—two faces separated by miles, yet joined by the weight of revelation.

"*Listen close,*" Arne said, voice dropping to a low, dangerous register. "*It wasn't a jealous courtier who exposed them. It was Soren—the Lead Aelfinn Emissary. He staged the reveal and rubbed it in with Human stink: a 'caught' Ravnborg courier, a planted ledger. Our read is simple: RIOS believes Soren—and King Aethor—meant to paint Humans as devious and sneaky so any peace would taste like a Human trick. The scandal gave them the fire they wanted for war."*

Bryn blinked, processing the scope of the conspiracy. "So you're telling me I'm supposed to groom the Aelfinn Doombringer, the literal cause of the war, as an asset?"

"You're the one who wanted her. She cost us extra to keep her out of the dungeon."

Bryn pinched the bridge of her nose, fighting a tactical headache. "Aaagghh."

"So what do you want to do? The political fallout of revealing this is astronomical."

A heavy pause. Bryn had to choose between protocol and the potential use of the asset.

Arne continued. *"We either cut her loose, right now, or let things play out. Maybe she'll resolve our problems for us."*

Bryn's stomach churned. "You mean die?"

"That's what warriors do, yes?" Arne countered, without inflection.

Bryn folded her arms, the subtle protectiveness rising. "She's still just a kid, Arne. And a liability now."

A dry chuckle echoed slightly. *"Well? She's your liability."*

She sighed, rolling a tense shoulder. "Let's wait and see. Girl's like a raging ram in a weaving room. She creates chaos, and chaos is useful."

"Your call—she's your project. You recruited her. Between you and me? We should've let her rot in the dungeon."

"Thanks. Thanks for your support," Bryn said flatly.

"By the way." Arne held up a stack of old, thick copper sheets inscribed with runes. *"We're burying Rylen's history.*

These sheets are headed to the forge for recycling. He will remain a ghost."

"You fukken skitkarl! I'm out here in the field, and you're taking away my leverage! You're stripping my bargaining power! Skitr!"

"*He was a Captain of the Guard. He's gone through enough. Let him fade away. You lost that leverage when the whole Keep saw them hug.*"

Bryn held the silence a heartbeat, jaw tight. The loss of the threat was palpable. "Vid hamri Thors!"

"*Bryn. Not everybody is a tool for you to use in grooming your garden. You should be thanking us.*"

"And you're not in the field," she shot back, her voice laced with venom.

She reached out and forcefully touched the Ravnborg globe, ending the connection. The image blinked out, the sphere settling back to its neutral, watchful shimmer, leaving Bryn alone with the monumental, terrifying chaos she had just guaranteed.

CHAPTER 17

HELSGAARD RANGERS

THE FAIRY AND THE DRAGON'S HEADS

THE INFIRMARY SMELLED SHARPLY of pine pitch and boiled linen. Oil lamps flickered, casting restless light over the cots and the scarred oak table where instruments lay in perfect order. Anja stood facing the door, sleeves rolled, meticulously washing a line of stitches from a Warrior's lucky escape in a training accident. Her movements were exact, the way a person moves who has taught their hands to obey when the heart will not.

Bryn paused at the threshold, her usual swagger replaced by a deliberate softness. "Anja?"

Anja continued her suturing. "You must want something that requires quiet."

"I do." Bryn came closer, palms open, her posture signaling deference. "About Soren."

A sudden stillness arrested Anja's shoulders. She finished the stitch, tied the knot, snipped the thread, and only then looked up, her blue eyes sharp. "You found something in RIOS. Something the ledger buried."

Bryn considered the easy lie—that this was just rumor—and let it die. "Ravnborg is burying Rylen. His copper sheets are headed to the forge to be melted. Arne made sure of it." She swallowed. "I have less leverage than I thought, and you are far more dangerous than I thought."

Anja's mouth tightened, a thin, bitter line. "That is how men like Soren win. They erase the ledger, then swear there was no debt."

Bryn pulled out the chair opposite, but remained standing. "Tell me about the man. Not the title. I need to know how he moves."

Anja dried her hands on a clean cloth, then hovered them above the Warrior's wound, summoning the faint, ethereal Aelfinn healing light.

After a moment, she took a deep breath. "He is neat. That is the first thing people miss. Nails clean. Ink never on the fingers. His words are sharpened until they do the cutting for him. He never raises his voice. He lets silence make you volunteer your own throat."

She glanced at the stitched Ranger, asleep. She lowered her tone. "He smelled of juniper and winter mint. He said 'please' when he ordered ruin."

Bryn waited, the unspoken question hanging heavy.

"The affair revelation?" Anja's gaze went far away, bright with a residual hurt she still refused to let settle. "He staged it like a ritual. A courier 'caught' with Human notes. Pages dressed in Human cipher, a scribe's hand mimicking Human's. Witnesses placed where they could gasp on cue. He wanted the stain to look Human—a trick, a snare. And when the court fed on it, he spoke the old words in the new way: treason, impurity, obligatory death."

Her fingers curled. "Then came the bounty. Mine. Rylen's. The unborn child's. He called it cleansing."

"Why the child? Lozen, you mean?"

"Yes, Lozen. Because Soren believes order is a bloodline and disorder is a contagion." Anja's voice roughened with deep contempt. "A half-Aelf is a breach in his wall. The harbinger of a silly prophecy told around campfires."

"You were his protégé. The star of his diplomacy."

"I was his example," Anja said, and now the pain showed; not tears, but the cold, flat exhaustion after them. "He smiled when he used it."

Silence held a moment. Outside, a cart rattled past the shutter.

"Truth, then," Bryn said, her voice steady. "If he is still moving pieces, where does his hand fall next?"

Anja looked to the door, to the Keep beyond it, to the sky past that. "On the story," she said. "He will not come with steel first. He will come with a directed narrative. A forged letter, a witness who swears, a stain that looks like ours. When the room is ready to believe it, then he sends the knives."

Bryn nodded, once. "Ah, yes. Disinformation."

Anja's eyes sharpened as she looked at Bryn. "You came gentle because you lost your tools. Don't lose your teeth with them."

Bryn managed a thin smile. "I came gentle because I need the truth faster than I need a win. Now I have the target."

"That is wise," Anja said, and it sounded like it hurt her to grant it. "Keep Lozen where witnesses are many and records are double-written. Make Soren do his work in a crowd."

Bryn pushed back from the table. "If he comes here?"

Anja picked up her cloth again, hands steady by force. "Soren prefers to win with paper. If paper fails him, he will use a knife. Seems unlikely he will—we're so remote. If he does, he's probably wielding knives, and lots of them." She met Bryn's eyes. "Do you know something you're not telling?"

"No. You're the only person in Ravnsríki that knew Soren. I'm just collecting information."

"The information is poison, Bryn. You can wear it like a tool, but it will coat your insides if you're not careful," Anja said, her voice dropping into a low, professional warning, like advising a patient about a strong-acting potions. She reached out, not to touch, but to offer a clean, folded square of linen. "Soren wins because he makes others as cold as he is. Don't let him take your heat along with his secrets. Guard your boundaries as fiercely as you guard your intelligence."

Bryn squared her shoulders and walked out toward the RIOS Communications Room, her mind already spinning a counter-narrative. If Soren fought with political disinformation, the King and RIOS needed her assessment—now.

⚠️⚠️⚠️

The sun beat down on the dusty training yard, turning dust to a persistent, blinding glare. A double rank of newly formed Warriors stood with bows in hand—too stiff, too slow, too Human.

Anja paced the line, correcting grips and shoulders. "Breathe on the draw. Hold the wrist steady. Again."

Lozen moved among them like a flicker of shadow—tapping an elbow, nudging a stance, adjusting a sightline. Her voice was cold and precise. "You're high. You're late. Fix it." Arrows thudded. The wild scatter began to tighten.

Olaf, broad-shouldered and smirking, waited until the moment was perfect. As Lozen stepped past him, his foot shifted.

Lozen's foot caught. She fell hard, hitting the ground face-first in the dirt.

A ripple of stifled laughter broke the silence. Lozen spun, eyes blazing, and met Olaf's smug expression.

"Oops," he drawled, utterly unapologetic. "Aelf should watch where she's going."

Petr broke from the line instantly, dropping his bow in the dust. He stepped into Olaf's space, fists clenched, his face flushed with a hard, dangerous anger.

"You want to try that with me? " Petr growled, shoving Olaf's chest. "Or are you only brave when they aren't looking?"

"Petr. Stand down," she said, her voice steady, refusing to let Olaf see her rattled. "I don't need a shield."

Petr hesitated, glaring at Olaf one last time before stepping back, though his muscles remained coiled.

Lozen pushed herself up, dusting off her tunic. Her instincts screamed for violence. Instead, she forced her rage into cold cunning. She snatched his bow, flipped it, examined his stance, and handed it back—just enough off-center to make him fumble the catch.

"Your grip's sloppy. You lose control faster than I lose my footing," she said smoothly. "Watch that, too."

The yard laughed at Olaf, not at her. He did not try that particular stunt again.

Days slid into weeks. They trained in wind and glare, in mail and leathers, on walls and slopes. Anja drilled precision until their fingers ached; Lozen taught them to shoot ugly—off-balance, under pressure, at targets that moved and feigned.

Lozen stepped behind Bjorn, whose knuckles were white with tension. "Loosen your fingers," she said. "You're choking the bow. Like a snake you're afraid of. Relax."

Bjorn exhaled sharply through his nose. "I got this... Aelf."

He loosed the arrow. The arrow flew wide, burying itself in the dirt an arm-span to the left of the straw man.

"My rass you got this," Lozen snapped. "You got nothing."

Bjorn gritted his teeth, his face flushing, but he held his tongue.

Hans, standing in the next lane, snorted loud enough for the line to hear. "Y-your m-mouth is sharp, Bjorn. T-too b-bad your aim isn't."

"Stow it," Lozen snapped, stepping between them. "Save the mouth for the tavern. On this line, the only thing that speaks is the arrow—and yours is silent."

Bjorn glared at Hans, then Lozen, but he turned back to the target, his knuckles white on the bow. The morning ground on, the tension in the yard rising with the sun. Heat radiated off the stone walls, turning the air heavy and suffocating. By the time the horn blew for the midday meal, patience had evaporated along with the morning mist, leaving only raw nerves and simmering aggression.

During a midday break, the heat shimmering, and the air was thick with the musk of sweat. Olaf barreled into her, shoulder-checking her hard as he passed. Lozen stumbled.

A fury ignited in her chest. She spun around, muscles coiled with rage.

A firm hand gripped her shoulder. She barely turned her head, but Petr's grip was enough. A silent command: Not here. Not now.

Olaf smirked, arms crossed. "What's the matter? Your friends have to save you?" His mockery, reducing her to a dependent child, hung heavy in the air.

Lozen didn't take the bait. Instead, she stepped in close—grabbing his crotch—her lips a breath from his ear. Her voice dropped to a whisper, cold as winter steel. "I know where you sleep. And don't think for a minute I won't cut off your manhood and feed it to you."

Olaf scoffed, but his gaze wavered. Lozen smiled—a slow, knowing thing.

◬◬◬

The heat of the day had not broken, and the dust in the yard was hot enough to sting through thin leather. During a transition drill, Hrolf paced the line, his sharp gaze sweeping the Warriors. He stopped.

Two figures stood out—not for their posture, but for their feet. Bjorn and Olaf stood in formation in their wool socks, shifting their weight uncomfortably to avoid the scorching, sun-baked dirt.

"Bjorn! Olaf!" Hrolf barked, pointing at their feet. "Where are your boots?"

Bjorn stared straight ahead, his face burning brighter than the sun. "On the roof of the longhouse, sir," he muttered. "Hanging from the Dragon's heads."

Hrolf followed his gaze. Sure enough, four boots dangled by their laces from the carved wooden dragon heads jutting from the roof peaks, swaying gently in the breeze like grotesque ornaments. He bit the inside of his cheek to suppress a smirk. "And how did they get up there?"

Bjorn and Olaf looked puzzled, remaining silent.

"Did we get a fairy infestation overnight? Tiny wings fluttering your gear away while you slept?"

Bjorn and Olaf shook their heads.

"That is community property, and you are responsible for it. Go get them!"

The bootless Warriors were perplexed. Bjorn asked "How do we get up—"

"—Find a fukken fairy. I don't care. GO GET THEM! RUN!"

The bootless warriors took off, bolting across the yard toward the longhouse, wincing as their stockinged feet hit sharp stones. The rest of the Warrior House howled with laughter behind them.

Hrolf turned slowly to the two Aelfs standing nearby. Anja was inspecting her fingernails. Lozen was watching a cloud. They looked back at him, the picture of wide-eyed innocence.

He exhaled audibly, rolling his eyes and shaking his head.

"Carry on," he grunted.

△△△

On the twenty-eighth day of archery training, the sun began to dip below the horizon, casting long shadows across the training yard. Exhausted but triumphant, the archers stood before Lozen and Anja, their faces beaming with pride. What was once a group of novice archers had transformed into a cohesive unit, their skills sharpened and confidence soaring.

Hrolf and Bryn approached the trainers, his stern features softened by a look of genuine approval. "I am impressed. Your methods have yielded remarkable results. Bryn observed your methods, measured the results, and I am pleased."

He moved to the raised platform, his steps purposeful and measured. Hopping up on it, he surveyed the archers with a keen eye. "All archers, circle up on me."

The archers' movements were crisp and efficient. They quickly circled, looking up at their Commander.

"I have received reports from your training team that in the last turning of the moon, you have mastered archery and, in some cases, shoot almost as well as any Aelfs."

Lozen and Anja exchanged smiles, their hearts swelling with a shared sense of accomplishment. Their hard work and dedication paid off, and the archers under their tutelage exceeded all expectations.

Hrolf gazed upon the assembled warriors, his voice steady and commanding. "Your mastery of melee and archery, your deep understanding of nature and the ways of the land—skills that will endure and grow under the leadership of Anja and Lozen—set you apart. You have embraced the mantle of protectors, thriving on the edges of society where others would falter. But you are no longer mere warriors. You have become something greater, something extraordinary."

He paused, letting his words sink in before delivering the momentous pronouncement. "From this day forward, with your mastery of the forest, axe, and arrow, you will be known as the Helsgaard Rangers. Well done!"

The crowd roared with approval as the newly christened Rangers cheered and clapped each other on the back. A sense of camaraderie and shared achievement permeated the air, confirming the bonds forged in the crucible of training. Petr and Hans both looked to Lozen with a silent "thank you," and she nodded in return.

Anja and Lozen shared a proud smile, their faces beaming. They trained a new generation of elite warriors, and Lozen discovered purpose within the walls of Helsgaard Keep.

"You are dismissed!" Hrolf bellowed with respect for the Rangers under his command.

As the Rangers dispersed, their laughter and chatter echoed off the Keep walls. Anja and Lozen stood amidst the fading sunlight, their faces illuminated by dusk's warm, golden hues. They savored the sweetness of their hard-earned victory, their hearts filled with triumph. Overcoming adversity and defying expectations, they emerged as formidable leaders, their bond strengthened by shared experiences.

CHAPTER 18

THE BLUNTWOOD

WOOD BLEEDS LESS.

THE CELEBRATION AFTER THE archery training completed had dulled to a low hum as the sun dipped lower, casting long, bruised shadows across the training yard. Most of the newly named Rangers had drifted toward the mead hall to toast their new titles, but Lozen remained by the weapon racks, checking her bowstring.

"Hey, Ranger Lozen," a voice called out.

Lozen rolled her eyes and turned. Petr and Hans approached, grinning like wolves who'd found an open coop. Petr held a long object wrapped in oilcloth.

"Don't call me that," Lozen snapped, though there was no heat in it. "Hrolf gave the titles. I just yelled at you until you stopped missing."

Hans chuckled, his blue eyes bright. "A-and now w-we're R-rangers. B-but Rangers n-need more than strings."

Petr stepped forward, offering the bundle. "We've been working on this. Since you were busy teaching us not to shoot our own feet."

Lozen took it, the weight surprising her. She unwound the cloth to reveal a wooden sword. It wasn't a crude stick; it was carved from heavy, seasoned oak, weighted with lead in the pommel to mimic the heft of steel. The edges were rounded, but the balance felt dangerous.

"A bluntwood," Petr said. "For practice. Anja showed us how to make it."

"I wondered what you two were up to." Lozen blinked, touched. She reached to her belt and unclasped Vonar Egg, the mírenstál sword Anja had given her weeks ago. She held the gleaming, blue-tinged metal in her left hand and the oak bluntwood in her right.

She tested the weight of both, tipping her wrists.

"Vid hamri Thors," she whispered. "It's... it's almost identical. The balance point, the grip length... how did you do this?"

"I t-t-told you," Hans said proudly. "Anja showed us. We w-watched. And w-we measured when y-you weren't l-looking."

"It's amazing," she admitted, sheathing Vonar Egg and gripping the oak handle with two hands. "Thank you."

"Don't thank us yet," Petr said, drawing a beat-up training shield from his back. Hans did the same. "Now we help you learn to use it."

"Yes," Anja's voice cut in from the shadows of the infirmary doorway. "I will teach her. You two will be the walls."

Anja stepped into the light, her movements fluid and predatory. She gestured to the open dirt. "Lozen, center. Petr, Hans—flank her. Shields up. Close the distance."

Lozen raised the wooden sword, feeling foolish. "I know how to fight, Anja."

"You know how to shoot," Anja corrected, circling them like a shark. "And you know how to brawl in a tavern or mud pit. This is different. Petr, Hans—press her."

The two men moved in. They didn't swing weapons; they simply walked her down, hiding behind the rims of their round shields.

Lozen stepped back, looking for an opening. There wasn't one. Petr slammed his shield against her right shoulder, knocking her off balance. Before she could recover, Hans checked her from the left, pinning her between the wood and leather.

"Hey!" Lozen yelped, trying to shove Petr away with the crossguard. "Get off! I can't move!"

"That is the point!" Anja barked. "In melee, personal space is a luxury you do not have. You are an archer; you crave distance. You want the clean shot from fifty paces. The sword is not a conversation across the room, Lozen. It is a whisper in the ear. It is intimate. It is suffocating."

Petr shoved harder, grinding the shield rim into her ribs.

"Ow. Fukk!" Lozen whined, driving an elbow into Petr's shield, which did absolutely nothing. "It's like wrestling a bear in a closet! How am I supposed to swing?"

"You don't swing!" Anja corrected, stepping in to adjust Lozen's grip. "You leverage. You create space. Use the pommel. Use your feet—back up. Stop trying to kill them and start trying to breathe!"

Lozen grunted, stomping on Petr's foot. He flinched, giving her an inch. She slipped out, panting, hair wild.

"Again," Anja ordered.

A small crowd of Rangers had gathered by the racks, mead horns forgotten in their hands. Most had never seen a sword used in earnest—axes and spears were the weapons of Ravn-sríki. They watched with fascination as the two men bullied Lozen around the yard, and the healer barked commands on angles and footwork.

The bruising became a daily ritual. For weeks, while the Keep prepared for war, Lozen spent her evenings getting crushed between shields, whining about the lack of air, and slowly, painfully, learning to turn her hips to slip the crush.

One evening, the air thick with the smell of ozone and impending rain, Anja halted the spar.

"Enough," Anja said. She looked at the bruised, sweating trio. "You are moving well, Lozen. You are finding the gaps. But you still treat the sword like a club. You do not trust the edge."

Lozen wiped sweat from her eyes. "It's a wooden stick, Anja. It doesn't have an edge."

"Then let us change the lesson." Anja pointed to a training dummy—a thick log post wrapped in old leather armor. "Petr, strap your shield to the post."

Petr looked intrigued, lashing his battered training shield to the wood.

"Lozen," Anja said, her voice dropping to a hush that silenced the gathering crowd of Rangers. "Draw Vonar Egg."

Lozen hesitated. She handed the bluntwood to Hans and reached for her belt. The mírenstál blade hissed as it left the sheath, glowing with a faint, ethereal blue light in the dusk.

The Rangers murmured. Up close, the metal looked like frozen starlight.

"Attack the target," Anja commanded. "Do not hold back. Strike the shield."

"I'll chip the blade," Lozen argued. "That's iron-rimmed oak."

"Strike it."

Lozen took a breath. She settled into the stance Anja had drilled into her—low, balanced. She stepped in, twisted her hips, and unleashed a two-handed cut, expecting the jarring shock of impact.

CRACK.

There was no shock. The mírenstál blade bit into the iron rim of the shield and didn't stop. It sheared through the metal, sliced through the oak planks, and buried itself deep into the log of the dummy behind it.

The top half of the shield clattered to the dirt, severed cleanly.

Lozen stood frozen, the vibration humming in her hands. The Rangers gasped, a collective intake of breath. Petr stared at his ruined shield, eyes wide.

"V-v-vid hamri Thors," Hans stuttered. "T-that... that went t-through iron like c-cheese."

Lozen pulled the blade free. The edge was unmarred.

Rylen stepped up beside Anja, his face grim as he looked at the shattered wood. He addressed the stunned Rangers.

"Aye," Rylen said, his voice carrying over the yard. "Take a good measure. Every Aelf in Aeldoria carries a blade like this. Your axes will lose their edge. Your shields will split like dry pine. Do not trust your wood to hold the line against that steel."

"Rylen!" one of the Rangers called out. "You act like the Aelfs are coming. Last I heard they're stickin' to their trees making logging difficult down by the border."

"The stone never stays still, friend," he replied, his voice dropping to a low rumble. "And we need to be ready when the mountain moves."

Anja nodded, her eyes on Lozen. "Archery keeps them away. But if they get close... this is the reality. That is why you train to not get hit. Because you cannot block this."

Lozen looked at the sword in her hand, then at the destruction it had wrought. She finally understood the desperation of Anja's lessons.

"Okay," Lozen whispered, sheathing the glowing blade. She picked up the wooden bluntwood. "Petr, Hans. Get new shields. We go again."

The rhythmic clack of wood against wood resumed, echoing off the stone walls as the sun died behind the western peaks. Lozen threw herself into the dance, sweat stinging her eyes, driving the image of the shattered shield from her mind with every strike. But as the twilight deepened, a cold wind swept down from the pass, rattling the iron rings of the gate and stirring the dust in the yard. It tasted of ozone and old earth, a restless draft that made Rylen's warning feel less like advice and more like a prophecy. The stone might not move on its own, but the storm was already hunting for its mountain.

CHAPTER 19

HAUSTBLÓT: THE FIRE'S WARNING

THE STORM WILL FIND ITS MOUNTAIN

THE BRISK AUTUMN AIR carried the scent of roasting boar and cloves, but on the edge of the training yard, the only smell Lozen registered was the ozone-tang of cut air and pine resin.

Hiss. Thwack.

While the rest of Helsgaard Keep huddled around the roaring bonfire for Haustblót, Lozen moved in the shadows. In her hand, Vonar Egg was a blur of pale starlight. The mírenstál blade, light as a willow switch but harder than diamond, sang a high, lethal note as she pivoted.

She didn't hack; she flowed. With a pivot of her hips, she drove the blade through a thick training post wrapped in hardened leather. The sword sheared through the wood with terrifying ease, severing the top half of the dummy. It clattered to the frozen ground, the cut surface smooth as glass.

"Lozen!" Hrolf's voice boomed from the firelight, cutting through her focus. "The boar is dead, the gods are fed, and the mead is pouring. Stop terrorizing the woodwork and join us!"

Lozen exhaled, her breath pluming in the chill air. She flicked Vonar Egg to the side—a habit to clear blood that wasn't there—and slid the blade into the scabbard at her hip with a sharp snick.

She stepped from the cold perimeter into the warmth of the feast. Long wooden tables were crowded with Rangers, their faces flushed with firelight and ale. It was a celebration of survival, of stores filled with venison and elk thanks to the archery training she and Anja had led.

She swung a leg over the bench between Rylen and Anja, dropping heavily onto the seat. Across from her, Petr eyed the decapitated training dummy in the distance, then looked at the mírenstál hilt resting against her thigh.

"You keep the trades clan busy," Petr grinned, tearing a chunk of bread. "That's the third post this week. They're starting to complain that Vonar Egg cuts faster than they can build."

"Then they should build them stronger," Lozen said, reaching for a trencher of venison.

Hrolf stood at the head of the fire, raising a massive drinking horn. "To Lozen and Anja!" he roared, silencing the chatter. "Without their skill, we'd be gnawing on bark and wishing for spring. Instead, we feast! Skål!"

"Skål!" The cheer rippled through the yard, horns clashing.

Lozen raised her cup, offering a tight smirk, but she didn't relax. Her hand rested instinctively on her sword pommel.

Rylen leaned in, his voice low enough to slide under the noise of the party. He nodded toward a group of younger Rangers who were eyeing Lozen's weapon with a mix of awe and hesitation.

"They see it, you know," Rylen murmured. "The blade. The way you move with it."

"They see a weapon," Lozen said.

"They see difference," Anja corrected gently, placing a hand on Lozen's arm. "They honor us tonight, but war leaves deep scars. To them, that sword isn't just steel. It's Aelfinn magic. It makes you... other."

Lozen's jaw tightened. She looked at the sword—Vonar Egg, Hope's Edge. It was a masterpiece of the Aelfinn smiths, lighter and deadlier than any heavy iron axe on the table.

"Let them look," Lozen said, her voice flat. "Iron rusts. This doesn't."

"True Nordlund kin," Rylen said, his fingers curling around Anja's hand but his eyes hard on Lozen. "Regardless of the steel you carry or the ears you hide. Never let them make you feel small for being sharp."

Petr leaned across the table, pouring more mead into Lozen's horn. "Ignore the looks, Lo. They're just jealous. You can cut a fly off a mule's ear without waking the beast. They're just wondering if you'll use that thing to carve the roast."

Lozen finally let a real smile break through. She drew Vonar Egg just an inch from the sheath, the exposed mírenstál gleaming with a cold, internal fire that outshone the bonfire.

"If I carve the roast," she said, "I'll cut the table in half, too."

Petr laughed, clinking his horn against hers. The tension broke, but as Lozen drank, she kept one hand on the hilt. The feast was for the living, but the sword was for what came after.

⧊⧊⧊

As the night wore on and the feasting slowed, the attention turned toward the central bonfire, where the Forest Seeress, Alva, sat with her piercing red eyes fixed on the flames. Wrapped in her deep green cloak, embroidered with silver runes, she had been silent for most of the evening, only sipping her tea, her presence alone keeping some at a cautious distance.

Without a word, she stood, her motion drawing the gathering into silence. From a small leather pouch, she withdrew a handful of dried herbs, murmuring in Aelfic, the lyrical cadence foreign to most—but not to Lozen and Anja. The words sent a chill down Lozen's spine, not for their meaning, but for who should and should not have known the words.

She tossed the herbs into the fire.

The flames roared high, shifting from their natural orange glow to shades of deep blue, then violet, then sickly green. Gasps rippled through the assembly as the fire twisted unnaturally, the shadows it cast dancing like wraiths against the stone walls.

Alva exhaled slowly, her voice carrying over the stunned silence. "The winds carry more than winter. The spears of men will gleam next Várblót—the spring sacrifice. War marches sooner than you would like."

Murmurs broke out, some in confusion, others in hushed dread. The Aelfs had never come this far into Ravnsríki before, and yet, the fire spoke of war at Helsgaard's doorstep. Eyes flickered toward Lozen and Anja, some wary, others merely curious, as if their very presence now carried new weight.

Hrolf narrowed his eyes. "What war? The Aelfs?"

Alva did not answer directly. She turned her gaze to Lozen. "The storm finds its way to the mountain, whether the mountain seeks it or not."

Lozen stiffened.

Rylen muttered, "I have no stomach for this, aye."

"She's not a mountain," Petr snapped, leaning forward to block Alva's line of sight to Lozen. "She's flesh and blood. Keep your storms to yourself."

"W-we have enough r-real enemies," Hans added, gripping his tankard until his knuckles turned white. "W-without inviting g-ghosts."

Hrolf stepped forward, his tone shifting back to command. "If there is danger, say it plain. Give us more than your Seeress riddles."

Alva turned back to the fire, watching as the colors shifted back to orange, the unnatural energy fading. "The fire has spoken. The runes remain unwritten."

Hrolf moved to her side and gently took her arm, guiding her back to her seat. "Then sit and drink your tea," he murmured, the authority softening to paternal care. "You've earned it tonight."

Lozen caught her gaze before Alva sipped, and for the briefest moment in the flickering firelight, Alva's features seemed to shift—less human, more ancient, as if she belonged to a time long forgotten.

The gathering, once alive with celebration, had turned thoughtful. The Rangers still had much to celebrate, but now, beneath their laughter, a profound shadow of unease had settled in.

Outside, the cool autumn wind rustled the trees, whispering its own secrets into the night.

⟁⟁⟁

The Haustblót fire was waning, the shadows stretching long, consuming the training yard. The Rangers had dispersed, leaving only the immediate circle around the scarred wooden tables, where Lozen, Anja, and Rylen sat in a tight, protective knot. Rohand and Hrolf were nearby, toward a watch tower, their voices low as they discussed keep operations.

Lozen sat motionless, the image of the fire twisting from blue to a sickly green still burned in her eyes. The Seeress's words, *The storm finds its way to the mountain, whether the mountain wills it or not,* were a cold, constant pressure against her chest.

"Alva called it a storm," she whispered, not to anyone in particular, but the fear was loud enough for both parents. "And it's coming here. Now."

Anja reached under the table and placed a hand on Lozen's wrist. Her touch was firm, but her eyes, wide and fixed on the dying embers, were shadowed with thought.

"She knows the kind of storm that follows war, but I don't think she knows we are the target yet," Anja murmured, her voice barely a breath. "Soren couldn't know we are here. If he did, you would already be dead. He will be focusing on the Aelf army movements, not ghosts in the west."

Rylen, whose posture was always ready for a fight, suddenly looked like the weight of the past sixteen years were resting on his shoulders. He glanced sharply toward Hrolf, who was still talking to Rohand, then leaned in close, ensuring the conversation was a private, desperate huddle.

His hand clamped down on the table's edge. "Alva speaks in riddles and double-tongues, aye. The war has been escalating, yes. But her turning to you, Lozen—that tells me the threat is already set and moving this way, even if we don't know its true measure."

The former Captain and pragmatist, saw the logistical and strategic vulnerability of the Keep. He continued. "Hrolf and Rohand will assume she means the Aelfs are finally throwing the line deep into the valley because of the King's new homesteading score. But that score is the true strategic fault, Anja. All this new settler noise in Helsgaard Frontier—it's a beacon. It's too easy for Aelf scouts or, worse, Soren's shadows, to root themselves among the homesteaders and merchants. We've gone from being a secure rock to a busy border. The perimeter is now soft ground."

Lozen nodded. "I spent three years hiding in plain sight just by wearing a cloak over my ears. Remember when I showed up and you told me to take off my hood? Are we going to walk up to everyone we see and demand to see their ears?"

Lozen wrapped her arms around her chest, trying to fend off the sudden, overwhelming dread that she was the lightning rod drawing the disaster. "The scouts. The spies. They could find us just by asking a question in a tavern."

"Confirmed," Rylen confirmed. "Soren doesn't have to hold the full measure of why he finds us here. He only needs to send his shadows to monitor the new population noise, and when they observe you two training the string, or at the market square, or walking the deep dirt, the score snaps together."

Lozen and Anja agreed.

Rylen nodded, rising to his feet with purpose. "The first action is bringing Hrolf into the tally on the settler risk, now. Not as the makers of the Prophecy Child, but as his tactical advisors. As Rangers."

He strode toward Hrolf and Rohand, his voice cutting through the remaining noise of the feast with the grave, professional tone of a former Captain delivering a critical field report. "Commander, a moment..." Rylen continued to deliver his assessment of Alva's warning, and the implications of an Aelfinn assault.

Anja watched him go, pulling Lozen closer. "The storm is coming. We just need to control where it hits."

CHAPTER 20

WINTER IN HELSGAARD

BEFORE EVERYTHING CHANGES

THE FIRST SNOW HAD fallen like ash—soft, quiet, and heavy with things unspoken. Lozen reminisced watching it settle over Helsgaard Keep from the tower, the flakes coating rooftops and ramparts like a burial shroud. Then the storm winds came. Roads vanished, the valley sealed, and the world shrank to firelit halls and fraying tempers. Weeks passed in a blur of drills, repairs, and too much silence.

She couldn't sit still anymore.

Lozen pulled her cloak tighter around her shoulders and strode through the winding paths of Helsgaardborg. The winter air bit at her cheeks, sharp and bracing, but it carried the earthy scent of woodsmoke and pine—familiar, grounding. The settlement had grown since she first arrived, yet the endless inactivity chafed her street-honed energy.

She returned to the Keep looking for Astrid, the Griffin Keeper.

Her boots crunched across the frozen path as she approached the Griffin Longhouse—the largest of its kind, looming against the pale sky in the northeast corner of the Keep. Built from thick timber and stone, its sloped roof was dusted in snow, and its gates stood open, inviting yet formidable. This was where the Griffins came and went, their sky-bound freedom stitched into the fabric of Helsgaard.

Inside, warmth met her first—then scent.

The musk of hay, leather, and something wilder wrapped around her, earthy and electric. The long central fire crackled low, casting flickering shadows that danced across rafters and walls. Lozen stepped quietly, her breath visible in the cool air as her eyes adjusted to the dim.

Three Griffins perched high along the beams, talons curled around thick timbers. They watched her—not with idle curiosity, but with the kind of intelligence that pinned you in place and weighed your soul. Feathered heads shifted slightly, wings rustling in their sleep-wake stillness. Her breath caught in her throat. Up close, they were more than majestic. They were muscle and myth, danger and grace wrapped in feathers and claw.

From one of the stalls, Astrid stepped out, brushing straw and dust from her tan tunic. Wiry and lean, with her pale hair in a loose braid and blue eyes sharp as a winter sky, she spotted Lozen instantly.

"Was wondering when you'd find your way here," Astrid said, wiping her hands on her trousers. "Not many come unless they have business with the Griffins."

Lozen stepped closer, still absorbing the presence of the massive creatures. "I was looking for you. I have questions. About the Griffins."

"Ah, curiosity finally got the best of you?"

Lozen admired the Griffins. "Something like that. Where did they come from? I've never heard of Griffins in Nordlund."

Astrid leaned against a wooden post, her gaze drifting to the nearest Griffin—a great storm-gray beast preening its feathers. "They're older than any of us, older than Nordlund, maybe even Midgard. Some say they came from Hrævfölnir's brood, the great hawk that perches atop Yggdrasil. Either way, they were here long before men built keeps and walls."

"So why are they here now?" Lozen frowned.

"Why do any of us stay where we do? Shelter. Food. Kinship. Helsgaard is safe, and they know it. Not all of them stay, but the ones that do..." Astrid gestured toward the Griffins watching from their perches. "They're bonded to us. To me."

"You can talk to them, can't you?"

"Not with words. It's... different. They send thoughts, emotions, images. Every Griffin chooses their bond, and once they do, it's for life."

Lozen shifted her weight. "Then how do you get them to fight?"

Astrid chuckled, looking at Stormchaser. "We don't. They fight if they decide the fight is worth it. If they see a threat to their bonded or their territory, they'll tear through it like a storm ripping through a valley. But if they don't care? Then you're on your own."

"So they're stubborn."

Astrid smirked. "You say 'stubborn' like it's a flaw. It's not. It's what makes them Griffins. They aren't beasts of burden.

They're warriors, same as us. If you want to partner, earn a Griffin's respect."

"So they choose everything," Lozen murmured. "Where they fly. Who they bond with. Whether they fight."

Astrid nodded. "They're free. Always."

Lozen fell silent, watching the Griffins in their effortless power. There was something about them that resonated deep within her.

⏃⏃⏃

The snow blanketed Helsgaard like a downy cloak, muffling sound and softening the sharp edges of stone and steel. Lozen stood just outside the Höfn House, rubbing her mittened hands together.

Rylen appeared from around the side of the house, grinning like a boy with a secret. His beard was dusted with snow, his cheeks flushed from the cold. In each hand, he carried a training shield—the old, rounded wooden kind that had their metal boss removed.

"Lo," he called, "I have a plan for ye."

She blinked at him. "An idea? Last time you had one of those, I ended up skinning rabbits for a week."

Rylen laughed, the sound echoing warmly. "That was the hard lesson. This is for pleasure, aye."

He tossed her a shield. She caught it with a grunt, eyebrows rising. "You want me to... what? Train in the snow?"

"Nay. Sled." He slung the other shield under one arm and started walking toward the west gate. "Let's go."

Lozen hesitated just a heartbeat before falling in beside him. She hadn't seen her father smile like that in weeks. If he needed this, she wouldn't say no.

They reached the road that led down the western wall—the supply path now buried in snow. Today, they'd turned it into something else.

Dozens of figures stood scattered along the slope. Laughter rolled up the hill. Sleds—makeshift and real—dotted the incline. Lozen's eyes widened. "Is this... authorized?"

Rylen gave her a sideways glance. "Only if we hold the truth from the HouseFathers."

"I can keep a secret."

"Good. Now, the rules are fixed. Plant yourself, lean back, and steer by the shoulder. And if ye strike Rohand, I'll clear your tally of the dirty work after náttmál for a full seven days."

No after-supper chores? That got a real laugh from her.

They trudged to the top of the slope. Lozen kneeled first, positioning the shield beneath her. Rylen crouched beside her.

"Will ye race?" he offered.

"You'll lose," she said with a grin.

They shoved off together.

The slope caught them instantly. The world became a blur of snow and cold air and unadulterated laughter. Her father whooped behind her, a sound so full of life it made her heart ache and soar all at once.

At the bottom, she tumbled off the shield into a drift, sputtering. Rylen arrived a moment later. "You alive?"

"Barely," she coughed. "But I won."

But before they could drag their shields back up, a snowball hit Rylen square in the back of the head.

Rohand stood ten paces away, another snowball in hand, smirking like a wolf.

Together, they armed themselves and opened fire.

They lost track of time. The battle was chaotic, brief, and glorious. Snow flew in every direction as more Rangers joined in. Petr showed up with a small sled and no shame, charging down the slope while pelting anyone in range. Lozen nailed him mid-ride and cheered as he veered off into a snowbank.

"Who taught you to throw like that?" Petr yelled, climbing out of the drift, his face split by a wide, good-natured grin.

"My Dad," she shouted back, ducking behind a drift.

Breathless and flushed, Lozen collapsed beside Rylen near a small fire pit. She stared up at the sky, heart pounding, laughter still bubbling in her chest.

"Ye be a true Ranger," Rylen said suddenly, his voice softer now.

She turned to look at him.

"You've got the hunter's instinct. You take the lesson quickly. You hold your stone." He nudged her shoulder. "Your mother carries the pride."

Lozen swallowed hard. "You think?"

"I ken it." He smiled, and there was no teasing in it. Just warmth.

The sky darkened to indigo. Lozen rose and brushed herself off. "Thanks, Dad. I needed this."

Rylen stood too, groaning a little. "Me, also."

At the top of the hill, just beyond the last torch post, two figures watched them in silence. Anja stood wrapped in her healer's cloak, a steaming mug in her mitten hands. She smiled as the pair trudged uphill, their laughter still lingering in the air like woodsmoke. Beside her, Hrolf crossed his arms and gave a small, approving nod.

"He's not as fast as he used to be," Anja murmured.

"No, but the girl's faster every season."

"I like seeing them like this," she said.

They walked back up the path together, the last golden light catching in Lozen's orange-red braids and her father's graying red hair. For once, there were no battles waiting. Just the crisp scent of pine, the squeak of snow, and the quiet bond between a father and daughter—witnessed, wordless, and strong enough to hold through whatever storms were coming next.

CHAPTER 21

FEAST OF VÁRBLÓT

SILENCE IS ACCEPTANCE

THE FOLLOWING SPRING, DURING the feast of Vár-blót—the celebration marking the return of life and the end of winter—the hall was raucous, fueled by too much mead. Lozen and Petr sat together, enjoying the feast. Their shoulders brushed occasionally, their legs touched beneath the table—small gestures of familiarity and warmth. Petr, in his mid-twenties, with dusty blonde hair and light-blue eyes, laughed at a joke from the next table.

During a moment when the music paused, Lozen heard the word "Dwaelf." She stiffened, the sound a physical shock that cut through the pleasant noise.

At the end of the table, Hrolf also caught the slur, and noticed the way both Lozen and Anja tensed at the word. A hush, cold and sudden, spread through the revelry. Petr looked visibly alarmed, his hand resting near Lozen's.

The silence thickened.

Hrolf rose swiftly, his keen gaze sweeping the gathering. "Who said it?" His voice cut through the quiet like a blade of ice.

The gathered Rangers shifted uneasily, moving away from Olaf and Bjorn, leaving them exposed.

Without hesitation, Hrolf stepped forward and drove an elbow into Olaf's jaw—a sharp, punishing blow that sent the man reeling and sprawling across the rushes. Groaning, Olaf tried to rise, but Hrolf's boot planted firmly on his chest pinned him in place.

Hrolf bent low, his voice cold and clear. "You'll hold your tongue in this hall—or I'll cut it out myself."

Then, gripping Olaf by his braided hair, he dragged him toward the Keep's gate, the other Rangers following in grim silence.

When they passed the outer gates, Hrolf barked at Petr. "Take off his boots. Throw them back inside."

Olaf groaned, still gasping for breath. "My boots—"

"—are community property," Hrolf snapped. "They belong to the Keep. You lost the right to them when you violated our honor."

Petr enthusiastically yanked off Olaf's boots and tossed them back through the gate, his action swift and devoid of courtesy.

Hrolf released Olaf's hair and took a step back. He spoke with measured authority. "Your life's journey has come to a fork, Olaf. To the left—stay on your path, you walk away, and leave Helsgaard Keep behind. To the right—you make amends and embrace the core values of Ravnsríki."

He crossed his arms. "Your choice."

Olaf stared at Hrolf, his eyes full of pain and defiance.

Hrolf's voice turned sharp. "Recite the core values."

Rather than comply, Olaf demanded, "I have rights! I demand a ting—a reckoning before the community!"

The crowd simultaneously gasped and went silent. The ting embodied the ideal of free speech and collective decision-making in a warrior society.

Hrolf paused, taking a couple of deep, controlled breaths. "You certainly have the right to be heard. I want you to take a moment and think about what could go wrong. I have reclaimed community property, so you have no boots until the *ting*—a convened public assembly—is convened, which will be days from now to allow proper notice to Helsgaardborg and the Keep."

The two men continued staring at each other.

"No boots? Like a thrall? Hrolf, you—"

"—At the ting," Hrolf interrupted, "the free men and women will decide your fate per the lawgiver's rules. You may be victorious. But as I look around, understanding you insulted the Keep's healer and her daughter, also a healer, I suspect the community will not side with you. You could be exiled, and where would you go? Helsgaard Keep is already the last chance for most of us here."

"So you backed me into a corner? And you get away with it? You think you can beat me and I have no recourse?"

"You have a choice, Olaf. Comply, ting, or leave. Choose wisely. Choose now."

Tense, silent moments passed as Olaf glared at Hrolf.

Olaf coughed and struggled to get the words out, yielding. "Independence, Self-Reliance, Loyalty, Modesty, Hospitality, Generosity, Compassion, Courage, and Wisdom."

"And tell me—where does insulting your former HouseSister fit into those values?"

Olaf had no answer. Only pain. His arms cradled his ribs, his breath coming in uneven gasps.

"You lacked loyalty, compassion, and wisdom," Hrolf stated. "So you're going to stay outside this gate and think about that."

Hrolf turned back to the crowd. "Everyone—back to the feast. Except the Rangers who sat with him and did nothing."

Five Rangers remained, including Bjorn.

"You should have stopped him," Hrolf growled. "It's your job to uphold our values. Since you failed, you'll run the perimeter of the Keep—twice. Consider it time to reflect. RUN!"

He looked at Lozen. "Pick up his boots."

Lozen's brows shot up. "Why are you involving me?"

Hrolf's stare remained unyielding. "You and Olaf have things to work out. If he chooses the right path, it's up to you if he gets his boots back. Maybe you two can clear the air."

Lozen grimaced but obeyed, scooping up the boots. "So I have the choice to not give them back?"

"That is a choice. We all have choices to make." Hrolf turned to Anja. "And you—stay out of it."

Anja scowled but said nothing. Rylen hugged her reassuringly.

Everyone drifted back to the festivities, leaving Olaf alone outside the gate.

⚠⚠⚠

A short time later, Olaf limped back through the gate, clutching his jaw. He found Lozen with Anja, Rylen, Petr, and Hans. His expression was pained, but his words were hollow.

"I'm sorry," he said stiffly. "For what I said."

Lozen stared at him.

Anja's gaze was piercing. "Go to the infirmary."

Rylen folded his arms. "Hrolf commanded ye keep your hands off the work."

Anja smirked. "I won't heal him—but I'll be there for Lozen."

Lozen handed Olaf his boots. He put them on without a word.

"See you two at the Höfn House," Lozen said to Petr and Hans. She walked toward the infirmary with Olaf, Anja, and Rylen trailing behind.

Once inside the infirmary, Olaf settled onto a sturdy wooden bed. Lozen helped Olaf remove his cloak and tunic, her gaze sharpening as she assessed his injuries.

"You need to lie back," she instructed.

With Anja's help, he eased onto his back, grimacing as pain lanced through his jaw and head. A low groan escaped him as Lozen placed her hands over the bruised jaw, the soft blue glow of healing energy illuminating the deep purples and reds of his injuries.

Anja stepped back, arms crossed, silently observing. Across the room, Rylen tended to the hearth.

Anja finally spoke, breaking the heavy silence. "The word 'Dwaelf' is a deep insult in Aeldoria," she said. "It's not just a slur—it's an insult to cast someone as nothing."

Lozen focused on the bruises beneath her fingertips. She paused, looked into his eyes, and asked quietly, "What did I ever do to you?"

The question hung in the air. Olaf stared at the ceiling, struggling with an answer. The person he had belittled was now easing his pain. He swallowed hard, shame obvious on his face.

He exhaled, his voice rough with guilt. "I was wrong. And I'm sorry. Truly."

Lozen continued her ministrations.

He looked at Lozen, his expression uncharacteristically raw. "What can I do to make up for it?"

The door swung open. Hrolf entered.

Hrolf's sharp gaze flicked to Olaf's bruised chest. "How's the patient?"

Anja gave a curt nod. "Healing well. He'll need more treatments."

Lozen tensed.

Hrolf sighed. "Olaf, you'll stand guard on the western tower from sunset to sunrise for a half-moon."

Anja's eyes widened. "Hrolf—"

He cut her off with a glare and a raised hand. "And since you just re-joined the Keep and were re-issued boots, you're no longer a senior member of the House, you will sleep at the far end, away from the hearth. Not that you're going to sleep much."

Lozen stiffened. "Why!?"

Hrolf met her gaze. "Because discipline is necessary. You don't get to apologize and move on like nothing happened."

Lozen opened her mouth to protest, "But—"

"—Lozen—outside. Anja, take over the healing," Hrolf ordered.

Outside, the night air bit at Lozen's skin.

Hrolf's tone was calm but firm. "Never challenge my authority in front of others. If you have a question, ask me in private."

Lozen swallowed and nodded. "Understood, sir. Can I say something?"

"Go ahead."

She hesitated. "I think his punishment is too harsh."

Hrolf folded his arms. "I told you months ago I had a zero-tolerance policy for this skitr. An offense was committed. It must be atoned for. If I show leniency, others will think they can get away with the same." He paused. "Someone must pay the price. Would you rather take his place?"

The question hung between them. Lozen's stomach tightened.

She exhaled slowly. "No, sir."

He nodded. "Then let him learn."

Lozen exhaled, letting the cold air steady her. She squared her shoulders. "I won't challenge you in front of the others again."

A beat of silence, then Hrolf gave a small nod of approval. "Good. Not many people know this, but Günther made that mistake. Challenging superiors in public. And now he's here, at the Last Chance Fortress."

"So... what did you do... to get sent here?"

"Ah," he chuckled, "that is a tale for another time."

Lozen inclined her head in respect, and returned to the infirmary.

The heavy wooden door creaked as she stepped inside. Anja looked up, her sharp blue eyes softening, while Rylen leaned back against the hearth. Olaf lay on the bed, watching her carefully. The earlier sneer, the bravado—it was gone.

Lozen pulled up her sleeves, placed her glowing hands over Olaf's ribs, and continued the healing.

CHAPTER 22

THE WESTERN TOWER

RUNNING FROM THE JARL'S FIRE

O N OLAF'S FIRST NIGHT atop the western tower, a little past midnight, Lozen climbed the stairs, her boots barely making a sound against the worn stone steps. The silence of the Keep was profound, broken only by the distant sounds of the wind.

At the top, she found Olaf huddled near the small fire, his arms wrapped tightly around himself against the mountain chill. His jaw was swollen, and he shifted uncomfortably against the pain in his ribs. His eyes widened in surprise when he saw her. He had expected a long, lonely night, not visitors.

Lozen hesitated, sitting down across from him, warming her hands over the flames.

Olaf narrowed his eyes. "What are you doing up here?"

She shrugged, keeping her gaze on the fire. "Figured you might want some company. The cold makes the punishment seem longer."

His shoulders relaxed marginally. "Huh," he grunted. "Wasn't expecting that."

They sat in awkward silence for a moment, the fire crackling between them. To break the tension, Olaf finally asked, "So... how did you and your parents get separated?"

Lozen exhaled, her breath curling into the cold night air. "Anja and Rylen have death bounties. They gave me up, sent me to live with a different family to keep me safe, then escaped to Helsgaard Keep. But when I was twelve, people started noticing my Dwarfinn traits. Hair stayed red, didn't grow tall, ears too small, broad shoulders."

She hesitated, bending the truth to focus on the easy injury—the one he could see. "I was exiled a year later."

Olaf's brows furrowed, and he winced when he moved his jaw. "Because of how you looked?"

She nodded. "Because of how I looked. Nothing I had control over. Like your swollen jaw now."

"You were just a kid."

"Yeah. Sucks. But I got lucky. Ended up in the same place as my parents, and we get along."

Lozen let the silence linger, watching him carefully. She saw the tension around his eyes every time he breathed shallowly.

She leaned forward, dropping her voice. "I know it hurts to breathe. Hrolf doesn't pull his punches."

Olaf flinched, surprised by the honesty. "It's fine. I don't need the healer."

"I'm not the healer right now, I'm Lozen. And you have fractured ribs," she corrected, her voice soft but firm. "I can help with the swelling and the pain. You won't be much use on guard duty if you seize up."

She extended her hand, palm up, revealing the fine silver scars along her wrist—old marks from training mishaps. Her expression was neutral, offering the help without demanding acceptance.

Olaf stared at her hand, then at the faint, blue glow beginning to gather around her palm. He knew what that light meant. It was the Aelfinn magic he had insulted. He looked from her hand to her eyes, searching for mockery, but found only quiet resolution.

After a tense moment, he gave a curt, almost imperceptible nod. "Just the ribs. Leave the jaw alone."

Lozen accepted the partial agreement. She shifted closer, placing her hands gently over his aching ribs. The faint blue glow pulsed, and the mountain chill around them seemed to recede, replaced by a deep, invasive warmth. Olaf closed his eyes with a low, involuntary grunt of relief as the heat began to dull the sharp edges of the pain.

When the glow faded, Lozen pulled back. "Better?"

He slowly stretched his shoulders, testing the movement, and opened his eyes. "Very much so," he admitted, his voice rough.

For once, Olaf had nothing to say. That night, he didn't thank her for coming, but he didn't send her away either. The healing was a silent contract, an exchange of vulnerability for compassion.

⚠⚠⚠

The next night, right after midnight, Lozen returned. She carried a small pot of green salve—a thick, pine-scented paste her mother had mixed for deep bruising and stiffness.

Olaf smirked as she settled in across from him. "You do realize I won't die from boredom if left alone, right?"

Lozen snorted. "You won't die, but the stiffness in your ribs will linger. Sit still." She pulled out the salve and, without waiting for permission, began gently rubbing the herb-infused paste into the bruises visible beneath his tunic at his ribcage.

Before they could finish, Bryn appeared, strolling up the stairs with her usual casual confidence.

"A mouse doesn't skitr—" she started.

"—without knowing how many turds it dropped," Lozen finished.

They laughed. The shared work, the shared insult, the shared laughter—it was the true beginning of their truce.

After a few minutes, Olaf shifted, looking at Lozen's hands, which were now resting in her lap. "That healing you do... the blue light. Does it hurt? Anja moves like it costs her nothing, but I saw you grimace... that... night. Two nights ago."

Lozen exhaled, leaning back against the cold stone. "It doesn't hurt, exactly. But it drains me. Like pulling the strength out of your bones."

"You mean like blood loss?" Olaf asked, his Warrior's mind searching for a comparison.

"Worse," Lozen corrected. "It's an emotional drain. I have to connect to the injury, to the pain and the fear of the person I'm healing. Anja, she can put up a wall. She's learned to separate the emotion from the job. Me? When I heal you, I feel the blow that Hrolf gave you. I feel the insult that made him throw it. I feel the fear of the person who is injured."

Bryn listened, arms folded. "So the cost is higher for the young."

Lozen nodded. "It's why I was angry that night. You've been harassing and tormenting me ever since I got here. Then Hrolf sets me up to heal you..." She looked toward the Warrior House and flipped a blótstafn to an imaginary Hrolf. "And now I use my energy to heal the man who insulted me. Who insulted my parents."

She stared into Olaf's eyes. "I had to heal my own abuser."

Olaf's face, still bruised, crumpled with a fresh wave of shame. "Faaahhh. I didn't think of that."

"Of course you didn't," Bryn muttered, breaking the tension, looking at Olaf with something that was almost pity.

"No, you didn't," Lozen agreed quietly. "But you asked, and I told you the cost. You now know what it takes for me to save your ribs. You owe me for that."

Olaf stared at her, the offer of a transaction—a debt—a concept he fully understood, replacing the uncomfortable shame. "A debt. I was wrong, Lozen. Truly. What is the price? What can I do?"

Lozen smirked, tapping his still-bruised jaw lightly. "The price is simple: You get smarter, Olaf. You learn to choose your enemies better. And when the real fight comes, you stand beside me. No insults, no second-guessing. Only loyalty."

Olaf's face hardened with determination, the shame replaced by the weight of the oath. "Done. You have my oath."

"Oath," Lozen affirmed, accepting the pledge.

Bryn lifted her flask, nodding approvingly at the clear, ruthless transaction. "That is a solid contract. A clear ledger is better than any apology."

◬◬◬

On the third night atop the tower, Lozen brought Rylen with her. The night air was crisp, and the fire settled into a low, steady glow.

Olaf had stopped questioning Lozen's appearances, though he arched a brow when Rylen arrived.

"Thought you were here to keep me company," Olaf grumbled.

Lozen grinned. "And I thought you might like a different storyteller tonight."

Curiosity flickered in Olaf's gaze. "Alright then," he said, stretching out by the fire. "How did you end up a King's Guard?"

Rylen leaned back against the cold stone, crossing his arms, the familiar weight of the past settling on him. "Aye, it's a long tale I carry, friend. It starts with m'father, who couldn't fight the pull of work far away, especially when the payment was richer than the rocks could give."

Olaf smirked. "Good. We have all night."

Rylen spoke of his early years: how his family moved to the Human capital, Ravnborg, because his father was sworn to the King's Guard. He was raised with the understanding that his own path was fixed—he would inherit his father's shield and duty. Growing up in the sprawling Human city, far from other Dwarfs, he poured all his energy into that sworn service, letting discipline replace companionship. He climbed the ranks swiftly, his focus absolute, until he earned the captain's mantle. Then, his voice dropped, turning serious.

"I held the rank of Captain of the Guard, assigned as Anja's shield during the Ravnborg peace summit," Rylen began. "For six full weeks, the score between us was clean. Protocol demanded the space. My standing duty commanded it."

He paused, looking out over the dark valley, remembering the moment the war began.

"Then came the breach, aye. The politics had brutalized Anja. She opened the door, silent. She used pure force to pull me across the line and into her quarters. It wasn't the diplomat's score; it was a raw, undeniable need to be blood—to be seen as Rylen and Anja, not the Shield and the Delegate. She set fire to the protocol with one look."

Lozen listened closely, understanding the fierce, desperate nature of the choice.

Rylen continued, his voice heavy with the weight of loss. "We were seven months carrying the child when the treaty was set for the sealing. Our plan was plain: once the peace was secured, we would simply cut the line and vanish into the West as humble wood-folk, taking our baby with us."

He paused, the silence stretching. "Soren, Anja's mentor, found the truth, aye. He didn't just expose the breach of trust—he revealed the half-blood kin and the Aelfinn deep lore. He used the very presence of our daughter to ignite the seventeen-year war. He used us as the match, aye, to start the war."

When dawn finally crept over the horizon, Olaf sat in quiet reflection, his smirk gone. The truth was heavier than any story he'd heard in the longhouse.

⬥⬥⬥

On the tenth night, Lozen arrived after midnight. The fire had burned low, reducing the tower to deep shadows and the scent of ash. Olaf stood at the crenel, arms resting on the ledge, his silhouette a solid, immovable block against the scattered stars.

Lozen joined him, leaning her elbows on the cold stone. For a long while, neither spoke; the silence was no longer awkward, but a shared, easy breathing.

Olaf shifted, breaking the silence with a soft sound of movement. He wrapped an arm around her waist and gently pulled her close.

She tensed for half a breath—her body's ingrained reaction to confinement—but didn't pull away. She allowed the contact.

He turned toward her, his proximity a warm demand in the cold night. Their eyes met, illuminated faintly by the waning moon, and he leaned in.

Lozen lifted a finger and pressed it lightly against his lips, stopping him.

She whispered. "We're friends, I hope. But, no—that's not happening."

Olaf's eyes flickered with something unreadable—disappointment, quickly mastered—but after a beat, he simply turned his gaze back to the vast expanse of the stars, keeping his arm firmly around her.

Lozen rested her head against his chest, feeling the slow, steady rise and fall of his breath and the solid, unyielding warmth of his body. The moment wasn't awkward. It was a safe harbor. It just was.

"Oh?" Bryn's voice rang out, sharp and delighted. "What have we here? Getting cozy for the rest of the winter?"

They jerked apart so fast, the violence of their separation made Lozen stumble, nearly losing her balance on the slippery stone.

"Nothing! We were just—" Olaf started, his voice a defensive roar.

"—Absolutely nothing," Lozen agreed, pushing her disobedient hair back and glaring at Bryn.

Bryn chuckled, lifting her hands in mock surrender, her eyes sparkling with malicious amusement. "Mmmhmm. I believe you. Thousands wouldn't."

She said nothing more about their embrace, but the smug, triumphant smirk she settled on her face told them she'd never let them live down the moment they were caught in the act of honest, unpoliticized warmth.

CHAPTER 23

THE SERPENT'S ENVOY

THE NEW PATH TO PROSPERITY

TENSION LINGERED IN THE air within the hallowed halls of King Aethor's throne room in the Aelfinn capital, Astraelyn. The flickering candlelight danced upon the ancient tapestries, casting shadows that twisted like tormented spirits. King Aethor, resplendent in his mírenstál crown, sat on his ornate throne. The visible stress around his eyes was not from weariness, but from the taxing nature of maintaining his pretense.

His trusted counselor, Idril, sat across from him, her face etched with deep, genuine concern.

"My King," she began, "the Council of Elders grows restless. Their whispers have become louder, their doubts more pronounced. They crave peace."

Aethor smiled thinly, a calculated mask of resignation. "I am well aware. Their contentment is purchased with Human land and Human resources. Their impatience does not escape me."

"Their concerns are not unfounded, my liege. The seventeen-year war has drained our resources, our people are weary, and the old ways of total conquest no longer seem politically viable."

Aethor nodded, his gaze fixed on the flickering flames, already calculating the next move on the grand chessboard. "The Humans, once considered barbarians, have grown in strength. Their technology, their sheer tenacity—they pose a risk we cannot conquer by slow attrition."

"Indeed, my King. Yet, the Council embraces the future, eager to forge alliances with the Humans. They see only opportunity, not the dangers that lurk beneath their goodwill."

Aethor rose from his throne, his tall figure casting an imposing shadow. His voice rang with false sincerity. "I will not let the Aelfinn kingdom stagnate. We must adapt—we must control their growth by consuming their resources. We must show the Council that total domination is the only path to true peace and prosperity."

Idril looked at her King with admiration, blinded by the perceived vision. "What is your plan, my liege?"

Aethor smiled, a hint of deep cunning now entirely replacing the weariness in his eyes. "I will send an envoy to propose a summit. I will placate the Council with the narrative of alliance and common ground. Perhaps, with their borders open, we can build a future where only our race truly thrives."

"It is a bold plan, my King. But I believe it is the right one—to end this war."

"Now is the time," Aethor whispered, his voice resonating with pure, cynical ambition. "To finally end their sovereignty." He called out for his messenger. "Summon Soren."

⚠ ⚠ ⚠

The chamber doors whispered open, and Soren stepped forward—a figure of chilling elegance and contained menace. His angular Aelfinn features were sharpened by the shadows. His silver-white hair, meticulously plaited, cascaded down his back, a stark contrast to the dark circlet resting upon his brow.

His robes of deep sapphire silk were embroidered with intricate silver runes, and a brooch shaped like a serpent eating a raven—a mark of his dedicated ruthlessness to the crown—pinned his cloak. His pale blue eyes were cold as a frozen fjord, flicking toward Aethor with calculating, ever-watchful intensity.

He moved with the poised precision of a fencer, each motion deliberate, controlled. As he reached the throne, he dipped into a flawless bow, his voice smooth as polished steel, yet carrying the weight of hidden ambition.

"My Lord King," he murmured.

Aethor nodded. "Dear friend, the time has come for us to proceed with our plan. The envoy of peace will be dispatched tomorrow."

"Yes, m'lord."

"Do you have a suitable and loyal army for the true mission?"

Soren replied, "I have recruited three hundred loyal to our cause. Every one of them is dedicated to our way of life and ensuring the prophecy never has a chance to be fulfilled."

Aethor gestured at a table. Retrieving the parchment, Soren presented it to the King. Aethor crafted a series of important notes, conscripting every ship needed for the invasion.

"I'm sure I don't need to inquire, but do you have a battle plan?" Aethor asked.

Soren, smiling confidently, nodded. "You know me well, m'lord. We aim not for a border skirmish, but the heart of their kingdom."

"We will land in Ravnsríki at the Nels River, follow that north, and take Helsgaard Keep. The Nels River inlet provides cover from South Shore and Fjördheimr. We will sneak in under the cover of darkness, far away from the Human cities."

"And Helsgaard Keep? Why that remote outpost first?"

"Ah, m'lord, excellent question. Our scouts have identified a pass through the Eastern Helsgaard Wall that opens up near the forest northwest of Ravnborg. It's a one-way pass—hard to ascend, but easy to descend. I plan to replenish our supplies from the war booty of Helsgaard Keep and Helsgaardborg."

Soren leaned in, his voice tightening with cold menace. "The Keep is also the fastest way to confirm the prophecy. Our scouts have heard persistent whispers of two Aelf women at Helsgaard Keep who look remarkably like mother and daughter. If that mother is Anja, my former protégé, then the daughter is the half-breed. I look forward to putting this prophesy to rest forever."

"Ah, good," Aethor said, satisfied with the dual purpose.

"Then we go down the pass, traverse Ravnsríki at the forest tree line, and take Sjóvarborg via a sneak attack. Once this is complete, Ravnsríki will be divided into two. Our forces will advance on Ravnborg from the north, compelling King Valdissen to yield to our demands as his defenses are all to the south. We will strike Ravnborg before Valdissen can recall any forces from the southern border. Victory is assured."

Aethor nodded his approval. "Very good, my friend. Let it be done. The envoy of peace will be sent on the dawn tide to mask your true departure."

Soren bowed deeply. "Yes, my Lord—as you command."

After casting a final, determined glance at his King, he turned and departed, his footsteps echoing through the empty corridor. Aethor sat alone, the impact of his treachery heavy upon him, resolving to see his vision of Aelfinn control over Human resources realized.

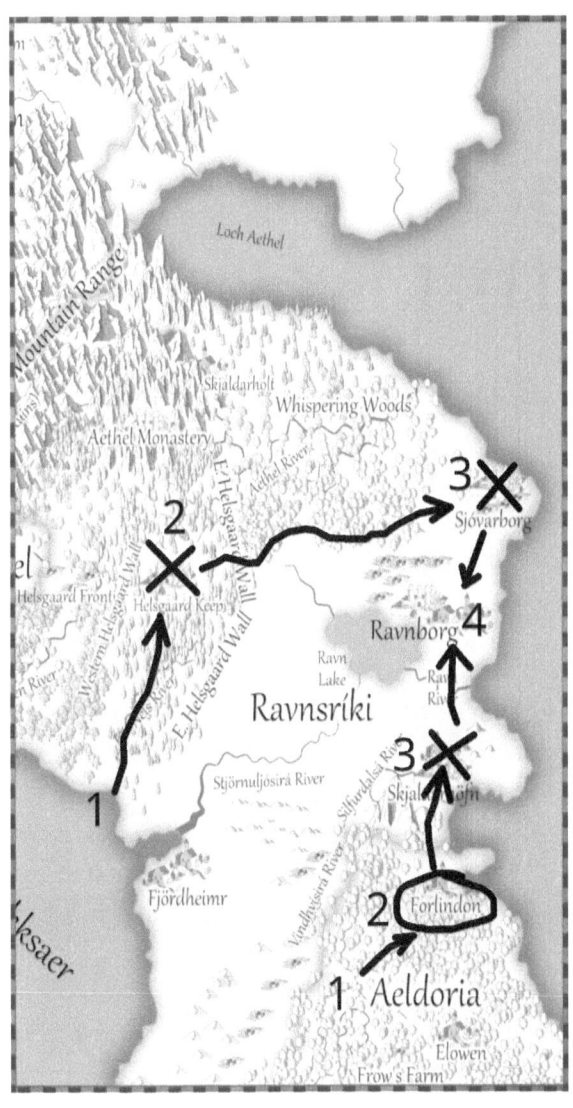

Strategy to Split Ravnsríki

CHAPTER 24

THE KING'S FALSE PEACE

THE NEGOTIATED DECEPTION

T HE AELFINN COUNCIL CHAMBERS exuded a solemn grandeur. The walls bore intricate tapestries depicting ancient battles and moments of unity, their heavy fabric absorbing sound and wrapping the space in profound silence. At the front of the room, two diligent scriveners sat at a polished wooden table, quills poised above fresh parchment, ready to capture every detail of the proceedings.

The air was thick with tension as the Elders gathered in a semicircle, their expressions set with concern. The grand wooden doors creaked open, and King Aethor entered in his formal court robes, the mírenstál crown gleaming atop his head. He stopped at the center of the chamber, the focus of the semicircle, his presence commanding but unwelcome in many eyes.

Rerendyl leaned forward, his voice laced with frustration. "The war has drained our coffers. Starvation spreads through the outer provinces. Trade routes have collapsed. Smuggling is rampant. And what is being done?"

Círdan scoffed, folding his arms. "Aelfs have endured hardship before. We are not weaklings to whimper at the first sign of struggle."

Faelar's emerald eyes locked onto Aethor. "Aelfs are not weak, but economies are. Farmers abandon their fields for the smuggler's trade because they can no longer afford to grow food. Merchants, once the pride of our ports, now raid Human shipping or worse—attack Orcish shore villages. Desperation makes fools of us all, and I wonder, my King, do you see this as clearly as we do?"

Aethor met her gaze without flinching, his practiced smile firmly in place. "I see it," he said. "And I have already acted. An emissary has been sent to Ravnborg to negotiate peace."

A murmur spread through the chamber. The shock of the diplomatic pivot was visible.

Lindir tapped a finger against the armrest of his chair. "A bold step, but peace alone does not repair a ruined economy. What guarantees do we have that the Humans will even negotiate in good faith?"

Thranduil's voice cut through the murmurs. "And if they do? Do we trust them to honor an agreement? Or will we barter away our sovereignty for a few sacks of grain?"

Maelon, his ice-blue gaze unwavering, nodded. "Aethor speaks of peace, but if that is truly the goal, why has it taken nearly two decades of suffering to pursue it? What changed, my King?"

The accusation hung heavy in the air. Aethor had taken the throne after his predecessor, Aelrindel, had died under mysterious circumstances. Now, Aethor spoke of peace?

Aethor inhaled slowly, letting the shadows of their doubts settle before responding with practiced rhetoric. "This war began before I took the throne, but I will be the one to end it. If we do nothing, our people will starve. If we let this war drag on, there will be no kingdom left to rule. I seek control of their resources to end our suffering."

Maeglin, revered for her pragmatism, interlaced her fingers. "And what terms do we offer? Do we have coin to bargain with? Ships to trade? Or do we expect the Humans to gift us peace?"

Aethor's lips pressed into a thin line. "The terms are being negotiated as we speak. Trade will resume. Stability will return. The Aelfinn Kingdom will prosper again under our full dominion of Human resources."

Legolas, who had listened in silence, spoke at last. "And what of the people suffering now? An envoy to Ravnborg will not fill their bellies today."

Aethor turned and walked toward the door, signaling that the discussion was over. "You will have your answers soon. For now, trust that I do what must be done to ensure Aeldoria's future."

Before he could leave, Celeborn's voice rang out, sharp as steel. "This meeting is not yet concluded, my King."

Haldir inclined his head. "There is more to discuss—"

Aethor cut them off with a glance. "Then discuss it. I have already made my decision."

Without another word, he passed through the doors, his cloak sweeping behind him. The Elders remained seated, some simmering with frustration, others grimly thoughtful. The scriveners, unshaken, continued to record every word, every shift of power.

And somewhere within those carefully inked lines, history was being written.

CHAPTER 25

THE SOFT PERIMETER

THE CAPTAIN'S WARNING

T HE MORNING AIR IN Mission Commander Hrolf's office was cold, carrying the faint, clean scent of cedar from the unlit hearth. The room was austere, its stone walls hung with intricate maps that were already being updated with new settler routes. Hrolf sat at the head of the heavy wooden table, his face stern and attentive. Rylen and Rohand sat opposite him.

Hrolf set down a copper sheet, a summary of the latest reports. "It has been two months since Várblót, and the promised invasion has not materialized. We have been granted time, but I do not trust this silence. What do you see, Rylen? Beyond the obvious."

Rylen, dressed in his Ranger leathers, pushed his hands flat on the table. His posture was focused and without excess movement.

"The why of the attack is war, Commander, but the method of the breach has shifted," Rylen stated, his gaze sweeping the maps. "The Aelfs, under Soren, rely on fine control and the spoken lie. They won't throw their line across the ground to begin. They will first send the shadows—spies."

Rohand nodded in agreement, leaning forward. "They will scout the Western Wall cliff face for weaknesses."

"Nay," Rylen corrected, his voice sharp. "The Western Line is only the choke. The Nels River Valley is the true line of breach. It gives cover and a direct, uncounted path to the Plateau." Rylen tapped a point on the map. "And they won't trust the deep dirt. They'll use the open weakness caused by the King's new policy."

Hrolf frowned, following Rylen's finger. "Weakness? A soft perimeter?"

"Aye. People. Settlers," Rylen replied simply.

"Please explain."

"The Keep was meant for fire-lizards and to fence off the high ground. We are not manned to track the rising dust of humankind," Rylen stated, his voice dropping to a harsh professional whisper. "The Humans flooding the valley—the shopkeepers, the dirt-scratchers, the opportunists—they are the finest screen. They are the background. An Aelfinn viper, hiding as a merchant or a desperate farmer, is lost in that crush. They can take every fact about our stores, our Warriors' paths, and the common mood, all while talking about the price of goods."

Hrolf stared at the map. "You believe they are actively spying and plotting against us?"

"Commander, the King's new settlement score is a beacon. Soren's shadows will exploit it. Their primary command is to gather the score to support the breach via the Nels River Valley. That means finding our soft ground. That is my final read, aye."

Rohand stiffened at the implication.

"And," Rylen continued, "as a piece of bad luck for us, if a viper happens to prove the whisper of an Aelf mother and half-breed lass training the arrow's flight here, that is all Soren needs to justify his heavy attack to his elders, assuming the price of lies is the same. But the numbers—the stores—that is the whole job."

Hrolf rose, walking to the narrow window overlooking the training yard. He sighed, the complexity of the political threat settling over him. "So our perimeter is no longer the stone wall, nor the threat of Dragons. It's the honesty of every Human farmer moving into the valley."

"Confirmed. We need to watch the shadows. We need Rangers outside the stone, monitoring the noise of the settlers, looking for anyone who doesn't fit the score of the land. Anyone too fixed on our patterns, or who asks too many questions about our deep stores and our tallies."

Hrolf turned back, his decision made. "Very well. Rohand, implement a daily rotation of two-person scouting teams. Roving patrols. Their primary mission is finding anything out of place. They focus on the routes connecting the new homesteads to the Keep, particularly those coming up the Nels River Valley. I'll meet with Bryn to discuss what RIOS has uncovered and what makes a spy look like a spy."

Rohand nodded. "Understood, Commander. The scout rotations start today."

"No armor. Low profile. Blend in. You are dismissed."

⚑⚑⚑

Several weeks of patrols had slipped by, uneventful and dry.

Now, the morning sun beat down on the unforgiving terrain. The heat shimmered in the air like an evil force, already collecting sweat beneath their leathers. Rohand and Petr, paired for the scouting rotation, emerged from the eastern gate of Helsgaard Keep and strode into Helsgaardborg, the adjacent settlement.

"Rylen's soft perimeter," Rohand grumbled, kicking at a loose stone. "Half day in, and all we've confirmed is that the price of chicken feed went up five öre this week."

Petr chuckled. "Be glad, Hersir. It means the farmers are busy complaining. And it confirms what Rylen said: we're just noise."

They moved quickly through the settlement, heading toward the edge of the forest that bordered the Nels River Valley. They soon reached a small clearing where Alva, the Forest Seeress, kept her tent.

"Hail, Alva," Rohand greeted. "Seen any trouble in the woods this morning? Anyone strange pass through?"

Alva turned her head slowly, her gaze sweeping over them before fixing on Petr. "The woods are quiet, Ranger. Only the young woman goes in and out without purpose. Not all who wander are lost, but not all who run are seen."

Rohand frowned at the riddle. "Thank you, Alva."

They left the clearing and plunged into the trees. They were a hundred arm-spans into the quiet, dappled light when Petr suddenly halted.

"Hold, Hersir. Not chicken feed this time."

Petr dropped to one knee. The ground told a violent story: a spray of fresh blood, dark against the damp earth, and broken branches, showing something large had come through the trees in a hurry. Rohand dropped beside him, tracing the blood trail.

"An armed fight," Rohand muttered, picking up a broken shaft of wood—an arrow, split cleanly down the middle. "And the target was running for his life."

Petr pointed to a faint mark beside the blood. "That's a boot print. Deep and clean. Never seen one like it before, and the stride is short, like stalking, not running."

Rohand stood, his eyes sweeping the dense, concealing forest. He looked from the blood to Petr. "Our mission is intel. We cannot risk compromising the scene or becoming victims." He made a quick tactical decision. "Petr, hold here. Watch the trail. If anyone approaches, conceal yourself and return to the Keep immediately. I'm taking this arrow and running directly to Hrolf."

Petr nodded immediately, gripping his axe tight. "Understood, Hersir."

Rohand turned and sprinted back toward the Keep. Just as he cleared the forest line, he intercepted Bryn and Lozen, who were walking and talking.

"Rohand, what in the Nine Realms?" Bryn snapped, seeing his urgent pace.

"Skirmish! We found blood and Aelfinn arrows a hundred arm-spans in! Go find Petr—now! He's back the way I came. I'm alerting Hrolf and getting the Rangers mobilized."

Rohand didn't wait for a reply, sprinting toward the Keep.

Lozen and Bryn turned and ran into the forest, following Rohand's tracks. They found Petr concealed, axe ready, guarding the clearing.

"Lozen, Bryn! Over here!" Petr called out in a low voice, pointing toward the undergrowth. "The injured party went that way. The pursuer is close."

Lozen, instantly focused, touched the ground. "Petr, stay on guard. Bryn, cover me... no weapon?"

"I'm a spy, not a warrior."

"Fukken useless Little Bird is what you are," Lozen quipped, taking pleasure at taunting Bryn. "You're going into a battle with no weapons!"

"Maybe my mind is my weapon."

"Now you sound like Alva."

Lozen followed the broken trail for a few minutes before her keen hearing picked up a labored sound. "Shhh! He's near, and he's not trying to be quiet. Injured."

A lone figure stumbled through the undergrowth. His armor was damaged, and his body bore the marks of a grueling ordeal. His long, pointed ears identified him as an Aelf.

They stood up and quietly approached the scout. He saw the humans and Lozen, with a confused look crossing his face before collapsing onto the ground.

Lozen knelt beside the injured scout, her fingers probing his wounds. "You're badly hurt," she stated in Aelfic. "But I can help. What is your name?"

He fought to find his voice. "Elros... King... Aethor... message."

She gently patted his shoulder and continued in Aelfic. "Rest, friend Elros. Your message will be delivered. But first, trust me."

She reached into her herb kit on her belt. She quickly applied a poultice to his deepest wound, giving Bryn updates in the Common tongue.

Bryn, concerned, asked, "Did he run into a raiding party?"

"That's the troubling part. I see evidence of arrows and these cuts on his armor—those are from Aelfinn swords." Lozen paused, pressing on a deep, precise gash.

Bryn raised an eyebrow. "How can you tell?"

"Human warriors don't have swords; they use bearded axes. mírenstál swords, which are standard for Aelfs of age, maintain an edge iron cannot match. These cuts are sharp and clean."

Bryn was impressed. "Aelf on Aelf? Petr, join me standing guard. Lozen, be quick."

Lozen applied her Aelfinn healing to soothe the worst injuries.

A few moments later, Bryn returned with Petr, her expression grim. "Time to go," she announced.

Lozen glanced up. "Is there a problem? I don't hear anything."

Bryn scanned the forest. "That's the problem. I hear silence where there shouldn't be any. His pursuers might be close. Let's move!"

Bryn knelt beside Lozen. "Petr, you take the right shoulder. Lozen, you take the left. We carry him fast. We are the soft target now."

Petr didn't hesitate. Lozen settled Elros's arm over her shoulder, and Petr immediately took the other.

The trio embarked on the arduous journey back to Helsgaard Keep. Lozen and Petr moved as fast as they dared, fueled by the conviction that Elros's message held the key to the Keep's safety. The relentless sun beat them with oppressive heat, and Elros's mostly-dead weight dragged them down, making every step a challenge.

They burst through the final line of trees, gasping for air. The Keep loomed ahead, its stone walls comforting yet immense.

But the Keep's gates were not open for a gentle welcome.

Instead, a sudden, controlled chaos erupted. The alarm horn and gongs were already ringing—a dull, rhythmic clang—and Rangers poured out of the main gate in a focused rush. Not in a disorganized mob, but snapping into disciplined formation. Rohand was barking orders from inside the formation. They spread out in a semi-circle outside the dry moats, dropping to one knee, axes and spears leveled in a shield wall facing the forest line the trio had just left.

Hrolf and Rylen stood at the mouth of the gate, their armor laced, their expressions grim.

The contrast was stark: the weary, mud-streaked trio supporting a bleeding enemy-turned-asset, welcomed by a disciplined, defensive wall of their comrades.

As Lozen, Bryn, and Petr stumbled toward the line, Rohand's voice boomed from the ranks. "Hold your spears! Make a hole! Incoming!!!"

The line parted instantly. Rylen, his face taut with fear and relief, locked eyes with Lozen's for a brief, critical moment, a silent acknowledgment of the danger they had just navigated.

"Rohand—fall back!" Hrolf's voice cut the air.

Rohand shouted "Fall back! Fall back!"

As the trio passed the gate, Hrolf said, "Lozen, straight to the infirmary! Bryn, report to my office—"

"—Not now." Bryn raised her hand, strutting by, ignoring Hrolf, her attention solely on the Elros.

Hands reached out—strong, steady, and clean—to relieve the trio of Elros's weight. Lozen and Petr, exhausted, were suddenly swept into the protective embrace of the Keep, leaving the open battlefield behind them as the Rangers closed ranks, their axes ready for the unseen pursuer.

Bryn grabbed Petr's arm. "Petr—bring Günther to the infirmary. Now! Tell him this is RIOS priority—immediate and absolute."

Petr, energized by the seriousness of the order, did not hesitate, immediately breaking into the fastest run his exhausted body could manage toward the Commandant's office.

Hrolf, infuriated by Bryn's public disregard for his direct command, stood rigid at the gate, his jaw and hands clenched, but the urgency of the moment outweighed his rage as he watched four Rangers carrying the injured Aelf escorted by Bryn and Lozen.

CHAPTER 26

THE UNSPOKEN WAR

THE PRICE OF
INDOCTRINATION

THE INFIRMARY WITHIN HELSGAARD Keep was a dimly lit yet surprisingly comforting space. The rough-hewn stone walls had a chill softened by thick tapestries, their designs depicting scenes of healing herbs. The air was filled with the mingled scents of dried lavender, chamomile, and a faint, antiseptic tang.

Elros lay on a cot, his armor removed to reveal the extent of his cuts and bruises. Anja hovered over him, her hands radiating a soft, ethereal glow as she channeled her healing powers to mend his wounds. The room's peace was broken only by his occasional hiss of pain. Lozen and Bryn stood on the other side of the cot.

Günther entered, his eyes filled with professional concern. "What news, Bryn?"

With an urgent tone, Bryn turned to Anja and Günther. "He says he carries a message from King Aethor, but we're a long way from anything that high up on the diplomacy scale. A message from the Aelfinn king, especially one delivered by a wounded scout, can only mean trouble is coming our way."

Anja looked at Lozen, hands still glowing with healing energy. "You translate. I need to focus here."

Lozen knelt beside the cot, her voice gentle and reassuring in Aelfic. "Well met, my friend, Elros. What message does King Aethor send?"

Elros visibly relaxed as he heard the familiar sounds of his native language. With each word, he gathered his remaining strength, his voice growing stronger.

"Aelfinn extremists," he gasped in Aelfic. "Preparing—massive offensive. Target—Helsgaard—split Ravnsríki in two."

Lozen's face went pale as she translated for the others. "It's not a message from King Aethor. It's a warning about King Aethor. He's planning an offensive to split Ravnsríki in two, starting with us."

Everyone gathered around the cot gasped. Elros's chilling prophecy of doom cast a pall of dread over the room. The implication was unmistakable: war was imminent, and Helsgaard Keep lay directly in its path.

Elros's voice rasped, "More—King Aethor—sending—peace message—to Ravnborg."

Lozen translated, disbelief heavy in her tone. "There's more. The Aelfs are sending a peace envoy to Ravnborg. That doesn't make sense."

Anja turned toward him, her Aelfic unpracticed and halting, yet imbued with heartfelt compassion. She said softly, "Rest now, brave one. Your message has reached us."

He closed his eyes, his body succumbing to exhaustion.

Günther's jaw locked. "Anja, guard this Aelf. He is an enemy combatant. Restrain him, but keep him alive." He looked at Bryn. "Bryn, go brief the Mission Commander, and I want a permanent guard on this Aelf until we know exactly what's going on."

Bryn's face showed she was racing through the political implications of the message. Disengaging from Günther, she pointed at Lozen. "You come with me. You're delivering the report."

Günther stepped out from the infirmary, grim and determined. He walked quickly to the courtyard, where the newly mustered Rangers were still holding their formation. Their expressions showed a mix of fear, anger, and resolve.

His voice boomed as he addressed his warriors.

"Helsgaard! We have received grave news. The Aelfs are preparing to march on our lands, to bring war and destruction to our doorstep!"

A wave of unease rippled through the crowd, quickly replaced by a hardening resolve.

Günther raised his voice, his words a rallying cry. "But we will not cower in fear! We will not let them take what is ours! We will fight. We are defenders of Helsgaard Keep, Helsgaard-borg and Ravnsríki!"

Shouts of agreement transformed into a unified roar. "We are prepared for the coming storm. We are strong. We will show the Aelfs that they cannot break our spirit, that they cannot conquer our land!"

A booming chorus rang through the courtyard, a defiant challenge to the encroaching darkness. Günther's chest swelled with pride as he surveyed his Rangers.

⚠⚠⚠

Bryn walked to the western guard tower with Lozen in tow, pushed a stone brick, and a secret door appeared. They went through the passage, and Bryn closed the door with a decisive thud.

The room was small, measuring about two arm-spans on each side, sparsely furnished save for a desk. Illumination came from glowing crystal balls placed in the corners, their ethereal light banishing any trace of shadow. A map of Ravnsríki dominated one wall, embedded with more glowing crystal balls, each displaying a fleeting face. These represented the various cities and towns: Ravnborg, Skjaldarhöfn, South Shore, and others.

"This is my communications center with RIOS," Bryn stated, her voice tight with professional urgency. "Now you see firsthand what you signed up for."

Lozen gazed in amazement at the silent, watchful faces. Overwhelmed, she managed a small wave and a quiet, "Hi."

"Team, meet Lozen. She's the primary intelligence asset for this report. We know there were some delays, and now here's her indoctrination."

The crystal ball voices spoke in cold, professional unison. "*Welcome, Lozen. Report.*"

Bryn leaned closer to the Ravnborg globe. "This is a high-priority alert. King's ears only. All others included for awareness and preparation. Lozen and I intercepted an injured Aelfinn scout. Lozen, since you interpreted his message, tell us about your conversation."

Lozen, instantly forced into a high-stakes role, started speaking nervously but quickly gained confidence. "The scout's name is Elros. His armor damage was consistent with Aelfinn mírenstál weaponry. He warned us about an impending attack by Aeldoria, targeting Helsgaard Keep to split Ravnsríki in two."

She paused. "He also advised us of a peace mission on its way to Ravnborg. Obviously, these are in conflict. However, our understanding is that both are true, and we believe the peace mission is a ruse."

The face in the Ravnborg ball asked, "*Confidence level?*"

"Near 100%," Bryn interrupted.

"*Confidence in your apprentice?*"

"100%."

"*Thank you for your report. We'll take it from here. And, Lozen, welcome to RIOS.*"

The faces turned and disappeared instantly, the globes settling back into their neutral shimmer, carrying a dire message to their superiors.

Lozen pointed to an empty space on the map. "I see a hole instead of a ball with Copperhearth underneath?"

"The Ironroot Mountains are virtually impassable, but that pass is our only land vulnerability from the west," Bryn explained. "RIOS is setting up a post there. My friend Helga is there on-site."

Bryn tapped Lozen on the arm. "Let's go. We are on our way to see Mission Commander."

⁂

In the heart of a moonlit forest clearing, a crackling fire cast a dancing light show upon Alva's aged features. Her wild, gray hair whipped about her face as she stirred a bubbling cauldron with a staff, its gnarled wood etched with ancient symbols.

She chanted in a raspy voice. "Spirits of the fallen, hear my call. Rise from your slumber and speak to me."

A shimmering, indistinct ghostly visage materialized within the swirling smoke, its ethereal form hardly discernible in the flickering firelight.

"What news from the realm of the other side?" Alva asked with a sense of urgency.

The ghostly visage flickered, its form shifting. A voice, mixed with the crackling of the fire, spoke from the smoky depths. "*The great usurper seeks to cleave Ravnsríki by striking Helsgaard.*"

Alva's eyes widened. "Who is this usurper?"

"*Aethor, and his right hand, Soren.*"

"Aethor, the King of Aeldoria? But why would he attack Helsgaard?"

"*He is unstable, needs to learn, and needs to return to the Halls of Mandos.*" Referring to the Aelfinn afterlife, its form dissolved into the swirling smoke.

Alva shook her head in disbelief. "This cannot be allowed. Ravnsríki must be protected. Is there any hope?"

The ghostly voice, its ethereal tones fading, offered hope. "*There is a warrior... of two worlds...*"

"Who is this warrior?" Alva begged.

The ghostly voice's final words were a faint echo in the forest, revealing the name of the one who could save Ravnsríki from impending doom. "*Her name is Lozen.*"

Alva, eyes gleaming, stirred the cauldron with a final, determined motion. "Lozen—she really is the one—just like I told her—she is our only hope."

CHAPTER 27

DEFENSIVE STRATEGY

ASSESSING THE THREAT VECTOR

T HE AFTERNOON SUN FILTERED through the narrow archer's slits, casting long shadows across the stone walls of the Helsgaard Keep Command Chamber. Günther sat at his desk, his brow furrowed in concentration as a small scriber etched runes onto a copper sheet with steady precision.

Hans stood outside the open door, shifting his weight from foot to foot. His blonde hair gleamed in the sunlight, and despite his youthful nerves, his posture reflected his determination to serve.

Günther's voice cut through the stillness. "Hans!"

The boy stepped into the room with brisk energy. His words emerged with a brief pause, his mild speech impediment causing a stammer that he tackled with obvious resolve. "Y-y-yes, Com-m-m-mandant?"

"Get Bryn," Günther instructed, his tone sharp but not unkind.

"Yessir!" Hans replied, turning and sprinting down the hall.

Günther returned to staring into the distance. His scriber flowed runes across the page, forming the message that would carry Helsgaard Keep's fate:

To His Majesty, King Valdissen of Ravnsríki,

Greetings from Helsgaard Keep. We have received grave news from a grievously wounded Aelfinn scout who arrived here. He bore a message of an imminent Aelfinn offensive, targeting Helsgaard Keep, Helsgaardborg, and further seeking to divide Ravnsríki.

While this news is dire, he also tells us of King Aethor's desire for parlay. He seeks peace talks, a chance to end this senseless bloodshed.

We urge you to consider his offer but with the utmost caution. This attack, if successful, could cripple Ravnsríki before peace talks can even begin, should the parlay be truthful.

The presence of the Aelf in Helsgaard urges utmost caution as the messages conflict. We humbly request reinforcements of warriors and supplies to bolster our defenses and prepare for any eventuality.

At Your Service, Commandant Günther of Helsgaard Keep

Satisfied with the urgency, Günther placed the letter on the table.

Bryn entered, concern obvious on her face. Her eyes locked onto the copper letter.

"Yes?" she asked.

Günther gestured towards the letter. "I want you to read this."

When she finished, she set the copper sheet down. "That was my assessment as well—a peace ruse masking an invasion."

Günther, a knowing smile playing on his lips, nodded. "May I presume you probably already sent your assessment to your intelligence net?"

"I would be derelict if I didn't. I assumed you would make a formal plea, and with our messages going out through two different channels, one of them will surely be received."

Günther chuckled, pleased with her initiative. He rolled up the copper sheet, sealed it with wax, and called out, "Hans!"

Hans burst into the room. Günther's face softened as he handed the sealed letter to the young warrior. "Take this to the Griffin stables immediately. Inform Astrid that this message must reach King Valdissen with all haste. One more thing—stop by Mission Commander and tell him I'm on my way to his briefing room."

Hans snapped to attention. "Yes-s-s-sir! It w-w-will be done!" He rushed out, his enthusiasm echoing in the hallway.

Günther smiled. "He's a good kid. Come with me."

Bryn merely offered a glare and followed.

⚠⚠⚠

The Mission Commander's briefing room was dimly lit, its walls adorned with strategic diagrams. Hrolf sat at the large table, his gaze fixed on a detailed map of Ravnsríki.

"Commandant Günther," Hrolf said. "I understand we're dealing with a covert Aelfinn offensive aimed at splitting Ravnsríki. I've considered the scout's report and see three potential approaches they might take."

Günther nodded, his face grim, and stepped up beside Hrolf. "I'm listening."

Hrolf outlined the first possibility: South Shore. "They could follow the Clarellen River up. That would take them roughly five days. But the Western Helsgaard Wall only has one way up, and that ends in a chokepoint at the Keep."

He shifted his finger eastward. "Alternatively, they could land here at the Nels River and follow it up. A shorter route, three to four days' march, and a day to prepare."

Finally, he pointed north. "Or, they could infiltrate the Whispering Woods. A longer route, at least six days, but one with ample cover."

Hrolf returned his attention to the map and tapped his finger near the mouth of the Nels River. "My instinct tells me this is their most likely path. It's the quickest and most direct route to split the Kingdom."

Günther nodded. "Have you considered the scout may be a ruse to get us to focus on the Nels River approach while they attack somewhere else?"

"We have a security expert in our Rangers. Based on his recommendations about the possibility of Aelfinn spies working their way up the Nels River Valley, I initiated roving patrols, focusing on Helsgaardborg and the forest to the south.

"A security expert? Dare I ask who?"

"It's Rylen. The healer's husband. Low key fellow, until recently."

"Is there any aspect of that family that is normal or sane?"

Hrolf and Bryn looked at each other. "No, not at all," they said in unison.

"Loki and the Norns must be enjoying themselves, right now. I have a security expert, his healer wife who's an expert archer, their healer daughter who has the only sword in the Keep and is spicier than all the horseradish in Nordlund, and the Seeress in the woods is in overtime spinning riddles. And somehow, this collective of misfits predicted where Aelfinn scouts would appear, one of whom we have in the infirmary at this moment. Does any of this seem sane to you?"

Hrolf and Bryn shook their heads.

"May the AllFather save us." Günther paused for a moment. "And your read on the totality of the situation?"

Hrolf nodded toward Bryn, "I have full confidence—"

"—We believe him," Bryn interjected, flatly. "No indicators of deception. Events align with expectations. RIOS agrees with our assessment."

Günther nodded in agreement. "Well, there's nothing we can do about a Whispering Wood offensive—Ravnborg will have to figure that out. So we focus on Nels River." He looked at Bryn, who agreed.

He remained fixed on the map, looking at the southern edge of the Eastern Helsgaard Wall. A spark of inspiration ignited, and a daring plan began to take shape.

Günther turned to Hrolf, filled with excitement. "If Aethor's forces choose the Nels River route, we can ambush them from the rear by coming in from this side." His finger traced a path. "They might expect resistance at the Wall, so we follow once they start up the Nels River Valley. Wait until they attack the Keep, come up behind them, and execute an ambush attack. There is no escape to either the east or west as the walls drop off."

Hrolf, impressed, nodded. "A bold plan, Commandant, but a risky one."

"Desperate times call for desperate measures. We must be willing to take risks." Hrolf confidently proposed, "We could also split Helsgaard's forces. And send them south of the Eastern Helsgaard Wall in case we don't get the King's warriors in time."

Günther seized upon the idea. "Can the Griffins carry a Ranger with equipment?"

"Sure they can."

"And you now have a corp of Aelfinn-trained Rangers proficient in archery?" Günther asked.

"Yes, and?" Hrolf inquired, curiosity piqued.

"Put the Rangers on the Griffins and come in from behind in an aerial attack. An arrow can only go so high shot from the ground. An arrow from the sky goes until it hits the ground. Fly high and pick them off as they exit the forest." Günther looked at Hrolf with wonder. "How did you get this assignment?"

"Bad luck, sir."

"You're telling me," Günther chuckled. "Isn't that how we all got here?"

Looking at Bryn, he asked, "What about you? What pile of skitr did you step in to be sent here?"

"I volunteered to be a spy for RIOS in Ravnborg, and they sent me here. It was the luck of the draw, I guess. Easy assignment—until now."

Günther, feigning surprise, raised an eyebrow. "So you're the only one in the whole damn Keep that's not running from something or being punished?"

Bryn's smile widened, shrugging. "Seems so. Or I haven't figured out what my crime was."

Hrolf interrupted to bring the conversation back to the task at hand. "Sir. Let us prepare for battle."

Günther smirked at the banter but quickly turned serious. "Hrolf's right. Enough talk. If we're going to surprise the Aelfs, we'll need precision and speed. Brief the Rangers on their aerial approach—no noise. We strike under the cover of darkness."

He paced the room, his boots echoing against the stone floor. "Timing is everything. The aerial team—the Griffin Rangers—distracts them while your squad pushes through their defenses from the Keep. If they split their forces to deal with us, it'll leave their flank wide open."

Günther stopped pacing and fixed Hrolf with a cold, unwavering gaze. "Remember, Commander: this isn't just about winning a battle. It's about sending a message that will travel through every Aelfinn court: Ravnsríki will not fall."

Hrolf nodded, his face hardening with the commitment of a soldier facing certain odds. He didn't offer a platitude. "Understood, Commandant. The Griffins will be airborne on my mark."

Günther gave a sharp nod in return, acknowledging the grim task ahead. "Good. Luck is a poor strategist, Commander. Go execute."

Hrolf turned, the heavy chamber doors swinging shut behind him, leaving Günther alone to stare at the map, tracing the thin line where the ambush would begin. The silence that followed was not relief, but the heavy, waiting quiet of a final decision.

CHAPTER 28

THE GRIFFIN RANGER CONTINGENT

THE AMBUSH COMMANDER

T HE MORNING SUN BEAT down upon the assembled Rangers. Their faces were etched with a grim determination that mirrored the gravity of the situation. Mission Commander Hrolf, Lozen, and Anja stood before them, exuding quiet confidence born of experience and honed skill. Hans held a billboard with a map nailed to it for the Rangers to see. The air hung heavy with anticipation, and the stillness was punctuated only by the occasional murmur or the rustle of feathers as the Griffins shifted nearby.

With his voice projecting across the assembled ranks, Hrolf addressed his warriors with a stern resolve, "This is not a drill. This is a combat mission."

A hush fell over the Rangers. They trained for this moment, their skills honed, and their bodies tempered, but the reality of facing the Aelfinn in open battle remained a sobering prospect. Hrolf became more somber.

"We've been at war with the Aelfs for over seventeen years. Their raids have become more frequent and brazen. We have word they intend to strike Helsgaard to split Ravnsríki and surround Ravnborg. Over the last two years, Helsgaardborg was built, and now we have families and workers here who need our skills and protection."

Hrolf pointed to the map on the billboard, his finger tracing a route through the Nels River Valley. "Our scouts, the Griffins, have confirmed that a large Aelfinn force just landed in Ravnsríki at the Nels River."

A murmur of apprehension rippled through the Rangers. The news of the Aelfinn forces landing so close to home made them tense. But a fierce resolution to defend their land and their people tempered it. Sensing the shift in the atmosphere, Hrolf raised his voice, his words a rallying cry that echoed through the training yard.

"Fortunately, we have about three to four days before they arrive." He paused, allowing his words to sink in before revealing his plan. "You will work in tandem with our Griffins. They will carry you aloft, allowing you to rain down arrows on the enemy from above."

Griffin Keeper Astrid called out from the back of the assembled ranks. Her brow furrowed with worry, "Commander, with all due respect, this is not how we've trained with our Griffins. They are not accustomed to carrying archers, and their flight patterns will be unstable."

Hrolf turned to face her. "We must adapt. The Aelfinn threat demands it."

With a calm yet firm voice, Anja interjected, "Big problem, sir. The trajectory of an arrow shot from an elevated position varies significantly compared to one fired from ground level. We never trained for that. It's one thing to shoot from an elevated tower, which is almost like flat ground. It's another to shoot downward from a moving platform thirty or forty arm-spans in the air."

He paused, considering Astrid's and Anja's words. The Rangers, while skilled archers, were not trained for the complexities of aerial combat. "What about when the Aelfs are inside the mote, at the gates?"

"At four or five arm-spans, it's not going to make a difference. At fifty arm-spans, it makes a difference."

Hrolf nodded and turned back to the Rangers, his expression thoughtful as he considered adjustments to the battle plan. He paused, weighing the obstacles that complicated his strategy. The silence stretched as he assessed the situation, prompting the Rangers to murmur among themselves. After a brief but intense deliberation, he straightened and announced the revised plan.

"Our initial plan will be modified. The Griffins will not carry you during battle. Instead, they will transport you behind enemy lines, where you will dismount and engage in a ground-based ambush. We only have five or six Griffins staying with us, so you'll be ferried in small groups."

He turned to Lozen with confidence. "Lozen will lead the ambush. Her wilderness skills and archery experience will be crucial to our success."

Lozen nodded in acceptance. "We are ready, Mission Commander."

"You'll get half the Rangers, which is about fifteen. The Griffins will transport you behind the enemy under cover of darkness. You will fly east, drop over the Eastern Helsgaard Wall, turn south, and circle up behind them in the Nels River

Valley. Once you're in position, destroy any supply chain you find, then follow them until they arrive at the Keep."

Astrid, with a concerned expression on her face, spoke up. "Mission Commander, this is a dangerous mission. The terrain is treacherous, and the Aelfs are formidable opponents."

"I understand your concerns. But we cannot allow the Aelfs to continue their invasion unchecked. We will ask the Griffins to ferry the Rangers along the Eastern Helsgaard Wall. No combat risk to the Griffins. Do you think they will help us with that?"

"That seems reasonable—I'm certain they will assist with that request. Let me ask."

He turned his attention to Anja. "Anja will remain here at the Keep, monitoring the battle from a watchtower and relaying archer attack orders to the other tower and the battlements. This makes you Hersir for the Keep Rangers as long as bows are in effect. You have a couple of days to figure out how you will communicate between the towers. Because you came from Aeldoria, you should understand their thoughts and tactics."

Anja nodded with confidence. "We will not fail you, sir."

Satisfied with Anja's response, Hrolf scanned the assembled Rangers and stopped on Rohand. "Since you're the lead combat trainer, you're Hersir leading the ground defense should they get past the moats."

"Yessir," Rohand said.

"When I say 'Muster at the gates,' that's when Anja will hand off Hersir to Rohand. Understood?"

Anja and Rohand replied in unison, "Yessir!"

Hrolf turned to address the Rangers who would remain at the Keep, his voice ringing across the training yard. "Those of you that stay at the Keep will lay down a rain of arrows as the

Aelfs exit the woods and approach the far side of the moats. We expect them to use a shield wall, so the goal will to keep them on the defense." He paused, looking at the faces of his warriors. "Circle up!"

The Rangers gathered closer to the bulletin board, where a map of the surrounding area was meticulously drawn on stretched animal skin and spread out before them. Rohand's position beside Hrolf advertised his status as a Hersir, and he listened closely as the Mission Commander detailed the potential battleground.

"Looking at the map," Hrolf said. His finger traced the contours of the Nels River Valley. "The Aelfs will come up this valley and come out of the trees south of the Keep at this point."

"Even if they try crossing the land bridge through the moats, they must know we have archers." A sly smile spread across his face as he added, "They don't know our archers are Aelfinn-trained."

Hrolf traced a wide arc on the map over the Western Helsgaard Wall and discussed the defensive advantages afforded by their strategic position. "Note, no viable access point exists along this formidable barrier, save for a solitary road descending to Helsgaard Frontier."

His finger moved deliberately, highlighting the topographical features that fortified the Keep. "This passage, however, falls under our watchful eye and constitutes a brú—chokepoint—by its very nature." His finger drifted across the animal skin, emphasizing the inescapable conclusion. "Thus, any approach the enemy might undertake inevitably converges upon the moat and this strategically vital critical juncture."

Hrolf's finger came to rest upon the land bridge that bisected the moat. "While a water-filled moat would be preferable, such a luxury is beyond our means due to water scarcity. Alas, it remains but a dry ditch."

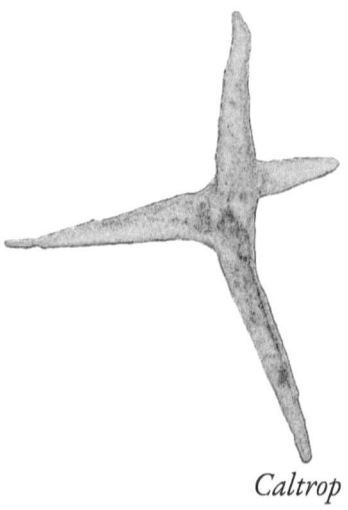

Caltrop

Looking up from the map, he addressed the assembled Rangers and the handful of settlers. His voice, though calm, carried an undeniable weight of authority. "Those of you not accompanying Lozen on her mission are charged with gathering every available stick and branch to obstruct the moat, impeding the attackers' progress. Furthermore, the field adjacent to the moat must be cleared of any obstacles that might inadvertently aid the enemy's shield wall. And I hope to have Torsten and his forge work up a couple hundred caltrops to deploy."

Hrolf looked at each of his warriors. "Prepare yourselves. This will be no easy feat, but I believe in your abilities. I have borne witness to your prowess."

He paused and drew in a deep breath. "One last thing for today. Helsgaardborg popped up in the last two years. These people have no idea what's coming. Spread the word to evacuate to inside the Keep. Keep them calm—we have a few days, but sooner is better to figure out where to put them. Tell them to bring their food and bedrolls."

"Helsgaard Rangers!" Hrolf shouted. "May Odin watch over you and guide your hands in battle!"

CHAPTER 29

NO REINFORCEMENTS, NO RETREAT

THE STORM SWALLOWS THE WINGS

T HE NEARLY FULL MOON loomed in the eastern sky, casting a cold, hard light over the stone battlements of Helsgaard Keep. Torches guttered in their iron sconces, flames twitching in the wind, shadows cutting across the yard like knives. Griffin Keeper Astrid worked fast, her hands raw from leather straps and claw scrapes as she saddled the restless beasts. The yard stank of sweat, oiled hide, old blood, and Griffin musk—thick enough to choke on, sharp enough to taste.

Lozen and her Rangers stood at attention. There were no speeches, no ceremony—just the weight of what lay ahead pressing on every shoulder. Bows slung across backs, quivers bristling, axes at their hips. Only Lozen wore a sword. The hilt caught the torchlight with a dull glint.

The yard held its breath. Even the Griffins were still, their great feathered heads turning to watch. Now and then, a wing rustled or a talon scraped stone, but otherwise, it was quiet—tense, charged, like the hush before a storm.

Günther stood beside Hrolf, his formal tunic creased from hours of wear. His voice was low but urgent. "Just got word from the King. He's keeping his warriors close. Doesn't want to risk them on a false flag. Bryn says the same. We're not getting help. Not tonight."

Hrolf scowled. His jaw clenched, teeth grinding. "Vid hamri Thors," he muttered. "The invasion's already here, not sitting pretty in Ravnborg's palace. Gods, we need more axes."

He stared at the dirt a moment, then drew in a sharp breath and faced the Rangers.

"Alright, listen up." His voice cut through the stillness. "You're heading into the dark with no reinforcements and no backup. Just your steel and each other. If the Emissary is a trap, you're the only wall between them and Helsgaard. Maybe the whole kingdom."

He let that sit. Not a soul shifted.

"You've trained for this. You know what's out there. But it's not just about survival. It's about stopping whatever this is before it gets out of control. Trust your instincts. Trust your team. Bring each other home."

Lozen stepped forward. Her voice was steady. "We won't fail you, Commander."

Hrolf looked at her—really looked. Two years ago, she'd been a half-wild street rat begging for refuge. Now she stood armored, armed, eyes sharp, spine straight, and in charge. He gave a dry, grim smile. "I know you won't. First mission leading a squad, and we drop the fate of the kingdom in your lap. Good luck."

Astrid finished checking the last of the saddles, giving Hrolf a nod.

He raised his voice. "First wave—mount up!"

The Griffins stirred, sensing the shift. Wings stretched wide with bone-deep power, feathers shaking out like war cloaks. One let out a shriek that cut through the night and echoed off the Keep's stone.

Six Rangers moved quickly: Lozen, Petr, grim Sigrid, broad-shouldered Arn, quick-tongued Kael, and silent Freydis. Just the tight, practiced efficiency of people who understood the weight of their mission. Lozen swung into her saddle, the mírenstál sword tapping against her thigh. She met Hrolf's gaze—steady, locked—and gave a sharp nod.

The Griffins launched.

Wings beat the air in a thunderous rhythm, torchlight flaring and sputtering in their wake. Wind tore past their faces as the yard fell away below, the night swallowing them whole. Above, stars bore silent witness.

For Lozen, the ascent was a violent, breathtaking rupture from the world she knew. The Griffin didn't just climb; it tore through gravity with a raw, surging power that vibrated through her thighs. The wind screamed in her ears, cold and sharp enough to scour the fear right out of her blood, replacing it with a wild, terrifying ecstasy. Looking down, the Keep was no longer a fortress of stone and duty, but a shrinking speck in the vast, velvet dark.

Hrolf watched until the last wingbeat faded. Then he turned to the ten Rangers still waiting in formation.

"Six hours. That's all the rest you get," he said. "Eat. Sleep if you can. Check your gear. When the Griffins return, the second wave will launch. You are dismissed."

They moved, gear clinking softly as they made their way to warmth and rest.

Hrolf stayed behind.

Astrid stood a few paces away, rolling her shoulders and rubbing a smear of something dark off her forearm with a rag.

He walked over. "Still standing, Astrid?"

"Barely," she said, not looking up. "One of them bit the saddle again. I'm sending the King a bill for repairs."

Hrolf huffed a quiet laugh. "Yeah, good luck with that."

She finally met his eyes. "They flew clean."

"They always do when you're prepping them."

Astrid waved off the compliment. "Seriously," she said. "Three waves in one night? That's a big ask. I don't take it for granted."

"Neither do they. They know what's riding on this. You saw how still they were? That doesn't happen unless they're focused."

Astrid gave him a mock glare. "Careful, Hrolf. You're sounding dangerously sentimental."

He smirked. "Don't let it get around."

She chuckled, then nodded toward the keep. "Get some rest. You look like Hela's bad side."

"You always know how to sweet-talk me."

"Truly!"

He lingered for a beat, then gave a nod. "Thanks, Astrid. For everything."

She nodded back, more serious now. "Bring them all home."

Hrolf glanced at the sky, where the last of the wingbeats had long since faded. "That's on Lozen now. I've done what I can from here."

He didn't wait for a reply. Just turned toward the Warrior House, boots crunching gravel, and walked into the dark.

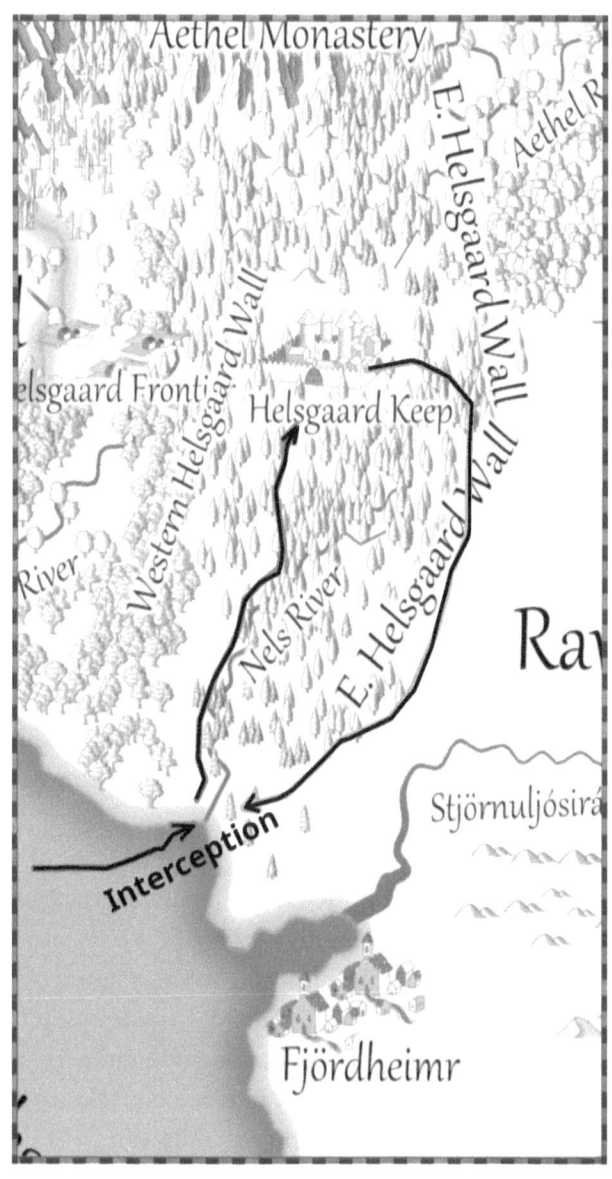

Interception at the Nels River

CHAPTER 30

GHOSTS ON THE NELS

THE HUNT BEGINS

T HE NOW FULL MOON, a luminous pearl high in the velvet sky, cast a silvery glow over the calm waters of the Nels River inlet. Under cover of night, four shadowy ships moved soundlessly, their sleek forms blending seamlessly with the darkness. The oar locks were cord-wrapped, and the oar blades were sheathed in leather, ensuring their approach remained undetected.

As the ships neared the shore, the gentle lapping of waves against their hulls grew louder. With a faint scraping sound, the vessels settled onto the sandy beach.

At the prow of the lead ship stood Soren, a figure of lethal grace. His high cheekbones and slanted, ice-pale eyes reflected the moonlight with an eerie brilliance, giving him an almost spectral presence. His silver-white hair was bound into a tight battle knot, revealing the sharp points of his ears.

He wore blackened leather armor, reinforced with míren-stál-threaded plating that clung to his lean frame without a sound. The runes etched into the vambraces pulsed faintly, whispering silent wards against detection. His long fingers tightened around the hilt of his mírenstál sword, his posture unnaturally still—like a viper waiting to strike. With an abrupt motion, he raised a clenched fist, a silent command.

Chaos followed. Oars dropped. Warriors surged over the sides, hitting the surf in unison. Water churned as they heaved the longboats farther up the beach with brutal precision.

In minutes, almost three hundred Aelfs stood assembled—silent, disciplined, deadly.

Soren moved to the front. "Warriors of Aeldoria," his voice cut through the night like a drawn sword: cold, commanding, and hungry for conquest. "Tonight, we embark on a mission of utmost importance. Tonight, we defy the twisted prophecy that seeks to bind us to a fate of servitude to the Humans."

He paused. "Tonight, we strike a blow for Aeldoria! Tonight, we avenge the injustices suffered at the hands of the Humans of Ravnsríki!"

They stood with stern, determined faces as they raised their swords and bows in a silent salute.

Soren mirrored the anguish and rage that burned within his warriors. "Ravnsríki's tyrannical and oppressive reign has plagued our lands for far too long. Their expansion threatens to consume all of Nordlund. Tonight, we seize the reins of our destiny! We will be the ones to shape the future, not some cursed prophecy!"

He paused, scanning their faces. "We will be swift, silent, and deadly. We will take them by surprise and not stop until Ravnborg, and ultimately, Ravnsríki is ours!"

A growl of agreement, a chorus of defiance, rose from the ranks. "Move out!"

Silent as whispers, the Aelfs melted into the shadowed embrace of the forest. Behind them, the boat crews stood vigilant, guarding the ships.

⚠⚠⚠

The moon hung low and full, casting a pale, merciless light across the Nels River delta. Lozen crouched in the underbrush, fifteen of Helsgaard's best Rangers fanned out in tight formation behind her. They'd been in place for hours, motionless and quiet, watching the water swell with the tide—and now, finally, the enemy had arrived.

Four sleek Aelfinn longships slipped into view like blades drawn from a sheath. The landing was a blur of disciplined violence. Within minutes, almost three hundred Aelfinn soldiers had formed ranks on the beach—silent, controlled, terrifying.

From the lead ship, a figure stood—tall, sharp-featured, wrapped in a black cloak. Even from a distance, his presence cut like a blade. Lozen narrowed her eyes.

"Soren," she whispered.

She didn't need to explain. The name alone sent a ripple of tension down the Ranger line. Lozen recognized the figure instantly: the unique silver-white hair, the lethal posture, and, most damningly, the Serpent-grasping-Raven Brooch—the symbol of treachery Anja had often described—pinning his cloak. He was the architect of the war, now standing on human soil, commanding an army meant to finish what he started.

Soren waited, letting the moment stretch like a bowstring. Then, with a sharp downward thrust of his fist, the Aelfinn warriors moved.

Lozen's pulse hammered behind her ears. She signaled her team to huddle behind a cluster of fallen trees.

"Our mission hasn't changed," she whispered. "We wait until they're deep inland—then we disable their ships, ransack what we can, and hit them hard at the Keep in a surprise attack. Petr?"

Petr, eyes fixed on the beach, didn't look away. "Exactly. We hit their ships first—cripple their escape route. Oars, sails, rudders—break it all. Once that's done, we circle back and set up the ambush near the Keep. We'll catch them between the walls and the woods."

Lozen nodded. "No oars, no sails, no retreat."

Petr tapped a rough-sketched map spread across a flat stone. "They'll move slowly through the woods. Our advantage is speed and terrain. Let them tire themselves hauling gear through marsh and slope. Then we bleed them dry near the Keep."

The Aelfinn force began to move inland, following Soren's silent signal.

She turned to her Rangers. Their faces were hard, focused. Still, the math haunted her.

She leaned closer to Petr. "Three hundred of them. Sixteen of us. Even at the Keep, it's thirty against three hundred."

Petr put a hand on her shoulder. "We're not here to win a fair fight. We're here to make sure they don't get one. We hit, we vanish. We're ghosts in the trees."

Lozen inhaled, slow and steady. Her fingers brushed the hilt of her mírenstál sword. The weight of command pressed down, sharp and undeniable.

"We wait until the last of them disappears into the forest," she said. "Then we follow. Quiet. Sharp. Fast."

The Rangers melted into the trees. The hunt had begun.

CHAPTER 31

NO OARS, NO RETREAT

THE AELFINN DECEPTION

THE FULL MOON BLED silver over four longships dragged high on the shingle, their tarred hulls hulking like beached whales. Salt wind whispered across the strand, carrying with it the reek of fish, pitch, and sweat. Three crewmen huddled near the prow of the closest vessel, their words hushed in Aelfic.

"Do you think this is really going to work?" one murmured, his voice brittle with doubt.

"Simple enough," said another, his hand resting on a curved blade. "Wear down the Keep. Our archers are better than theirs. We pick them off, bleed them out. After that? Numbers. Always numbers." He stared out over the dark water, trying to believe his own words.

The third smirked. "I'm just glad I drew boat guard du—"

The rest was swallowed by a sharp gasp and a wet crack. An arrow jutted from his eye, the shaft quivering as he crumpled.

The other two had time only to blink before more shafts hissed through the night. Thuds followed—one struck in the throat, another through the chest—their bodies thrashing briefly before falling still. Across the beach, a dozen more Aelfs dropped in the same heartbeat, arrows sprouting from skulls, ribs, and bellies. Sand drank deep as Aelfinn blood flowed.

A silence followed, broken only by the gulls screaming off-shore.

Petr stepped from the tree line, bow still drawn, face pale in the moonlight. He scanned the beach. "Check them," he called.

Lozen's hand snapped out, her voice cold as forged steel. "I give the orders. You tell me what needs doing, I decide. Clear?"

He dipped his head. "Yes, Hersir."

The Rangers spilled from the shadows, axe blades glinting. They stalked between the twitching Aelfs, boots crunching on shells and rocks. One by one, they drove knives across throats still bubbling for breath, sending the last survivors to the Halls of Mandos. The air filled with the copper stench of fresh blood, sharp and undeniable.

A twig cracked. From the foliage, a lone Aelf stepped into view, drawn by the dying cries. "What's happening?" he called in his own tongue.

Lozen dropped her bow with a curse. "Skitr!" Her gaze flicked to Petr, then back. She forced her voice calm, answering in Aelfic, "An oar crushed Arien's foot. Bastards didn't stow them right. We need help."

She angled her head, letting the moonlight catch the point of her ear. The Aelf faltered, suspicion softening into trust. He stepped forward.

Lozen gave the faintest nod.

The Rangers loosed their bows. A dozen arrows struck him at once, turning his chest into a stag's hide. He staggered, arms twitching as though trying to embrace the air, then crumpled to the sand.

Petr let out a shaky laugh. "That was close."

Lozen ignored him, eyes sweeping the tree line. "More?"

He shook his head. "Hard to say. Let's not wait to find out. Search the boats. Strip them of everything. Sabotage is priority. Kael, Arn, Freydis—you strip the boats of sailcloth, and shatter the rudders. Sigrid, Petr, axes to the tholepins. Make them useless to row. The rest of you loot the bodies, pull arrows."

Lozen split the team with a flick of her hand.

Kael, Arn, and Freydis worked quickly, slashing through the thick leather bindings holding the rudders and sails in place, destroying the essential control and wind power.

Petr and Sigrid moved along the gunwales, driving their axes—not into the hulls, which would be loud—but into the tholepins, the wooden pegs that hold the oars. They snapped and splintered the pins, making rowing impossible.

Crates thudded to the sand—sacks of dried fish, bundles of salted meat, quivers heavy with Aelfinn arrows, and a sword that glowed faintly blue in the moonlight.

"Load it," Lozen ordered. "Petr gets the sword. You don't have to use it, but it might come in handy."

A shadow rippled across the beach. The Rangers froze, heads snapping upward.

Against the moon's pale face, a shape glided: vast wings stretched wide, a silhouette like a nightmare stitched into the night sky.

Petr squinted. "That's the biggest bat I've ever seen."

Lozen's whisper was iron. "Not a bat. Too steady, too large. Bats bounce when they fly. That was a Dragon. Víd hamri Thors!"

He gave a half-snort, half-gasp. "Dragon? Winged beasts? That's tavern talk."

Lozen's eyes never left the sky. "Tavern stories don't leave behind claw-marks in stone. I've seen the tracks. Rohand showed me the footprints after a cow disappeared one night. They're real. They're hunting again." She pulled her cloak tighter. "And we're exposed. Back to cover."

The Rangers grabbed what they could and sprinted for the tree line, hearts pounding, loot clutched tight. Behind them, the beach lay desecrated, bodies sprawled like broken dolls, crates smashed open, blood soaking into the tide. Moonlight washed it all in ghostly silver as the waves crept in, steady and indifferent, erasing the slaughter grain by grain.

But the sky above still carried the shadow of wings.

CHAPTER 32

HELSGAARD PREPARES

THE CALTROP IMPERATIVE

H ELSGAARD KEEP, ONCE A quiet wall against the wilds, now throbbed with the tension of impending war. The air reeked of sweat, smoke, and palpable fear. Settlers and merchants flooded the courtyard, arms loaded with whatever they could carry—tools, blankets, heirlooms—pushing past each other in a desperate tide toward the gates. Guards barked orders over the din, their voices cracking, trying to keep panic from boiling over.

In the heart of the chaos, the forge burned like the center of the world.

Inside, heat blasted off the stone walls as iron rang under hammer blows. Torsten worked in a sweat-darkened linen shirt, the fabric clinging to his frame, soaked through from the furnace heat. His blonde hair was shaved close to avoid stray embers, and his face was set with grim focus as he hammered a glowing rod into shape with brutal precision.

Beside him, two apprentices hammered arrowheads in rhythm, their arms a blur of muscle and urgency. Leather aprons smoked at the edges. One paused to wipe the sweat from his eyes, knuckles trembling.

"How many more?" he asked, breath ragged.

Torsten didn't look up. "Until every quiver's full," he growled, "or my arms fall off. Whichever comes first."

Hrolf approached, yelling to be heard over the forge. "Can you make up some caltrops?"

They looked at each other, a silent understanding passing between the seasoned warriors.

"How many, what size, and how soon?" Torsten asked.

"Two or three hundred, small ones for feet, and immediately, so I can get them deployed."

His back ached from the relentless pounding. Torsten arched backward, stretching his weary muscles. "Send me three more helpers, and I can get you a hundred by nightfall. If you want two hundred, I have to stop making arrows. Caltrops are a pain in the rass to make."

Hrolf understood the blacksmith's predicament. "I'll get you helpers. Do the best you can."

With that, he strode off, thoughts already racing through the endless list of tasks. At the forge, Torsten drove the hammer down again, muscles screaming with every swing. The rhythmic clang of steel on steel echoed through the stone chamber—relentless, unbroken—a sound that promised Helsgaard wouldn't fall without a fight.

⚠⚠⚠

The ramparts of Helsgaard Keep rose like jagged stone fangs against the iron-colored sky. In the courtyard, Rangers, assisted by the residents of Helsgaardborg, moved like a war machine—hauling crates, sharpening axe blades and spear tips, testing bowstrings. Fletchers—arrow makers—worked at a brutal pace, turning shafts and feathers from the forge into weapons. Arrows piled up in crooked stacks, ready to blacken the sky.

Hrolf stood at the center of it all, scanning the work with a battle-hardened gaze. Every second counted. Every idle hand was a liability.

"More arrows to the south rampart!" he shouted. "If they come through there, I want them crawling over their dead before they touch the wall!"

A sharp clatter of boots on stone drew his attention. A young woman, barely more than a girl, ran toward him, her breath ragged, eyes wide with panic.

"Commander!" she gasped. "The Aelfs—they're a day out! Maybe less!"

Hrolf didn't blink. "Not likely. They're three days. We'll be ready for them. What are you doing right now?"

The girl faltered, trembling. "I—I don't know what to do. I'm just... scared."

"Good," he said flatly. "That means you're paying attention. Come with me. I'll show you how to turn fear into something useful."

He gripped her shoulder—firm, steady—and led her through the Keep until they reached the forge, where heat rolled out like a volcano.

Inside, Torsten hammered steel. Hrolf raised his voice over the din. "Torsten! You've got a new set of hands."

The blacksmith didn't look up. "He got arms?"

"She's got fear. Use it."

The girl stared around, stunned by the noise, the heat, the raw purpose in every movement. For the first time, she didn't look like she was about to bolt.

Torsten looked up and grunted. "Apron's by the wall. You burn yourself, you keep working. Do what the apprentices say."

Hrolf watched her move—hesitant at first, then faster, pulled along by the relentless momentum of the forge.

He nodded once. Then turned, muttering as he strode away, "One down. Two more to go."

CHAPTER 33

TRAILING BEHIND

THE STAGE IS SET

O N THE SECOND NIGHT after the Aelfinn landed, the Rangers crouched in a ragged circle, shadows moving in the fireless dark. The smell of unwashed bodies, damp leather, and blood gone sour clung heavier than the mist.

Lozen and Petr sat apart, backs to a fallen oak. Lozen's eyes were sharp as flint despite being weary.

"You know," she said, voice rough, "you've a decent mind for strategy."

Petr gave a humorless snort. "Just because I prefer wet-work doesn't mean I don't think, Hersir."

"And can thinking win this?" Lozen asked. "The Aelfs outnumber us ten to one."

"The land favors us." He stabbed a finger at the hide-map between them, rough ink glistening in the moonlight. "The valley cloaks us. The plateau exposes them."

A scoff came from the shadows. Kael, quick-tongued and sharp as broken glass, leaned forward. "You speak as if trees fight wars for us. The Aelfs will march, and we'll bleed. And when we do, will the half-blood lead us home?" His gaze slid to Lozen, mocking.

A few Rangers muttered—some in agreement, some in warning.

Lozen's jaw tightened, but Petr spoke first, his tone like a knife. "Careful, Kael. Words cut deeper than arrows, and you're not quick enough to dodge both."

She leaned in, her voice low, cold, leaving no room for jest. "You'll follow because I say so. Or you'll rot in the trees with the ravens picking your eyes and beetle eating your nethers. Which would you prefer?"

Kael's smirk faltered, but he spat to the side. "We'll see if your plan keeps us breathing."

The tension snapped like a drawn bowstring, then eased, leaving the night heavier than before. Plans continued, but now they were edged with unease.

⩘⩘⩘

After another day of silent pursuit, the late-rising moon emerged in the eastern sky, its pale, silvery glow filtering through the canopy to illuminate Lozen and Petr. They stood amidst the towering forest, where the air was heavy with stillness, broken only by the occasional chirp of hidden insects. Three nights of relentless planning and careful preparation had left traces of exhaustion on their faces. Yet, an unspoken resolve now bound them, a quiet testament to their shared determination.

Lozen's murmur barely disturbed the stillness of the night, and she spoke with confidence. "The Norns have spun the thread. We stand ready."

Surprised by her sudden shift in confidence, Petr looked up at her, his eyebrows raised in curiosity. "Ready?"

"Ready," she said. "The plan is solid, the Rangers are prepared, and the terrain is on our side. We'll give those Aelfs a surprise they won't forget."

A smile spread across his face. "I'm glad to hear you say that. I'll admit, I was starting to worry about your doubts."

She laughed. "Doubt? That was three nights ago. Now, all I feel is anticipation. The hunt is about to begin. And if my reckoning is correct, the battle should be upon us by the morrow's next."

"Then let us rest while we can, Hersir, for we fight in two days."

They settled beside the fireless camp, where the Rangers lay in scattered silence—half-asleep, half-alert. Petr laid down first, shifting under his cloak with a quiet sigh. Lozen followed, settling beside him with her back turned.

For a time, the night wrapped around them in stillness.

Then Petr's voice drifted through the dark, quiet and thoughtful. "Lo... you invoked the Norns earlier."

She didn't move. "I did."

"But the Aelfs preach of the Halls of Mandos—of reflection, training, and the eternal return. Why call upon the Weavers if your spirit is meant to cycle, not end? It seems... contradictory."

Lozen exhaled slowly, watching the mist curl around the tree roots. "In Aeldoria, they teach that time is a river—it flows, returns to the sea, and rains down again. But here? In the mud, with steel in my hand?"

She paused, her fingers brushing the hilt of Vonar Egg in the dark.

"This doesn't feel like a river, Petr. It feels like a knot. Mandos is for the soul that has eternity to learn. The Norns... they are for the warrior who might only have this heartbeat. Tonight, I don't feel like an immortal waiting to learn a lesson. I feel like a thread waiting to see if I will be woven or cut."

Petr was silent for a long moment. "Then let us hope the Norns have steady hands."

She turned back and closed her eyes.

The space between them stayed quiet, but no longer felt distant.

⚠⚠⚠

The moon, still below the horizon on the fourth night, lit up the eastern sky, silhouetting them as they finalized their plans. Lozen posed a crucial question to her trusted comrade. "Petr, how are we fixed for arrows?" she asked.

With his mind already attuned to the practicalities of their mission, he said, "I distributed the loot we found on the Aelfinn ships. Everyone should have around thirty arrows."

Lozen, her mind swirling with calculations, started to count their available resources. "Thirty arrows each—fifteen Rangers and me—that's three 16's with a zero..." she trailed off as she began counting on her fingers, muttering to herself. "Sixteen and sixteen is two-three—and sixteen is eight-four—add the zero—zero-eight-four." Her voice rose with surprise and satisfaction as she arrived at the sum. "Four hundred eighty arrows!"

Petr nodded and said, "Not bad for a night's work."

"Not bad at all. And with Helsgaard's Rangers adding to the volley, it should be like spearfishing in a barrel," she said, quoting Petr from two nights before. Gleaming with anticipation,

Lozen said, "Three hundred Aelfs against at least a thousand of our arrows from all sides? This is going to be a good fight."

Wrapped in their concealing cloaks, Lozen and her band of Rangers lay nestled amongst the trees, their forms indistinguishable in the dappled moonlight.

A twig cracked in the blackness, and the Rangers surged to their feet, weapons flashing in the half-light. The night held its breath.

From the tree line came Alva, her cloak dragging like a shadow behind her, her red eyes burning against the dark. She lifted her hands, slow, deliberate.

"Peace, warriors," she said, her tone silk laid over steel. "I seek Lozen."

Lozen said. "Alva! This is no place for you. Go back to your field."

Alva's mouth curved, faint and cold. "This is exactly my place."

The Rangers shifted uneasily. Petr's voice carried, tight. "And what of the Aelfs? Are you not afraid of their attack? Or of capture, or death?"

Alva's smile sharpened. "The Aelfs hold no power over me."

A ripple of unease ran through the circle.

Kael's laugh broke it—harsh, cutting. "And why do you not fear the Aelfs? A stranger, slinking in the night, claiming fate in her pocket? More likely leading us to slaughter."

Alva's gaze slid to him, and for an instant the air seemed to still, the forest leaning in. "You fear what you do not understand, Ranger."

Kael spat into the dirt. "Better to fear a lie than kneel to one."

Lozen snapped her head toward him, her voice low and dangerous. "Enough, Kael. Hold your tongue or I'll nail it to a tree."

Silence followed, brittle as glass. Kael smoldered, but he said no more.

Alva stepped closer, her red eyes fixed only on Lozen. " I have a message for you. His name is Soren, and you will hold him up for all to see. The winds have spoken."

The words struck like a knife of ice. Lozen tightened her grip on her sword hilt, unable to look away. "I know his name. And what do you mean I will hold him up?"

Alva tilted her head, her expression unreadable. "You will know. When the blood runs and metal sings, you will know."

Then she turned, her shape dissolving into the forest, until only the echo of her words clung to the night.

The Rangers stood in taut silence. Whispers stirred—witch, Seeress, traitor—carried just beneath the breath.

Lozen sheathed her blade, her hand shaking as it met the scabbard. Her voice cut hard to cover it, "Forget her. We march as planned."

But Petr watched her too long, seeing the unease she tried to bury. And in the quiet of the camp, the Rangers whispered—not of the Aelfs, but of the red-eyed Seeress who walked among them.

The two guards stood alert, returning to their positions for the night watch, scanning the surrounding forest for any signs of movement. The stage stood ready, the players in position, Ravnsríki hanging in the balance.

CHAPTER 34

THE BATTLE FOR HELSGAARD

THE GHOSTS IN THE TREES

Morning bled into the pine forest without cere-mony. Sunlight seeped through the needles in broken shafts, more smoke than gold. The air was too still, the hush of it unnatural. Lozen lay awake long before the first call, her nerves strung taut. Sleep had been shallow, threaded with nightmares that smelled like ash.

Two Rangers slipped into the camp shadows, their faces pale, breath shallow.

"Lozen. Petr. Up."

Her eyes snapped open before the words finished. Petr's hand went to his axe, his knuckles white.

The whisper came, sharp and expected. "The Aelfs. They're moving."

The camp stirred. Weapons rattled. Boots scuffed. Lozen rose, spine straight, eyes sweeping the trees as if she might catch the first shadow herself.

"You two—back to post. Keep your eyes open," she ordered, her voice low, steady.

The Rangers obeyed, vanishing as quickly as they'd come.

Lozen's voice cut through the camp, cold and clipped. "Up. Now."

Axes hissed free of sheaths. Arrows thudded into quivers. The men and women moved with practiced economy, but there was no hiding the pallor of their faces. They knew.

Lozen let her gaze rake over them. Her heart thundered like a smith's hammer in her ears, careful to not let it show through.

"When the Aelfs reach the field, Helsgaard will sound the alarm. That's our signal. We fan out like Mjölnir and strike—silent, sudden. Shadows and teeth. Sixteen arrows, sixteen corpses. Take the rear guard, split them apart. One arrow, one kill."

She met each gaze in turn, until the silence became unbearable. "Questions?"

None. Only grim nods.

Lozen and Petr lingered for a breath. Their eyes locked—a spark of shared resolve and something darker, quieter.

"Good. Then move."

The Rangers melted into the trees, ghosts with teeth. Lozen and Petr lingered for a breath. Their eyes locked—a spark of shared resolve and something darker, quieter: the unspoken truth that not all of them would return.

Then Lozen stiffened. She raised a hand, head tilting.

"Shhh."

Petr froze, listening, breath shallow. "What?"

"Bryn," she whispered. Her ear twitched. "She's scream-ing."

"I don't hear—"

"—She's not screaming in pain. She's screaming a warning."

Then the sound hit them both—distant, ragged, carried by the morning wind.

"They're here," Petr said. His voice was flat, certain.

The first war cries rose, a tide breaking against the walls of Helsgaard.

⚠⚠⚠

The early light bathed Helsgaard Keep in a false calm, gold dripping down stone like honey—a promise the day had no intent of keeping.

Then Bryn tore from the tree line.

Her face was white, her eyes wide, mouth open on a single word that carved the silence apart, "AELFS!!!"

Her scream rolled across the field, high and broken.

On the battlements, Rangers snapped awake. Quivers clattered. Fingers tightened on bowstrings.

Bryn flew across the grass, feet dodging instinctively around hidden caltrops, lungs burning. "They're coming!" she gasped, her voice shredding. "Hundreds!"

As if her voice had summoned them, the forest vomited forth an army.

They came in ranks, shields gleaming, blades raised. Their discipline was terrifying—cold faces, no war cries, just the unified rhythm of boots pounding earth. Archers slid to the rear, nocking shafts with mechanical grace.

The sight alone was enough to freeze breath in throats.

Then the world screamed.

Aelfs fell as if the ground itself betrayed them. They shrieked, their feet skewered by caltrops that tore through boot-leather and tendon alike. Some went down hard, caltrops piercing hands, knees, and tripping comrades in a cascade of broken formation. The charge faltered in a ripple of confusion. Shield walls shattered. Orders were swallowed in chaos.

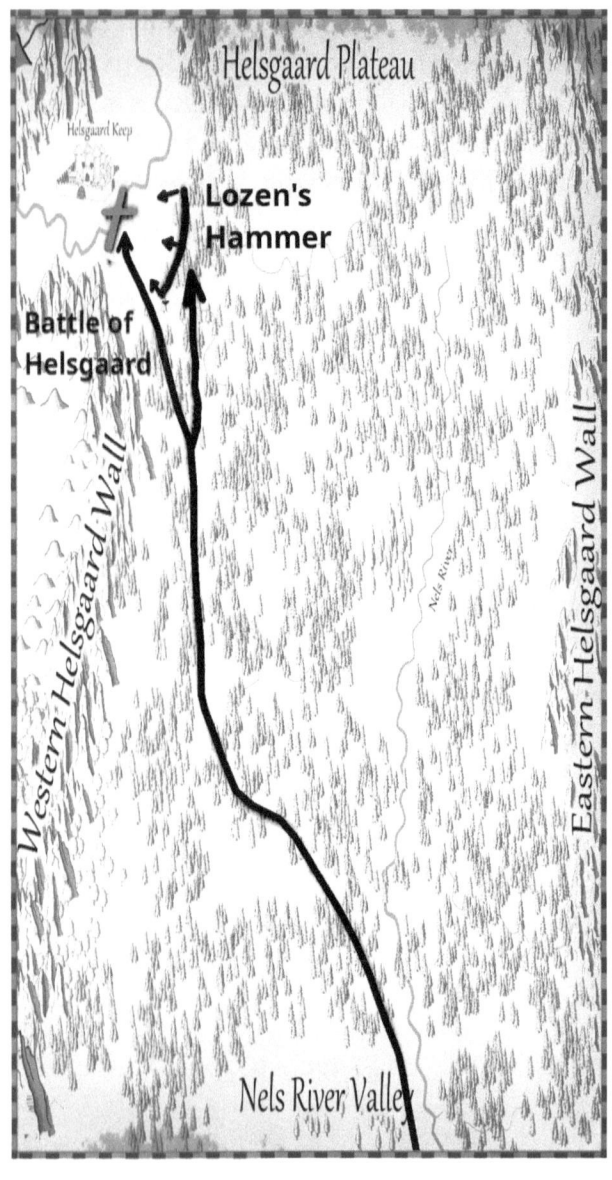

Lozen's Trailing Ambush

Arrows began to fly—Helsgaard's first answer.

The gate guards panicked into motion. Bryn barreled through the opening, lungs searing, legs threatening to buckle. She nearly crashed into one of the guards before stumbling to her knees, gasping as she wasn't used to running that far and that fast. One seized the alarm horn and blew until his face turned purple, the horn's wail raking the air raw. The other heaved the massive gate shut behind her with a groan of wood, the hardwood bar slamming home with a teeth-rattling crack.

The gong sounded—deep, booming, final. The countryside shivered with its echo.

Within the walls, chaos bloomed. Rangers pounded toward their stations, leather rubbing, axes flashing. Shouts overlapped, footsteps hammered the stone. Fear was a taste in the air—sharp, metallic, like blood sucked from a split lip.

Anja climbed the tower with her bow already strung, her fingers trembling only until they touched the string. From her vantage she saw them—the endless surge of Aelfs filling the field, blood streaming behind them where caltrops had done their work.

Her lips moved. A prayer, maybe. Or a curse.

"For Lozen."

The arrow left her hand with a whisper. It split the air, true and merciless, punching through the skull of an Aelf officer. He dropped without a sound, his helm pinned to his head, before he rolled into the mud.

Anja lowered the bow, her chest heaving as the weight of the kill settled on her soul. She squeezed her eyes shut, a single tear cutting through the dust on her cheek.

"*Goheno nîn, Mandos*," she whispered the ancient words. "Have mercy on me, Mandos. Forgive the hand that was sworn to heal. I send him to your Halls not out of hate, but out of love. Weigh my broken vow against his life, but let my daughter live."

A omen.

The towers erupted. Rangers unleashed volley after volley, shafts hissing down like black rain. The Aelfs staggered under the onslaught, their shield lines splintering as warriors toppled, shrieking, clutching at arrows that sprouted from throats and eyes.

The cries of pain, the wet cough of pierced lungs, the iron stink of blood—they rose together, drowning the morning in ruin.

And still Helsgaard's defenders did not cheer. They stood in silence, grim as executioners, raining death with steady hands.

The first trap had snapped. The second was already waiting.

The Aelfinn advance shattered as caltrops bit deep into flesh. Aelfinn warriors screamed, stumbling forward on ruined feet. Shields wavered. Tight ranks sagged like a breached dam, and the momentum of the charge dissolved into chaos.

Then the sky darkened.

Arrows rained from the Keep. The shafts fell like hail, thudding into skulls and ribcages, snapping spines, punching through eyes. Aelfs dropped mid-stride, collapsing in the churned mud. One Aelf clawed at the shaft jutting from his throat, gagging as blood poured between his fingers before he fell twitching.

The survivors had no time to recover.

From the tree line came a new storm, arrows hissing like serpents through the morning air. Lozen's Rangers had loosed their arrows. Hidden among the pines, they unleashed a merciless volley into the rearguard. The first line of Aelfs staggered back, shields raised too late, bodies jerking as shafts drove into backs and lungs. Panic flared.

"Ambush! Turn and face them!" Soren's voice split the din. Too late.

Lozen's Rangers fired again. Another wave of arrows buried themselves in soft flesh, pinning warriors where they stood. Aelfs cried out in shock and fury, falling into the dirt with arrows sprouting like quills. In moments, sixty bodies littered the rear, staining the earth red.

Soren's face twisted as he saw the battle slipping through his fingers. He cursed, eyes flicking between the faltering front and the slaughter in the back. "Retreat!" he bellowed. "Fall back! The Keep can wait—kill the ghosts in the trees!"

The order cracked discipline. The Aelfinn force splintered, lines dissolving as men turned to run for the forest.

And Lozen's Rangers were waiting.

"Charge! For Helsgaard!"

They erupted from the shadows, axes flashing, voices raised in raw defiance. The first clash was sickening: blades splitting bone, shields shattering under the weight of steel. A Ranger hacked clean through a thigh, dropping his foe into the dirt where he was trampled by his comrades. Another buried an axe in a neck and had to kick the body away to free the weapon.

The forest edge became a charnel ground.

From the Keep's walls, Anja's bowmen added their own rain. Arrows cut down those fleeing, shafts punching into exposed backs, dropping warriors like hunted deer. Screams tore the air apart.

What had once been an army now writhed in panic. Broken formations scattered, shields thrown aside, blades dropped in flight. They were no longer warriors, only prey.

Above it all, Lozen's Rangers fought with ruthless precision. No hesitation, no mercy. Throats opened, skulls split, blood sprayed across bark and stone. The field became a place of slaughter.

On the battlements, Hrolf saw the enemy falter beyond arrow range. His voice thundered, "Melee charge!"

Anja echoed from her tower, her voice like steel on steel. "Gather at the gate! Close combat!"

Rohand roared across the wall, "Muster at the gate! Axes ready!"

The Rangers surged to the gates, fear mingled with exhilaration, hearts pounding like war-drums. The massive timbers swung wide, iron hinges groaning.

Hrolf's cry shook the earth. "Charge! For Ravnsríki!"

"Keep formation! Go, go!" Rohand barked, driving them forward.

The defenders burst through the narrow bridge across the dry ditch, boots running through the ditches, axes raised high. They cut down stragglers with brutal efficiency, chopping into spines, cleaving skulls, splitting shields apart.

Hrolf seized Hans by the shoulder. "With me! Axe in hand!" He glanced back to Anja. "Stay. Hold the walls." Then he plunged into the chaos with the boy at his side.

Anja's voice rang clear, harsh as a raven's cry. "Press on! No mercy!"

The battle devolved into madness. Aelfs were trapped between Rohand's charge and Lozen's ambush, crushed in the vise of blood and steel. Once-perfect formations dissolved into one-on-one struggles, each fight raw and desperate.

Steel crashed on steel. Boots slipped in blood-slick mud. Screams and curses were heard over the curses and din of the chaos. The air stank of sweat, iron, and skitr—the reek of the dying.

What had begun as a battle was ending as a massacre.

CHAPTER 35

VONAR EGG'S JUSTICE

YOU WILL HOLD HIM UP
FOR ALL TO SEE

T HE BATTLEFIELD GROANED BENEATH the steel and
axes clashing as voices rose in screams and curses—but
amid the chaos, a silence seemed to coil, waiting. All the blood
spilled, all the bodies strewn, had led to this single thread in the
weave of fate.

As the sun crested the trees, the dappled light highlighted
the dim forest. Then Soren saw her.

He was cutting down a Human Ranger, his mírenstál blade
a silver blur, when he spotted the figure leading the ambush
near the tree line. The fighter was small, quick, and deadly—using low leverage and striking with unnatural speed using
a mírenstál sword.

Soren paused, his pale eyes narrowing. He recognized
the fierce, copper-red hair bound in braids, the deliberate,
low-to-the-ground fighting stance of a half-Dwarf, and the
unmistakable, sharp angle of the Aelfinn ears peeking beneath

her braids. The half-breed. The scout's whisper was true. She was here.

But then, as she turned, stepping over a collapsed log, a memory—old, clean, and polished by court propaganda—slammed into him.

He saw not the blood- and mud-streaked Ranger, but the small, fierce-eyed girl who used to hide behind Faelar's robes in the delegation halls. The one who brought flowers from the Astraelyn gardens. The child he had calculatedly sentenced to death before she was even born.

Lozen.

The name hit him like a physical shock. She wasn't a rumor or a strategic piece on a map. She was alive and leading the force that was currently crushing his army.

His eyes locked on her. The battlefield faded—the clash of steel, the shrieks of dying men—all drowned beneath the roar of blood and betrayal in his ears. He wrenched free of the melee, sword in hand, stride long and hungry.

Lozen felt him coming. Felt the weight of his hate like a spear hurled through the din. She did not rush to meet him. Instead, she fell back, dragging him away from his remaining warriors, isolating him in a desolate ring of trampled mud and corpses. He was the serpent; she would be the stone.

Their blades met with a sound like splitting stone. Sparks flew. mírenstál shrieked. The impact rattled her bones.

Soren pressed forward, blow after blow, his strikes merciless and precise. A lifetime of killing honed into every swing. Lozen's arms burned, her feet slid in the blood-slick grass, but she turned each stroke aside with desperate speed.

"Die!" he snarled in Aelfic, eyes wild.

She weaved, countered, a sheen of sweat on her face, the world a blur of flashing mírenstál. He was more experienced, his hate driving him forward.

Then fate stumbled.

His boot caught a root. He lurched, weight pitching forward. In that instant, Lozen's blade flashed, severing his fingers to the bone.

Soren's scream tore the air. His sword dropped, clattering into the pine needles, severed fingers still clutching the hilt before falling limp. He stared at the ruin of his hand, pinky finger dangling by a thread of skin, blood pouring down his wrist, his face a mask of disbelief and rage.

Lozen leveled her sword at his throat, breath ragged, eyes cold.

"Finish it," he rasped. Defiant even in ruin.

She held, blade steady, the mírenstál edge trembling for more. Vonar Egg pulsed in her grip, hungry. She demanded, voice harsh in Aelfic, "Your name. Say it."

His teeth bared in something between a snarl and a grin. "Remember it well. Soren. The last name you'll ever hear."

Her lip curled. "Bold words for someone with half a hand." She pressed the blade, nicking flesh, drawing a bead of blood that slid down his neck like a crimson thread.

Vonar Egg thrummed, eager to plunge deeper. But Lozen faltered, doubt cutting sharper than steel.

"Why?" she demanded. "Why seek my death?"

His eyes burned with scorn. "You don't know? You're filth. The half-Aelf spawn of a mistake. The abomination our seers warned of. The Dwaelf."

The word was a lash. Lozen's knuckles whitened on the hilt, fury clawing through her chest. Vonar Egg flared in her grip, as if the blade itself demanded vengeance.

"I am not an abomination," she growled. "My name is Lozen."

More blood welled at his throat. Soren sneered through the pain. "Look at you—stunted, thick, ears wrong. You're a Dwaelf."

Her vision blurred red. "Don't call me that!"

He leaned close into the blade, lips curling with spite. "Your mother's sin wasn't bedding a Dwarf. It was keeping the cursed Dwaelf brat that crawled out of her womb—"

Rage erupted.

"DON'T CALL ME THAT!"

Her scream split the battlefield as Vonar Egg plunged for his throat.

Soren, choking, resistant to the end, lashed upward with his left hand, clawing for the blade as if he could tear it from her grip. The instant his fingers closed on the glowing mírenstál, the sword answered. Its edge bit hungrily, severing them clean, scattering blood and knuckle-bones into the dirt.

He convulsed, a strangled cry ripping from his chest, blood pouring from both neck and hands. Vonar Egg drove through flesh and spine, pulsing with savage joy as it drank him dry.

"You fukken skitkarlr," she spat, voice shaking. "I already know everything about the prophecy from my parents."

He collapsed, dragging the blade with him. Lozen held firm as his body hit the ground, Vonar Egg carving deep but not clean. His neck split wide, half-severed, the head lolling grotesquely against his shoulder. Blood flowed from the ragged wound, soaking the earth in pulsing, steaming rivulets.

For a heartbeat, silence pressed down. The prophecy's words thundered in her skull: *You will hold him up for all to see.*

Vonar Egg pulsed in her hand, urging her to finish it.

Lozen's chest heaved, her veins alight with something savage, intoxicating. Shooting from shadows had always been detached, impersonal. This was different. This was close, warm, real. Her first kill by hand. The blade still hummed with blood, and her lips tasted of iron mist.

It was almost enough to make her laugh. Almost.

But the laughter died before it reached her throat. Alva's words crawled back through her skull, sharp as glass: *His name is Soren, and you will hold him up for all to see.*

Her hand trembled. Not from weakness, but from the weight of prophecy grinding down on her spine. She had never wanted destiny, never wanted to be the fulcrum of some ancient whisper. Yet here she was—standing over the corpse prophecy demanded.

Her eyes fixed on his ruined face, pale hair matted with gore. Her grip tightened on her sword until her knuckles ached. Then, with a grunt, she dropped her shield, crouched, and seized Soren by the hair. Flesh tore. Sinew stretched, stringy and stubborn. She wrenched harder, boots sinking in blood-soaked mud as she ripped. She tasked Vonar Egg to caress Soren's flesh one more time and the head came free, heavy and dripping in her fist.

Blood poured down her arm, hot and slick, pattering onto her battered shield.

She rose.

And screamed.

It was not a woman's cry. Not even a warrior's. It was raw, broken, a sound ripped from marrow. A scream stitched together from rage and triumph, grief and bloodlust. It cracked across the battlefield like thunder, echoing off stone and forest alike.

"Who's next!?" she howled, her words a mangled tangle of Aelfic and Common, guttural and jagged.

The fighting faltered.

Axes paused mid-swing. Blades hovered, dripping. Human and Aelf alike turned toward her, drawn as if the scream itself had seized their throats. She stood there, sword still glowing in her right hand, severed head in her left raised above her head, her armor painted in blood, her face streaked like a death-mask.

She marched forward, step by step, the head swinging above, splattering the grass red. Behind her shield bore streaks of gore like a banner.

"Who's next!?" she rasped again, this time in Common. Her voice cracked, but it carried. Then louder, in jagged Aelfic, "*Man dîn na-chaded?*"

Silence crushed the field. Only the groans of the dying broke it.

The Aelfinn lines wavered. Soren's death had gutted them. His head dangling from her fist drove the knife deeper. Feet shuffled backward.

Lozen's eyes swept over them, hard and empty. "Look around you," she said in their tongue, voice cutting like frost. "Hundreds dead. This is all that remains."

Weapons sagged. A tremor passed through the ranks. One by one, swords clattered to the dirt.

"We yield!" a voice cried, ragged with terror. Another followed, "No more!"

Three Aelfs dropped to their knees, hands raised, trembling as if they stared at something more than mortal.

Lozen raised Soren's head higher, blood dripping down her elbow in rivulets. Her words rang cold, final, "Drop your weapons and live. Raise them—and follow him to the Halls of Mandos."

The field went still. One by one, swords kissed the earth. Aelfinn warriors sank to their knees.

No cheer followed. No chant of victory. Only silence. The silence of carrion birds circling overhead, of bodies twitching in the dirt, of blood soaking deep into hungry soil.

Lozen stood unmoving at the center of it all, her face a mask of blood and shadow. Vonar Egg pulsed faintly in her grip, its glow rising like heat from a forge. The severed head dangled at her side. The world itself seemed to hold its breath.

Prophecy fulfilled. Destiny claimed. And Lozen—whether she willed it or not—had become something to be feared.

Across the field, Rylen strode toward her, axe dangling, his armor slashed and shield splintered. Blood ran freely down his arm from a gash that painted his knuckles red. He stopped a few paces away, eyes flicking to the kneeling Aelfs before settling on her.

"Daughter," he said, voice low, almost reverent. "Close the score. Put the head down, aye."

Lozen didn't move. Her chest rose and fell in shallow bursts, eyes locked on the churned earth as if she couldn't see past it.

"They've laid down the arms," Rylen said, stepping closer. "The fight is done. We hold the ground."

Still she said nothing. Her arms sagged. The severed head slipped from her grip, thudding wetly into the dirt. Vonar Egg stayed steadfast in her hand.

From the perimeter, one of the older Rangers muttered hoarsely, "Soren's head. By the gods."

Another—his face blackened with mud and spilled blood and his hands slick with it—stared at her not with triumph, but with unease. "She didn't even flinch," he whispered, awe curdled with fear.

Rohand limped forward next, blood soaking through a rough bandage at his thigh. He halted beside Rylen, eyes lingering on her before he finally spoke, voice softer than the battlefield deserved. "Lozen."

Her head turned at the sound, slow as if through water. Her face was unreadable beneath streaks of blood.

"You broke them," Rohand said, the words careful, weighted. "You cut down their Hersir. But you are not just a blade. You're still ours."

She blinked, jaw tightening. "They would've burned everything."

"And you stopped them," he said.

Around them, the Aelfs knelt in the dirt, wide-eyed, hollow. Some wept quietly, shoulders trembling. A few pressed their foreheads into the dirt as if to disappear.

Hrolf's voice cut across the silence. "Prisoners for now. Thralls tomorrow. Any who resist—kill them."

Rohand glanced at Lozen, but it was she who answered, voice raw, scraped thin, "Build biers for the pyres. All of them. Ours and theirs. And no binding. Chains break faster than fear."

Hrolf paused, his eyes narrowing. Lozen lifted a bloody finger to the tip of her pointed ear. He understood. She knew what bound Aelfs better than steel. He gave a curt nod and stalked on.

Stillness lingered like smoke. Rohand reached out—not to drag, not to restrain—just resting a bloodstained hand on her shoulder.

She did not pull away.

"We'll gather the bodies," he murmured. "We'll honor them, then move on."

For a moment, something in her gaze flickered—softened. But when she spoke, her Aelfic words were iron, clear and merciless. "You dared strike us on our soil. We've spared you. That mercy is a leash. You are our thralls, not prisoners. If any of you run, I will hunt you down and carve a blood eagle into your back, pulling your lungs through your back to become your wings."

The words hit like steel on bone. Then she said it again in Common, her voice cracking like a whip. Even hardened Rangers flinched. A few paled.

Rohand just stared, stunned, as if he no longer recognized the girl before him.

Lozen's voice cracked, raw now, "Where's Petr? Petr!"

Hrolf stood a few paces away, gazing down at a still figure. Blond hair clung to a face soaked red. Lozen's breath hitched. *No—no, not him.* Her chest clenched as if something inside her had caved in. Hrolf looked up, met her eyes, and gave a slow shake of his head.

She didn't scream. She didn't weep. Only a numb hollowness spread through her body.

When she finally spoke, her voice was flat, drained. "Rohand. I yield my team to you, Hersir."

And she walked away.

She left the field caked in gore, dragging silence behind her like another blade. The Rangers moved around her, cold and efficient—binding wounds, stripping the dead, corralling the kneeling survivors. The Aelfs obeyed without bindings, broken not by chains but by shame, beaten into thrall by one of their own who had been cast out.

No songs would be sung of this day. Only whispers.

And in every whisper, her name.

CHAPTER 36

THE HERALD OF A NEW DAWN

FIRE'S CRYPTIC WARNING

THE BATTLEFIELD SPRAWLED BEFORE her, a wreckage of shattered bodies, splintered steel, and red-stained earth. Human and Aelf lay dead, twisted together in the blood-soaked grass, indistinguishable now in death. Lozen stood alone in the middle of it all, sword still clenched in her trembling, blood-slicked hand. Her breath came in short, ragged bursts, chest heaving beneath the weight of it.

The stench was everywhere—iron-rich blood, sweat, piss, skitr. It clung to her nostrils and crawled down her throat. She turned in place, scanning the wreckage, eyes moving from face to face, name to name. Few friends. Many strangers. All of them gone.

"So many lives lost—so many families broken—for what?" she whispered, her voice a silent echo in the desolate landscape. "Hatred over something a person has no control over? How tall they are? Color of their hair? The shape of an ear?"

Nausea rolled through her, starting in the sides of her mouth, rolling down to her belly, twisting with guilt and despair. She dropped to her knees and retched. The sour sting of bile seared her tongue, and she spat it onto the dirt, strands of spit clinging to her lips.

"Was this the only way?" she asked, her voice a tormented whisper. "Was there no other path to peace?"

Looking down at her bloodied hands and the puddle of vomit at her knees, she suppressed a scream building in her throat. Tears of grief, rage and anguish, flowed from her eyes.

This can't be my fate.

A flicker of defiance ignited within her, a spark of hope amidst the darkness threatening to consume her. The prophecy, the ancient words that haunted her since childhood in campfire stories, reverberated in her mind, reminding her of the destiny that awaited her.

The half-Aelf, a child of two worlds, destined to unite their warring races. I will not let their deaths be in vain. She said, "I will honor their sacrifice."

She raised her head, focusing on the beauty of the forest. *I will bring peace to these lands. I will unite the Aelfs and the Humans. I will forge a new future, a future free from the shackles of bias and hatred.*

Determination surged through her, a powerful current that washed away the doubt and despair. She took a swig of water to rinse the bile out of her mouth and cleaned the blood from her hands and sword, a symbolic gesture of cleansing and renewal.

No longer was she the lost girl wandering aimlessly, burdened by her past and labeled the outcast. Gone were the days of being known only as the Shadow Archer, lurking in the darkness. Now, she stood confidently as Lozen, a fierce warrior of light, radiating strength and purpose. Her transformation marked the beginning of a new era, as she emerged as the herald of a new dawn, ready to inspire hope and change in a world that desperately needed both.

In the heart of the forest, under the cloak of night, a small clearing bathed in an eerie, flickering light served as Alva's sanctuary. A cauldron filled with a mysterious, bubbling brew hung suspended over a crackling fire. The atmosphere in the secluded grove crackled with an unholy energy, an intense magic that permeated every corner. Alva stirred the cauldron's contents with a gnarled wand, her eyes reflecting the dancing flames and her face framed by wild, gray hair.

With a practiced hand, she sprinkled a dark enchanting powder into the fire, the flames responding with a sudden, vibrant surge. "Spirits of the fallen, hear my call. Rise from your slumber and speak to me."

The flames danced, their movements growing more erratic and frenzied. A shimmering and indistinct ghostly visage materialized within the swirling smoke, its ethereal form a chilling display of the unseen forces surrounding them.

"What news from the realm of the dead?" Alva asked.

The ghostly face flickered, its form distorted by the swirling smoke. A voice, barely audible above the fire's crackling, emerged from the spectral figure.

"The great usurper has fallen," the voice announced, its tone hollow and otherworldly. "A half-Aelf, her blade stained with the blood of her kin. Her power grows. She is the one to unite the fractured kingdoms."

"Please—is it Lozen?"

The ghostly image wavered, its form dissolving into the smoke before reforming. "Her name is—not Aelf. Not Dwarf. Neither, yet both—Lozen."

Alva stirred the cauldron with renewed vigor, rambling in her native tongue. "Yes. Lozen. A child of two worlds, she may be the key to fulfilling the prophecy."

The ghostly visage began to fade, its form growing more indistinct. The flames in the cauldron, having spent their energy, died down, casting long, dancing shadows across the clearing.

"She lives... with her parents," the ghostly voice revealed a horrific prediction. "An Aelf and a Dwarf... they will soon join us... all of them... Lozen, too."

Disturbed by the prediction, Alva reached out with her staff and stirred the fire, her movements agitated and uncertain. The ghostly visage, its message delivered, faded into nothingness, leaving Alva alone with her thoughts.

"Nooo!" she whispered urgently. "No. No. No. No. She can't join you. She's the one. She has to live!"

Alva began to pace back and forth in the darkness, the silence of the night amplifying the relentless churning of her thoughts. The ramifications of the prophecy, entwined with the ghostly visitor's cryptic warning, painted a grim and uncertain future. The fractured kingdoms, once bastions of unity and prosperity, now teetered on the brink of chaos, their fragile peace threatened by the shadow of war. The pressure of her people's hopes and fears pressed upon her, a burden she embraced.

But the destiny of the young half-Aelf, Lozen, occupied the forefront of her mind. Alva sensed a profound power within the girl, a potential that could either heal the rifts that plagued their world or plunge it further into darkness. The prophecy spoke of Lozen's pivotal role, but its cryptic verses offered no clear guidance.

Alva refused to stand idly by while the world edged closer to ruin. The balance of Jörð—Earth—was unraveling, and with it, the fate of all who called her home. She would seek answers—not just for Lozen, not just for the prophecy, but for the very land beneath their feet. If the path to salvation led through darkness, so be it. She had walked that road before. Peril awaited, but Alva would meet it without hesitation. If sacrifice were required, she would pay the price—not for power, not for glory, but for the world itself.

CHAPTER 37

MESSAGE OF COMPASSION

SEVERANCE OF THE OLD WAYS

IN THE QUIET INFIRMARY of Helsgaard Keep, the Aelfinn scout, Elros, sat up on his cot. His wounds were bandaged, and his strength slowly returned. He stared at the floor, his expression mixed with shame and awe. Anja, gentle in her movements and compassionate demeanor, approached him with a bowl of nourishing broth.

"Here," she offered in the lilting cadence of Aelfic, her accent weathered by years of disuse. "Eat. You need to regain your strength."

Elros accepted the bowl with a silent gratitude that spoke volumes.

"Thank you," he murmured.

"You are welcome. You have served your king well."

The scout shook his head, his appearance one of profound regret. "I have failed. I allowed myself to be blinded by the hatred and fear of others. I almost became part of a great evil."

She sat beside the young warrior on the cot, her heart filled with compassion. "You were following orders. You did not choose this path."

He returned to looking at the floor, his shame evident in his slumped shoulders. "But I witnessed the truth. I saw the courage of the Humans, the skill of their archers, and the... the compassion of their leader."

Anja's surprise melted into a warm smile.

"She is not the abomination they claim her to be," Elros said. "She is a warrior of light, a beacon of hope in this dark war."

She listened, her heart swelling with pride. The scout's words affirmed her belief in the possibility of reconciliation between their warring races.

⚠⚠⚠

The dimly lit command chamber of Helsgaard Keep was thick with tension. The low fire cast flickering shadows across the rune-marked brass sheets and worn maps spread across the wooden table.

Günther stood at the head of the table, hands braced on its surface. Across from him, Elros, still wrapped in fresh bandages, stood stiffly, his shoulders squared despite the pain. His Aelfinn features—angular cheekbones, tapered ears, and piercing emerald eyes—were tight with barely contained dread. Lozen stood between them, arms folded, her face unreadable.

Günther turned to her and spoke with quiet authority. "Tell him: You have seen the truth. Now, return to Aeldoria and share it."

Lozen translated, her voice steady.

Elros's breath hitched. His eyes widened in horror, and a stream of Aelfic tumbled from his lips.

Lozen frowned and turned back to Günther. "He says returning means execution. They will never forgive his betrayal. He asks for asylum—he says he has nowhere else to go."

Günther studied Elros in silence, his gaze weighing the young scout's desperation. The command chamber remained deathly still except for the crackle of burning embers. He exhaled, his voice steady yet firm. "Elros, you risked your life for truth. That is not forgotten here. Returning would mean your death, and I will not hand you to your executioners. Helsgaard Keep offers you sanctuary. Here, you live. Your fate will be decided in time."

Lozen relayed the words, watching as Elros stood frozen—as if his body refused to believe his ears. A moment later, with a sharp inhale, his shoulders collapsed, and he sank to his knees. His voice trembled as he rushed through a string of Aelfic, his words nearly lost between half-sobs and deep bows of gratitude.

Lozen, affected by the raw emotion, swallowed before translating. "He says: Thank you, Commandant Günther. Your mercy is a beacon of hope in these dark times. I pledge my loyalty to Helsgaard Keep and will serve you in any way I can."

Günther moved beside the table and extended an arm. After a brief hesitation, Elros clasped it firmly. In that grip, unspoken understanding passed between them—a bond shaped by war and hard-won respect.

As Elros stood, it was clear—he was no longer just an Aelfinn scout. He was a bridge uniting two peoples, a symbol of hope. And Helsgaard Keep would not take him for granted.

△△△

The first warrior among the former Aelfinn thralls stepped into the Council Chambers of Aeldoria with the posture of one who had endured fire—and learned to walk through it. The chamber, wrapped in towering tapestries of ancient glory and unity, swallowed his footsteps in silence. But his presence stirred the air like a blade unsheathed.

He did not bow. He only stood—scarred, upright, unbroken—and every Elder saw it.

The Council of Elders sat in a crescent of carved thrones, robed in glacier-blue, each garment embroidered with the script of their dominions. Their eyes, cold and unblinking, tracked his every move. Beneath the elevated dais, two scribes waited with inked quills trembling above pristine parchment, ready to capture history.

Elder Faelar broke the silence first. Her voice rang soft as windchimes, but tension threaded every syllable. "You return from Ravnsríki. Tell us—how did the Humans treat our warriors?"

The warrior's mouth twitched, not quite a smile. "With discipline. And precision. We were healed by two of their own. One named Anja. The other... Lozen."

That name hit like a dropped blade.

"Lozen?" Faelar repeated, her tone uncertain.

"Yes. A half-Aelf." His gaze swept across the Council. "The same one who executed Soren with a single stroke."

Disbelief swept the chamber. Haldir scoffed, fingers drumming on the carved arms of his throne. "A half-blood commanding humans? Killing Soren? You expect us to believe this?"

The warrior didn't flinch. "I saw her blade burn through his spine. Saw her lift his head and call out 'Who's next?' In Aelfic. And the line broke."

Faelar leaned forward. "She spoke our tongue?"

"Yes," the warrior said. "Then turned and addressed her Humans in Common. Gave the command that we were now thralls."

Murmurs flared. A few Elders sat back as if struck. One began to protest, but the warrior raised his voice—not loud, but clear.

"She enthralled us, slaves, not prisoners. No bindings. No chains. Just the promise that if any of us fled, she would carve the blood eagle into our backs. And none of us tested her."

Faelar stared at him, pale. "Please, tell me about your release?"

The warrior nodded. "Yes, Elder. It was Lozen who negotiated our return. She spoke for Ravnsríki. Made it clear we were sent back only because she campaigned for us."

Silence swelled, thick and oppressive.

At last, Elder Arwin whispered, "The prophecy..."

Faelar's knuckles whitened on her staff. "The halfling blade-bearer. The one who walks both paths."

"She is no one's path," Haldir spat. "She is a warning."

"Or a weapon," murmured another.

Haldir dismissed the warrior. "Thank you for your report. Send in the next warrior."

The warrior bowed. "By your leave, Elders."

He turned and strode from the chamber with the same un-wavering step, the scent of battle still clinging to him. Behind him, the council dissolved into a storm of murmurs and dread.

No one moved. The name hung in the chamber like smoke.

Lozen.

Not conqueror. Not kin.

Something else entirely.

The ancient timbers of the Aelfinn Council Chambers groaned under the gravity of unspoken dread. Elders, their faces etched with worry, formed a silent semi-circle. King Aethor's entrance, heralded by the creak of grand doors and the glint of his guard's mírenstál, shattered the fragile quiet. Sunlight, sharp as a drawn blade, illuminated the tension, a tangible force that hung heavy in the air.

This was no mere courtly debate. The King's presence, the rigid stance of his guard, and the barely suppressed murmurs hinted at a deeper conflict, a struggle for the very heart of the realm. The council's decision, would shape not just policy, but the fate of their world, a weight felt in every stifled breath and shadowed corner of the chamber.

Arwin, whispering, leaned toward Faelar and asked, "Are all these guards loyal to our cause?"

Faelar, her lips pursed, nodded. "Yes, loyal."

Irritated, Aethor surveyed the assembled Elders with disdain. "At your service," he sneered. He was displeased to be summoned without an appointment, and he held contempt for the current composition of the Aelfinn Council, which caused his voice to drip with sarcasm as he offered a perfunctory bow.

His voice rising to fill the chamber, Arwin addressed the King with a sternness that brooked no argument. "After reviewing eyewitness reports from your secret and unsuccessful invasion of Ravnsríki," he began. His words were a condemning accusation. "The failed attack on Helsgaard Keep, and the deceitful use of false peace talks at Ravnborg have led us to address this escalating problem in the Kingdom."

Aethor's face paled as he realized his precarious situation. "You would presume to judge my actions for Aeldoria? How dare—"

"—Two hundred dead." Faelar snapped. "You would presume to challenge the Council?"

She nodded a subtle signal to the guards and calmly said, "A mere forty-nine returned of the almost three hundred Aelfs you sent on your invasion. You sent over two hundred of our people to their deaths. For what? The Humans out-maneuvered your invasion force and destroyed it. Two hundred Aelfs that will not be coming home to their families."

Pausing for dramatic effect, she looked around the Council. "The council has voted and has rendered a decision. Due to your less-than-honorable actions—"

The guards, swift and quiet, moved in behind Aethor, their hands closing on his arms in a firm grip.

"What?!?—" Aethor exclaimed.

Some of the Elders looked down, avoiding Aethor's glare.

"—What are you doing? Take your hands off—"

"—and the tragic loss of life in your misguided invasion while deceiving this council with talks of peace, your service to this Council and the Kingdom is, at this moment, terminated."

Aethor's muscles strained against the guards' unyielding hold, and his expression twisted into fury and hopelessness. "What do you know about Humans?!? Their deceit! Their desecration of our forests! You don't understand them like I do!"

Arwin muttered, "He would know about deceit."

Faelar continued. "You are to be taken to Astraelyn Square for a public beheading. After that, your head will be displayed with Soren's as a message to the Kingdom that we are an honorable race. The Humans healed our warriors and sent them back to us to show their compassion and respect for our people."

Faelar paused, staring at Aethor as he realized the futility of his resistance.

"You will, of course, have the option to accept your 'severance' gracefully," she offered as a double entendre, "or be bound and gagged."

Another pause as she awaited the disgraced King's response.

Bearing the Council's decision, Arwin announced, "The Council has voted on your successor—Aelric—and he will assume the throne effective immediately, with a coronation ceremony following your departure to the Halls of Mandos."

Haldir, somber yet resolute, added, "Most of the Council now feels the last eighteen years were a mistake, and it is time to reach out to the Humans and create a truce. No more war. No more useless death. It's past time for healing and changing course." He paused, looking at Aethor with pity and disappointment. "I was a staunch supporter of your beliefs in the old ways for a long time," he confessed. "So it pains me to say this, but the world is changing, and the old ways aren't working."

Aethor's face contorted with anger and desperation as he spoke through clenched teeth. "Allow a condemned man answers to some questions?"

Legolas coldly cut him off. "No answers. As you reflect upon your life in the Halls of Mandos, see if you can find your own answers. And when you come back, come back better."

Aethor's voice rose in a desperate plea. "All I was trying to do was protect Aeldoria from the filthy Human encroachment. They're cutting our forests. It's them! Can't you see that?"

Legolas turned to the guards and commanded, "Gag him."

A guard stepped forward, a gag in hand, and forced it into Aethor's mouth from behind. The former King, his protests muffled, struggled in vain against his captors with defiance.

Faelar said, "Remove the crown. His entitlement to it has ended." A third guard moved in, removed it, and handed it to Faelar.

Silence fell over the Council Chambers, with the only sound being the gentle rustling of the scriveners' parchments as they recorded the events. The Elders, sad and resolute, exchanged somber glances.

After a long, tense pause, Arwin spoke with a tone of finality. "We'll take silence as consensus. *Ael va'rin*—the verdict stands. These proceedings are concluded. Let us adjourn to the Square, sever our ties with the old ways, and commence with the Coronation."

The scriveners collected their papers, and the Elders filed out of the room, their footsteps echoing in the sudden stillness. The guards dragged Aethor, whose mouth was gagged and body bound, behind the Elders. Now slumped and disheveled, his once-proud figure presented a pathetic spectacle of defeat and disgrace. Each step he took reflected the loss of his former status and the depths to which he had fallen. The guards, indifferent to his plight, hauled him along like a common criminal, their rough handling a further testament to his humiliation. His struggles were futile, his cries for help muffled by the gag. The sight of him, a formerly respected leader, now reduced to this state, sent a chill through the onlookers. It was a stark reminder of the fickleness of power and the harsh consequences of failure.

CHAPTER 38

AWARD CEREMONY

THE WEIGHT OF THE TORC

THE SUN BORE DOWN on the gathered Helsgaard
Rangers, their faces lined with exhaustion and pride. A
low murmur of anticipation filled the air as settlers, merchants,
and craftspeople drifted toward the courtyard's edges, drawn
by the announcement.

Atop a raised platform, Commandant Günther surveyed
the crowd, his presence commanding. Beside him, Lozen
stood at the platform's edge, trying to appear regal and
strong—but her downcast gaze betrayed the war within her.
She could feel the force of countless eyes, judging, measuring,
expecting.

Günther's voice cut through the din like a war horn.

"Helsgaard Keep! Helsgaardborg! Distinguished
guests!" His words echoed off the ancient stone. "Today, we
celebrate our triumph over the Aelfinn invaders!"

A thunderous cheer erupted, the warriors' voices unified,
their victory still fresh in their minds.

"We faced a grave threat," Günther continued, "an army that sought to divide our kingdom, to bring chaos to our lands."

From the ranks of Rangers came the booming war cry, "WHO'S NEXT?!"

The stomp of boots followed, a deep, rhythmic sound like rolling thunder.

Günther raised a hand for silence, a slight grin tugging at his lips. "But this victory was won by more than just numbers. It was won by courage, skill, and leadership." He faced Lozen. "And today, we honor one among us who turned the tide of battle."

The crowd murmured, excitement building.

"Lozen of the Helsgaard Rangers," he called, "step forward and be recognized."

The warriors erupted again, "WHO'S NEXT?!"

She hesitated—for a heartbeat—before stepping forward with measured grace.

As she reached his side, Günther rested a firm hand on her shoulder, looking out over the assembly.

"This Ranger, a true daughter of Helsgaard, led a daring ambush behind enemy lines, disrupting the Aelfinn ranks and forcing their surrender."

"WHO'S NEXT?!"

Lozen swallowed. It was almost too much. The roars of approval, the waves of admiration—it was like standing at the edge of a storm. She felt pride rise in her chest, but also discomfort.

Günther powered through the interruptions. "For her courage and service, I hereby award her—"

"WHO'S NEXT?!"

A laugh rippled through the crowd, the energy electric.

Günther sighed. "Two Odin's Merks—"

"WHO'S NEXT?!"

His eye twitched, but he pressed on.

"—And the title of Helsgaard's Heroine!"

A fresh roar of approval tore through the courtyard, mixed with laughter and cheers.

"Drinks on Lozen at the tavern!" someone shouted, sending the crowd into a frenzy.

Behind her, Günther set the torc upon her neck, the twisted circlet biting cold against her skin, heavier than she had imagined.

He leaned in, whispering. "Smile, girl. This isn't death sentence. If can make you Helsgaard's Heroine—let's see what the King can do with you."

Lozen forced a small, practiced smile.

"Yes, sir," she murmured, grasping at the politics in play, fearing she just became an unwitting piece on the Hnefatafl board.

As the celebration swelled around her, Lozen let herself breathe, enjoying the moment. For the first time in her life, she didn't feel like an outsider.

Her eyes swept the crowd, taking in the sea of familiar faces—Warriors who had once doubted her, now cheering her name. Rangers who had fought beside her, now calling her their own. Somewhere in the throng, she spotted Anja and Rylen, their expressions full of pride.

Her parents—that word was still strange, but not unwelcome.

Her gaze drifted again and locked onto Olaf. To her surprise, he nodded and smiled—not mockingly, not begrudgingly, but with something like respect.

A challenge won. A place earned.

She lifted her chin, acknowledging him, before letting her hand rest on the torc around her neck. Its weight was solid. Real.

This was her home.

With family and friends, she felt like she belonged.

⚠⚠⚠

The waning sun cast a warm glow over Helsgaard Keep, painting the sky in a breathtaking palette of orange and purple hues. Lozen, perched atop a guard tower in the crenel between the merlons, her legs dangling over the edge, stared at the sprawling landscape. The wind, gently caressing her skin, carried the distant sounds of the Keep's evening activities: the clatter of dishes, the murmur of conversation, the occasional burst of laughter.

The rhythmic thud of heavy footsteps on the stone stairs announced Rohand's arrival. He emerged onto the platform, his broad shoulders filling the narrow space, and leaned against the battlement beside Lozen.

"How's my favorite Aelf?" he greeted her.

She spun around to face him, a wry smile playing on her lips. "I hope I'm your favorite. One is married and the other one's a guy. Unless you're into that sort of thing."

He laughed. "Over my corpse, I favor the curvy ones."

She smiled. "Good, the competition is eliminated."

"By the way, you've been summoned to Ravnborg to meet with the King and his court. Something about single-handedly stopping the invasion of Ravnsríki. Lots of pomp. It sounds like the Helsgaard Heroine is getting her recognition."

Lozen's smile faded, replaced by frustration. "That's not how it happened! Petr did it all—he was the brains behind the ambush."

"I know. Petr helped you, and he was a great Ranger. I am sad about his passing. But politicians like to hold up their heroes for the people to admire. Please, Lozen, be their heroine."

Lozen's shoulders slumped with an audible sigh.

"Do you believe in prophecies, Rohand?" she asked.

The unexpected question raised Rohand's interest, and he leaned forward. "Prophecies? Not really. Prophecies are for superstitious folk, and I believe what I see."

"Soren was so convinced I'm the one in the prophecy," she murmured, still fixed on the distance. "And their king was so convinced that he sent three hundred Aelfinn warriors and archers to kill me."

Rohand scoffed. "Hardly! Your meeting was a coincidence. Helsgaard Keep was their target—how would he know you were here, even if you are the one they were looking for?"

Lozen nodded, a thoughtful expression on her face. "Right," she snarked. "Coincidence. His look was one of recognition, like he was looking for me, not like he stumbled upon me accidentally. I've been thinking about it a lot lately. About what it means for me and my future. Am I 'The One'?"

He studied her face, noting the turmoil within. "You're 'The One' until you're not," he said. "Run with it—you already have the King's ear."

Lozen shook her head. "I can't ignore it. Something big is coming. I feel it in my bones, in every fiber of my being. I can almost hear it in the wind."

Rohand, sensing her growing anxiety, placed his hands, reassuring, on her shoulders.

"I puked," Lozen confessed, changing the subject.

"Huh?" Rohand was confused at the sudden change in topic.

"After the battle. I dropped to my knees and puked. How can I be 'The One' if I'm so weak that I puked after battle?"

Rohand chuckled, a deep, hearty sound that dispelled the tension in the air. "I was there. I would worry about you if you didn't meet Ralph after your first battle."

"Ralph? Hrolf? I don't get it."

"Ralph." Mimicking a vomiting noise, "Raaaalph!!!"

She scowled and said, "You're a pikk."

He paused, both hands on her upper arms in a comforting embrace. He looked into her glacier-blue eyes and said, "Here's how you're 'The One.' Anja and Rylen kept to themselves until you arrived, and then suddenly, Anja wants to teach everyone archery with your help."

"Right..."

"All of us in the Keep were able to take out half their invasion with arrows when they turned on you—that would not have happened if you and Anja hadn't trained us beforehand. Anja wouldn't train us—if she wanted to, she would have done it before you showed up. So you were the trigger for the archery training that saved your team, Helsgaard Keep, and maybe even all of Ravnsríki. Dunno—not a strategist, but it seems likely."

"Hmmm..."

"So you see—you're the one that got Anja motivated. You're the one who ambushed the invasion force. You're the one who beheaded Soren and stopped the battle. You're the one that stopped the invasion. Without you, they would have sieged the Keep and maybe captured it. You're the one that stopped it. You're 'The One.'"

Lozen smiled. "Thank you, Hersir—Rohand—Roh—I needed to hear that. And you're still a pikk."

"And you're still my favorite."

"Aelf?" She asked.

"I didn't say that. Just my favorite."

They stayed quiet for a moment, looking into each other's eyes. Her legs were spread as she sat on the stone block crenel of the guard tower. Rohand stood between her knees, their foreheads together, arms wrapped around each other in an embrace. Their breaths mingled. The only sound was the gentle rustling of the wind through the trees and the distant chirping of crickets. He pulled her close, hugged her tight, released her, and walked away, dropping down the stairs. "Good night, Lozen."

The final rays of sunlight slipping away, plunging the landscape into velvety darkness. Stars began to twinkle like diamonds scattered across the vast expanse of the night sky. The cool evening breeze whispered through the trees, carrying the essence of earth and grass. In this serene moment, her heart ached with longing, yearning for the warmth and security of Rohand's arms, a comforting embrace that felt like home.

THE END

PARTING WORDS

Before you go...

Indie authors don't have war chests—we have readers.

If this book earned your time, please leave a quick review on Amazon, Goodreads, or wherever you bought it. Even a single line helps **The Helsgaard Chronicles** find its next ally.

ROSETTA STONE

T HE ROSETTA STONE, AS ancient as time itself, served as a key to translate words and define ideas, enabling communication between people of different languages. The Rosetta Stone (Glossary) will assist in the language used in the stories of Hel.

Aeldoria (AL-do-REE-a) — The Aelfinn Kingdom where the Aelfs live.

Aelf (Alf) — Original Norse texts refer to them as Álfr. In this context, they are a race of humanoids whose notable characteristics include platinum blonde hair, tall stature, slender build, extreme physical coordination, long pointed ears, and a general disdain for all other races and cultures. They are excellent healers, adept at Reiki and the use of crystals, and their archery skills help them develop an innate mastery of geometry and mathematics.
Note: Álfr is the authentic Old Norse term from the Eddas.

Aelfs (Alfs) — Plural form of Aelf.
Note: Álfar is the authentic Old Norse plural form.

Aelfic (ALF-ick) — The language of the Aelfs.

Aelfinn (ALF-fin, with a prolonged "n") — Possessive form of Aelf.

Annarrslag (AN-narr-slahg) — A disciplined martial technique that condenses Qi/Ond (life energy, "spirit-breath") into a dense, visible sphere between the hands, then drives it forward as a physical impact rather than spellcraft. When released—often with a sharp syllable and a palm-thrust—it strikes like lightning made solid, delivering a concussive shock that can scramble nerves and hurl a target backward.

Ást mín (AST MEEN) — Term of endearment. Literally "my love."

Bikkja (BIK-kya) — A common word in modern Icelandic (meaning "female dog" or "bitch"), and it comes directly from Old Norse.

Bier (BEER) — A bier is a wooden platform or frame—often made of logs or heavy timbers—used to support the body before or during cremation. In Norse traditions, it might be elevated and interlaced with herbs, branches, or symbolic items, depending on the status of the deceased.

Blood Eagle — A brutal form of execution where the victim's ribs are separated from the spine through a long incision in the back on either side of the spine and the lungs extracted through the incisions. This term doesn't appear in surviving Old Norse texts verbatim, but the concept and its descriptions show up in sources like the Orkneyinga saga and Norna-Gests þáttr, especially relating to the legendary execution of enemies (e.g., Aella of Northumbria).

Blótstafn (BLOHT-stahvn) — A raised fist with index and pinky fingers extended (like the metal "rock on" sign). Meaning: In Norse culture, this would be used to mock someone as a follower of Loki, a Jötunn-lover, or a dishonorable oath-breaker.

Bretahaf (BRET-a-HAHF) — The Breta Sea, which surrounds the land of the Britons and separates it from the Norðrsær.

Briton (BRIT-on) — One who inhabits Breta (later known as Britain, then England).

Brú (BREW) — A chokepoint, usually a land bridge over a moat, river or ravine.

Crenel (KREN-el) — One of the open spaces or indentations in the top of a battlement or fortified wall, used for shooting or observation. Essentially, it's the gap between the solid parts (merlons) of a battlement.

Dagmál (DAG-mahl) — The first meal of the day, similar to breakfast. It was usually eaten around 8 or 9 o'clock in the morning, after the day's work had begun. Dagmál often consisted of leftovers from the previous night's Náttmál, such as stew, along with bread, fruit, porridge, or sometimes buttermilk.

Dagmark (DAGH-mark) — The Scandinavians divided the day into eight sections, marked by the sun's position relative to the horizon, which varied widely between summer and winter.

Draugr (DROW-gr, with a guttural "G" and a trilled "R") — The reanimated corpse of the deceased inside the burial mound. Said to retain some intelligence and had the ability to swell up in size, the only way to kill them (again) was decapitation or burning.

Draugar (DROW-gar, with a guttural "G" and a trilled "R") — Plural of Draugr.

Drekahǫnd (DREK-ah-hond, with a nasalized or long "o" sound) — Dragon's Hand or Hand of the Dragon. A Dragon's emissary. AKA Drekahond.

Dûrgath (DOOR-gath) — Dwarfinn Kingdom where the Dwarfs live.

Dwaelf (dw-ALF) — A contraction of Dwarf and Aelf – a pejorative term that can lead to violent physical confrontations, up to, and including death.

Dwarf (DWAR-f) — A race of humanoids whose notable characteristics include short stature, thick build, innate understanding of metallurgy, mechanical creativity, and excellent vision in the dark mines.

Dwarfs (DWAR-fs) — Plural form of Dwarf.

Dwarfinn (DWAR-fin, with a prolonged "n") — Possessive form of Dwarf.

Fukk (FUK) — Imperative conjugation of Fukken. AKA "Fuck!"

Fukkr (FUK-ker with a rolled "R") — Old Norse word meaning one who breeds, derived from the proto-Germanic word "Fokken. It applied to animal breeding but grew to be used with vulgarity. AKA "Fucker!"

Fukken (FUK-en) — A contraction of "Fukkandi," the present participle of Fukken, AKA "Fucking."

Fyrnrót (FURN-root, furn with a rolled "R") — A mystical herb native to the cold, untamed regions of Norðrlönd that can induce visions.

Gasthaus (GAST-house) — A tavern with simple guest accommodations, usually above the tavern.

Goðar (GO-thar, with a soft "th" sound and rolled "R" sound at the end) — Plural of Goði. Also spelled Gothar.

Goði (GO-thee, with a soft "th" sound) — Someone responsible for overseeing local religious practices, including conducting rituals and maintaining sacred sites. Also spelled Gothi.

Goðlaus (GOHth-louse) — "Godless / without the gods," i.e., someone who doesn't blót (offer sacrifices) and doesn't put trust in the gods and "believing in their own might."

Gorathökk (GOR-a-THECK) — The land of the Orcs on the other side of the Gorathökk Sea. The Orcs are viscous and live to fight.

Granat (GRAH-naht) — Grenade. Small handheld explosive. Based on the Latin "Granatus."

Half-moon (Half moon) — 1. The state of the moon when it appears to be half-full. 2. The time it takes to go from a full moon to a no-moon and vice versa, or about 14 days.

Haustblót (HOWST-bloht) — Autumn feast celebrating the fall harvest and animal sacrifice to appease the gods through-out the winter.

Hnefatafl (NEF-uh-Tah-full) — An ancient Norse strategy board game, often referred to as "The King's Table." It was widely played in Scandinavia before chess was introduced. Some reports indicate it goes back to the 4th Century.

Hel (HELL) — 1. Hel, or Hela, is a goddess who presides over the underworld realm of the dead, also called Hel. She is typically depicted with a face that is half-beautiful and half-de-cayed, reflecting the duality of life and death. Due to the drag-on wars with Ravnsríki, it was believed that the volcanic plain far west of Helsgaard, which was home to Dragons, was the entrance to Hel. 2. The domain of Hela where those who died of old age, illness or cowardice. Inhabitants were known as Hel-walkers or draugr.

Helgrindi (HEL-grin-di, with a rolled "R" sound and a dental "d") — Refers to the great gate or fence that serves as a primary entrance to Helheim, the underworld realm ruled by the goddess Hel.

Helsgård (hels-GARD) — This name refers to the entire region encompassing both the Helsgaard Plateau and the verdant valley that lies to the west, between the plateau and Hel. This valley is known as the Helsgaard Frontier. A clerical error a century ago corrupted the original runes. This changed the name from Helsgarðr ("Hel's Yard") to Helsgård ("Hel's Homestead").

Hersir (HAIR-seer) — The leader of a small group of warriors. Later, during the Viking Age, it included being a landowner and executing administrative duties, such as collecting taxes and enforcing laws.

Höfn (HEW-fn) — A haven or safe place.

Hvelpr (HVOL-pr, a breathy "HW" ending with a rolled "R" sound) — Whelp, or puppy, and by extension a cub (e.g., lion's/tiger's/wolf's young). Figuratively it can mean "urchin/brat." Can be used as a nickname/term of abuse in some contexts.

Ísdolkr (EES-dolkr, with a soft "K" and rolled "R" sound at the end) — Means "ice dagger," a famed but never-seen dagger made of quartz crystal that can be used to overcome the evil magic of the Dark Stone.

Jarl (YARL) — An elite, landowner, or wealthy person.

Jarnøskahrafn (YARN-uh-ska-RAHF-en with a rolled "R" sound) — Literally, "Iron Raven." It is a radical secret society in Jarnborg driven by revenge to exterminate the Dragons in retribution for losing the war 300 years earlier. The difference in spelling and pronunciation of Ravn versus Rafn is due to geographic isolation.

Jörð (YER-th, with a soft "th" sound) — Means "Earth" in Old Norse. Norse mythology describes her as a giantess (Jötunn) and personifies the Earth—a similar concept to Gaia in the Gaia Theory.

Karl (KARL) — An ordinary person.

Karlar (KARL-ar) — Plural of karl.

Kobold (KOH-bold) — A mischievous and evil spirit inhabiting mines and caves. While often depicted as small and goblin-like, they could be powerful and vicious when angered.

Kunta (KUN-tah) — This is another term with ancient Germanic roots, found in Old Norse and many other Germanic and Scandinavian languages. Like "cunt" in American-English, it is a vulgar term for the vulva.

Kvik (KVIK) — Alive, quick, living.

Loki (LOH-kee) — A cunning trickster god in Norse mythology. He is known for his chaotic nature and aiding and hindering the other gods.

Miðgarðr (MI-th-garth-er, with a soft "th" and rolled "R") — Also known as Midgard, it is centrally located among the Nine Realms, serving as a pivotal point that connects the various worlds. Its position is crucial to the overall structure of the Norse cosmos, which is often visualized as a vast tree, Yggdrasil, with its roots and branches extending into different realms. Its central position underscores its importance as the realm where humans reside and interact with the divine and the supernatural. It is a bridge between the various realms, reflecting the interconnected nature of Norse cosmology and the belief in the interplay between the mortal and immortal worlds.

Miðsumarblót (MITH-soo-mar-blote) — A blót (sacrifice/ritual) to honor the gods, ancestors, and spirits at the height of the sun's power.

Míren (MEER-en) — The Aelfinn afterlife realm, where the soul reflects on their previous life before reincarnation.

Mírenstál (MEER-en-STAHL) — A special metal alloy forged only in Aeldoria. Characteristics include being lighter than iron and high strength and hardness. When crafted as a sword, it has a high resistance to losing its edge.

Moon (Moon) — A unit of measure that is approximately one month long. AKA "month."

Náttmál (NAT-mal) — The last meal of the day, similar to

dinner or supper. It was typically eaten around 9 o'clock in the evening, after the day's work was done. Náttmál often featured freshly prepared food, such as stews made with meat or fish and vegetables. Wealthier households might have had more variety, including different types of meat. Ale was a common drink served with Náttmál.

Necro (NEC-row) — Short for Necromancer.

Niðingar (NEE-th-ing-ar, with a soft "th" and a rolled "R") — A word for "those without honor," or "cursed cowards," or "men damned by shame."

No moon (No moon) — The time of the month when the moon is not visible. AKA "new moon."

Nordlund (NOR-th-ewnd) — The peninsula encompassing Aeldoria, Ravnsríki, and Dûrgath.

Norns (NORNS) — The Norns were the Norse goddesses of fate, represented by three sisters named Urd, Verdandi, and Skuld. They lived underneath the world tree and wove the tapestry of fate.

Odin (Óðin) (OH-thin, with a prolonged "O" and a soft "th" and prolonged "N") — Formally written as Óðinn. Chief deity of the Norse pantheon. God of war, wisdom, death, poetry, and prophecy. Óðinn is invoked during oaths, curses, war cries, and sacred rituals. He is both revered and feared, representing the complex duality of fate and battle.

Odin's Merk (OH-thins Merk, with a prolonged "O" and a

soft "th" and prolonged "N") — One of the currencies of Ravnsríki. It's a coin made of gold, stamped with Odinn's face, weighing about 30 grams, or 1 ounce.

Ond (OND)
Life energy or "spirit-breath."

Pikk (PICK) — A vulgar slang word for a penis. It's also an insult to someone you don't like, especially a boy or man.

Rôst (ROHST) — How long one marches before taking a rest - about a mile.

Rass (RASS) — A vulgar slang word for the posterior that refers to a jerk or an idiot.

Rasshol (RASS-Hole) — A vulgar slang word for the posterior and used about a jerk or an idiot.

Ravnsríki (RAVNS-ree-kee, with rolled "R"s) — The name of the Human kingdom, which roughly means "Raven's Realm" or "Raven's Domain."

Sambúð (SAHM-booth) — Means living together or cohabitation. It can imply a domestic relationship or union, possibly even without formal marriage. It's the closest term to describing a long-term partnership or committed domestic life.

Seithr (SEY-ee-thr, with a trilled "R") — A type of magic involving communion with the dead practiced in Norse society. AKA Seeress.

Skål (SKOHL rhymes with "bowl," but with a shorter, crisper "o" sound) — A traditional Scandinavian toast, meaning "cheers" in modern usage. Historically, it was more than just a drinking salute, it symbolized camaraderie, respect, and good fortune. The word originates from Old Norse skál, meaning "bowl," referencing the communal drinking vessels shared among warriors and friends during feasts.

Skalds (SKAHLDS) — The poets and storytellers of the Norse world, skilled in composing and reciting verses that praised kings, warriors, and gods. They preserved history, recounted heroic deeds, and wielded words as both entertainment and political influence.

Skitkarl (SKIT-karl) — Translates to "shit-fellow" or "dung-man." It's a fancy Old Norse way of calling someone a "jerk" or a "good-for-nothing." AKA "Bastard." See also Skitr and Karl.

Skitkarlar (SKIT-kar-lar) — Plural of skitkarl.

Skitr (SKIT-er, trilled "R") — Means "shit" or "dung." It can also be used figuratively to mean something worthless or contemptible.

Tagelharpa (TAH-gel-HAR-pa) — The name means "horse-hair harp because the strings are made from horse hair.

Tanrite (TAN-rite) — A combination of an unknown white crystal and a shiny metal powder that explodes when exposed to sudden impact.

Ting (TING) — An assembly or governing council in Old Norse and other Germanic societies. It was both a political and legal institution—a mix between a parliament, a court, and a public forum. The þing was central to Norse identity. It embodied the ideal of free speech and collective decision-making in a warrior society. Participation was both a duty and a right of free people. AKA Þing.

Thrall (THRAWL, rhyming with brawl or maul with a strong "TH" as in thorn) — The actual spelling is þræll. Means "slave." Enthralled is to be enslaved.

Torc (TORK) — A torc is a rigid, typically metal neck ring, often open-ended, that was historically worn by various Germanic cultures.

Unter (UN-ter) — Meaning "below" or "under." When used as a prefix to a city name, it denotes the ghetto or an impoverished area.

Valknut (VALK-noot) — Three intersecting triangles representing the Knot of the Slain. It is associated with death, rebirth, the afterlife, and the journey to Valhalla. See Valknut.

Várblót (VOR-bloht) — Spring feast celebrating emerging from winter's embrace and animal sacrifice to appease the gods and bring good fortune and abundant harvests. See also Várblót.

Vid hamri Thors (VID ham-ree THORS, with a soft "TH") — By Thor's Hammer–a severe curse.

Rosetta Stone - Aelfinn Addendum

Ael va'rin (Ayl-VAH-rin) — "It is done." Spoken with finality, especially after killing a Necromancer, sealing a fate, or making a painful decision.

Berio nin (BER-io NIN) — Literally, "Shield me." It is an invocation of protection.

D'ra vel Aenn (Drah-vel-AYN) — "Let it be undone." Used in grief, regret, or desperation. Said quietly, like a prayer.

Goheno nîn (go-HEN-oh NEEN) — Have mercy on me.

Haerathen (HAIR-uh-then) — A sacred term: "The price is paid." Used after loss, vengeance, or sacrifice. Often spoken over a fallen ally.

Hrindr (HRIND-er) — "Strike!"

Myrren sol thae (MEER-ren sol THAY) — "I am of two worlds."

Nareth (NAH-reth) — "No! Stop! Danger!" Rooted in older Ælfinn warning cries. Often used to halt a charge, warn of incoming danger, or break a spell of madness. Has an emotional bite somewhere between "No!" and "Abort!"

Ni'valrenn (Nee-VAHL-ren) — "I am not ready." Whispered when overwhelmed, facing visions, or the approach of fate.

Skaldvárr (SKAHLTH-var) — "Oathbreaker of the old blood." A brutal insult. Used for betrayers, cowards, or horrors.

Skylda mér (SKYALDA mer) — "Shield me."

Téla sil Naevarr (TAY-lah sil NAY-var) — "Daughter of the silence."

Tharnak (THAR-nahk) — A quiet, venomous curse AKA "Damn the stars" or "Damn this fate."

Vael akthrúen (VAYL ack-THROO-en) — "I walk between." Implies becoming something else, such as a Seithr, changeling, or hybrid.

Vétskorr (VET-skorr) — "Desecrator." Used for Necromancers or anything that perverts natural life.

ALSO BY

Titles by the Author

Helsgaard's Heroine
Helsgaard's Fury
Helsgaard's Storm
Helsgaard's Wrath
The Drekahǫnd Rises

For the latest information, visit www.helsgaard.com
Sign up on the mailing list for promotions and freebies.

ABOUT THE AUTHOR

George writes grimdark military Norse fantasy with the kind of brutal precision you'd expect from someone who spent 20 years in the military. Raised in snowy Colorado but allergic to cold and complacency, he now lives in Phoenix, Arizona stirring the pot—because hellfire heat is still better than shoveling snow or getting buried in an avalanche. Don't ask.

His debut novel, Helsgaard's Heroine, didn't just storm the gates of fantasy—it earned a spot on the Grand Prize Shortlist Award for the 2024 Novel90 Writing Challenge. He's also the mind behind several grimdark screenplays (too raw for daylight), and a stack of technical articles written in a former life when things still made sense.

When he's not forging blades and betrayals on the page, George can be found camping off-grid, overlanding into nowhere, road-tripping, or helping people who just figured out they're in trouble.